SCARLETT FINN

Also by Scarlett Finn

GO NOVELS
GO WITH IT
GO IT ALONE
GO ALL OUT
GO ALL IN
GO FULL CIRCLE

EXILE
HIDE & SEEK
KISS CHASE

WRECK & RUIN
RUIN ME
RUIN HIM

**THE BRANDED
SERIES**
BRANDED
SCARRED
MARKED

**FORBIDDEN
PREQUEL DUET**
ALL. ONLY.
ONLY YOURS

TO DIE FOR...
TO DIE FOR TRUTH
TO DIE FOR HONOR
TO DIE FOR VIRTUE
TO DIE FOR DUTY
TO DIE FOR LOVE

**LOVE AGAINST THE ODDS
STANDALONE COLLECTION**
SWEET SEAS
HEIR'S AFFAIR
RESCUED
MAESTRO'S MUSE
GETTING TRICKY
THIRTEEN
REMEMBER WHEN...
RELUCTANT SUSPICION
XY FACTOR

NOTHING TO...
NOTHING TO HIDE
NOTHING TO LOSE
NOTHING TO DECLARE
NOTHING TO US
NOTHING TO SAY
NOTHING TO GAIN
NOTHING TO YOU
NOTHING TO THIS

THE FORBIDDEN NOVELS
FORBIDDEN DESIRE
FORBIDDEN WANT
FORBIDDEN WISH
FORBIDDEN NEED

KINDRED SERIES
RAVEN
SWALLOW
CUCKOO
SWIFT
FALCON
FINCH

THE EXPLICIT SERIES
EXPLICIT INSTRUCTION
EXPLICIT DETAIL
EXPLICIT MEMORY

MISTAKE DUET
MISTAKE ME NOT
SLEIGHT MISTAKE

**RISQUÉ & HARROW
INTERTWINED**
TAKE A RISK
FIGHTING FATE
RISK IT ALL
FIGHTING BACK
GAME OF RISK

LOST & FOUND
LOST
FOUND

ONE

"THIS IS YOUR BIG plan?" Oakley Orion asked the boardroom table occupied by three of his colleagues.

"It's perfect," Taylor said.

Taylor was his baby sister and one of his most-trusted employees. She'd only graduated college last year, but she was a vital part of the MatchMate family and had worked for him part-time and through summers since she was in her mid-teens. Beautiful, tenacious, and always willing to take a risk, his sister was more like a daughter than a sibling. Usually, he loved her positive attitude, because she would be the first one to jump on with any of his schemes or ideas. This time... not so much.

"MatchMate is the biggest dating company in the world," Ian Blundell said. Again, this guy was supposed to be his man, his wingman, his buddy, what the hell was he doing subscribing to this insanity? "We're so successful because we think outside the box. Like Taylor said, this is perfect. I can't believe we didn't think of it sooner."

MatchMate didn't start out as an online agency,

but they had moved with the times and now retained fifteen different international websites. Their USP was their safe approach to connecting members. The company owned several venues across the US and franchised across the world. Each MatchMate site had a restaurant, usually a couple of bars, and hotel rooms. They'd even branched out to rural retreats where members could try different activities on organized vacations either as singles or MatchMate couples.

They prided themselves on not only matching people but nurturing relationships from beginning to… sometimes, end. Hosting events, they didn't just match profiles using algorithms; they did it in person, offering all sorts of options for meeting. Speed-dating and drinks mixers were held at every venue several times a week. Weekend breaks were offered to new couples getting to know each other, and counselling was offered for those thinking about embarking on marriage as well as to MatchMate couples who had wed and were experiencing marital difficulties.

Oh, and they did the odd wedding too.

For couples who met through events or the website, they could use the restaurants and bars to meet, holding their dates in safe, secure environments. Food and drinks were free during MatchMate organized events, but members paid as they would anywhere else at other times. The hotel rooms were also available to couples who might want to take advantage of the opportunity to get more intimate. Again, it was all about giving members a safe place to enjoy each other. Security was always on site, discreet, but always there, and they had lawyers and counsellors on staff too to offer all kinds of ongoing support to members.

"You wanted a radical marketing strategy," Kody said. "Something to mix things up. Something that would make headlines. That's what you said. Interest the media and we get a bunch of free advertising. In this day and age, with the competition—"

"Okay, okay," Oak said, waving a hand at Kody Aitken, his head of marketing. "Media coverage, I get that, but how the hell do we market this without making it look like just that, a strategy?"

"What's the number one question you're always asked when you do interviews?" Ian asked, clasping his fingers together on the desk.

"Why am I still single?" he said, focusing on the surface.

Taylor took her turn to taunt him. "Because it doesn't look good that the CEO of our massive dating company, a company who prides themselves on producing strong relationships, can't find love."

"I date," he said to Taylor who was using her pitying eyes on him again. Their mother had taught her how to use those eyes against him, he was sure of it.

"Once in a blue moon," Ian said.

Oak huffed, he knew it was petulant, but really, he got enough of this from his mother and the media. "It's time you settled down," Taylor said. "Don't you want marriage and kids, you know, stability? You're thirty-five, you should—"

"I'm thirty-three," he said, scowling at her, though the discrepancy was hardly worth noting given that his next birthday was just a few months away.

Taylor must have felt the same, because she rolled her eyes toward the ceiling and exhaled. "Fine, you're thirty-three, but you started this company when you were in college." And he'd done it as a joke; he could never have known what it would become. "You shouldn't live like you're still there. You can't be a bachelor forever."

"I'm waiting for Ian's eyes to meet mine at midnight over the coffee machine in the breakroom."

Taylor could do unimpressed better than anyone he'd ever met and her growling expression forced him to lose his deadpan delivery and smile. "You think this is a big joke, Oakley," she said. "But one day you're going to wake up in that breakroom alone and realize we're all happy and settled down."

Oak straightened his back. "Wait, are we here to discuss a marketing strategy or my life plan?" he asked, flattening his hands on the table.

"The former," Ian said.

"Both," Taylor said at the same time.

He didn't know which of his colleagues he should believe, but if anyone was going to convince him to go along with this crazy plan, it was going to be these two.

"All we have to do is prove the product works," Ian said. "We find a girl who's been on the books for a while and convince her to play your girlfriend for a few months. We toss you both out on the TV; you do the chat shows, interviews in the papers, easy. Signups will go through the roof."

"But," Taylor said, drawing her eyes off Ian. "To make it look good, you should go to a few events, meet a few women, make it look like, you know, you're actually trying."

Taylor was so transparent, but she meant well so he couldn't be mad. "And if I happen to fall crazy in love by accident, all the better, right?"

Taylor grinned and shrugged. "Mom does want grandchildren."

"Yeah, you feel free to get started on that and I'll catch up."

At only twenty-three, Taylor got plenty of interest from men, and he hated every single one of them. But their age gap meant he'd always felt a strong need to care for her. Since their father had died when she was just eight, Oak had been the dominant male influence in her life.

Taylor had been a major reason for his drive, and his need for success. He'd almost dropped out of college when their father passed in the accident, but his mom had insisted he finish his studies. He did, after starting MatchMate, and the rest was history.

He'd taken care of both women ever since.

"Okay, I will," Taylor said, and he didn't like the way her chin went up.

What the hell? He'd been kidding and expected his sister to get offended, not cocky. "Who the hell are you going to have kids with? I thought you dumped that Edgar idiot."

"Ethan," Taylor corrected him. He'd known the fool's name, but Oak didn't want anyone to think the guy even pinged on his radar. "And we're talking again."

"Well stop talking. Talking leads to… not talking."

"Oh, so you do remember?" Taylor asked and slid an arm under her chest as she slanted toward him. "Tell me, brother, when was the last time you spent a night 'not talking' with a woman? Huh?"

At least her attitude made it easy for him to return to deadpan. "My sex life, really? That's what this is about? Faking a relationship I can get on board with, but you want me to sleep with this woman? Will that be in the contract? 'Cause that would make it much easier for me."

Taylor sneered out a faux laugh. "I'm sure once she's literally forced to spend time with you, you'll be able to wear her down. You've worn women down before. Unless…" She gasped. "You're not a virgin, are you?"

"Yeah, I am," he said. "You should try it."

She laughed again. "You'd like that, wouldn't

you?"

"I tried sending you to a convent when you were fifteen, Mom wouldn't sign the paperwork."

Her next laugh was more genuine, but he wasn't really kidding. If he'd been able to get away with it, he probably would've done exactly that. "That's 'cause Mom knows the value of a good lay."

"Okay," he said, revulsion making him recoil. "You've taken it too far. You've officially found my banter boundary… Mom? Sex? Really?"

Taylor shrugged. "Her and Henry have been not talking for a while."

His lip curled in disgust. "How do you know that and I don't? Why would you even want to know that?"

"I listen when people talk, and she's into him… they've been travelling together for a year. Did you think she was going to be celibate forever?"

"Celibate? Yeah, I'd have been okay with that."

"So, the women in the family have to be celibate, but you can go out there spreading your seed? Who's going to take over your great empire when you're six feet under?"

"This is about my legacy?" he asked, searching for the truth. "You need to pick an argument and stick with it, sis."

"I think we're getting kind of off-topic here," Ian said, spreading his arms to draw attention away from the siblings and onto himself. "Marketing? Remember?" Giving him a look and then sharing it with Taylor, Ian was really telling them to finish this argument later. "We'll set you up at a couple of events so you can meet some women. Meanwhile, we'll work behind the scenes to find the right one and we'll bring her in. Once she's signed up, we'll have the two of you meet… by accident at a MatchMate event."

By accident? This couldn't be further from an

accident. Oak didn't mind being involved in schemes; he liked to have fun. At least, he used to, but Taylor's griping was irritating him.

He dated… sometimes.

Yeah, okay, it had been a while, but the company needed his attention and he was bored of the dating scene. As soon as women knew what he did they expected him to be some sort of relationship genius. He wasn't. Far from it. He had an incredible team and a wealth of technology to assist the company in what they did. He knew no more about women than the next guy.

Oak was open to having a relationship, he just wished he could skip over the whole awkward dating part and jump right into the commitment. He was good at commitment. Once he was sure something was right, he'd give it his all.

And that was where he stumbled.

How the hell did someone know who they were supposed to spend the rest of their lives with?

***

SPEED-DATING.

In all the years Oak had talked about it in meetings and how it could be mixed up or marketed, he'd never actually taken part. Now he knew why.

Twenty women.

Twenty men.

Well, nineteen—he wasn't sure he counted.

The bar was busy. It was the smaller of the two bars on the premises and had been designed specifically for this purpose. Another good thing about MatchMate was that every venue they had was modelled for exactly what they needed.

So, twenty two-seat tables were arranged in their own individual booths. The wooden screens between the tables were only six feet high, but that was enough to conceal each table from the other when the couple was seated. Oak got the strangest feeling like he was in a confessional every time he sat down, which was weird because he wasn't even Catholic. But it made him uneasy all the same.

The women were nice.

There was nothing overtly wrong with them.

Some tried far too hard. Others were too nervous to make much of an impression. But he couldn't judge them; the whole contrived situation didn't give anyone a chance to relax enough to be themselves.

Ding.

Next table.

Woman number thirteen.

Leaving the table of woman number twelve, Oak shook her hand and she giggled. Great, a giggler. He'd met a few of those tonight. The IT guys had taken his picture down from the websites, but it was too little, too late. Most of the women here knew exactly who he was. So much for the anonymity everyone else was afforded. Maybe this was exactly why he'd never used his own company to find love.

At the start of the evening, the men had been put at one side of the bar with the women at the other because they weren't supposed to mingle. The men hadn't known who he was and he got a boost of confidence. Good, he didn't want to be recognized.

Then he'd sat at the first table and he was reminded that women were far more thorough when it came to dating. They knew who owned the company they were entrusting their future happiness to.

Shuffling down to the next table, Oak expected a smile, a handshake, a cheek kiss, just like he'd received at every other table. Instead, he saw the top of a head.

The petite brunette was typing something into

her phone and didn't even look up. Okay, maybe she was taking notes on the last guy, maybe she liked him, maybe they'd exchanged numbers. Members weren't supposed to contact each other outside the MatchMate system, but he and his colleagues weren't naïve to the fact that it did happen.

"Can I sit down?" he asked, tilting the neck of his beer bottle toward the seat opposite hers.

When she tipped her head back, she sort of sagged as she exhaled. Her keen eyes slowly began to glitter. A smile curled her lips at such an excruciatingly gradual pace that he thought he might wait the entire six minutes to see it. Eventually, when it lit her whole face, it hit him full-force, grabbing him so deep he couldn't inhale.

He sealed his lips tight, flat.

Shit.

"I would absolutely love to say no," she said, losing none of her glee. "But my car isn't due to pick me up for another hour, so… what the hell? Let's go crazy."

Gesturing toward the vacant chair with a flat hand, she slipped her phone into her purse as he sat down.

"So…" he said.

Linking her fingers, she rested her forearms on the table, parallel to her body and bobbed her head. "Going with the awkward opening, okay… do you want me to giggle or bat my eyelashes? Or is it your preference that I lean forward and…"

Pushing her breasts together with her upper arms, she bowed forward, plumping them behind the low neckline of her dress, leaving little to the imagination.

"Whichever you prefer," he muttered, finding himself transfixed by her cleavage for a good few seconds.

Damn. He'd seen boobs before, plenty of them, and he never leered… Why were Thirteen's breasts so interesting?

She pondered aloud with a short hum. "I could ask you what you do for a living, but I already know that, so that would be a waste of time. I could sit quietly until you ask me what I do, but I'm going to lie, so that's no better."

That took him aback. "You're going to lie?" he asked, finally managing to stop staring at her breasts for long enough to make eye contact and drink some beer. Good, yes, he was pulling this back, take control. She was nodding. "Why would you lie?"

"Because what I do is not very interesting and it won't give you a hard-on."

Coughing out the beer he'd just tipped onto his tongue, Oak didn't appreciate how one side of her lips tipped higher than the other. Wiping his mouth with his hand as he choked down the liquid that had managed to make it past his lips, he kept his eyes on hers.

Who the fuck was this woman and why the hell was she here?

Being hot, smart, and confident, Oak couldn't see how she'd ever have any problem finding a guy to lead around by the balls. "Okay, I guess you want to play," he said, compelled by a need to hold onto this conversation. Too many men were probably overwhelmed by her; she was undoubtedly used to making them blush and stutter. Oak wasn't going to be one of those men. "Is that why you're here? For sex?"

Mirroring positions on each side of the table, he copied her move of linking his fingers to lean over his forearms. He didn't have boobs to distract her with, but if he kept his eyes on hers, he could win this.

She lifted a shoulder. "I'd say that's why everyone's here. Some might want all the love and romance bullshit that goes with it. But ultimately, yeah, everyone who signs up to your scheme really just wants to be fucked good and hard."

"Good and hard," he muttered and broke his own rule because while his teeth stayed clenched, his eyes descended to her mouth. "You don't want love and romance? Have you heard of Tinder?"

Her smile was quick and she exhaled a laugh. Why did it give his pride a boost to make her laugh, especially such a pathetic little one that might not even have been genuine?

"Tinder is good," she said. "But there's less charming conversation over there."

Did she really use that website to hook up with strangers? Her? A woman who could walk into any room, snap her fingers, and probably receive fifty marriage proposals in thirty seconds?

"MatchMate members are supposed to be serious about finding love."

"Are they?" she asked, tipping her head to the side like he was educating her, but didn't believe him for a second. "Have I been naughty? Am I going to be punished by the handsome, rich CEO?" Her eyes darted around like she was searching for something in her head. "I think there's a movie about that."

The only thing Oak heard in that statement was that she thought he was handsome. A point for him. "Do you exchange numbers with guys at these events? Go home with them?"

"Maybe," she said like it was no big deal and it shouldn't be, except for some reason, it was. Recognizing that he was pissed because he felt like his company was being violated, Oak had to concede that as long as she paid her membership fee, he shouldn't give a damn. "If I do, I'm not the only one… Would you judge me more harshly than the men who invite me back to their beds?"

Actually, yes, but not because he held double standards. Oak found it hard to imagine a guy who would refuse her.

"You know how to manipulate men," he murmured, searching her eyes as he tried to figure her out.

She laughed again. "Oh, so it's my fault? I'm an evil siren, singing to men who are helpless to resist my charms?"

"I think if you tell a guy you're not interested in love or romance, and flash your tits at him, he's going to make assumptions about who you are."

"And what assumptions have you made?" she asked, narrowing her eyes and losing her humor. "That I'm a whore out to play with men's emotions?"

"Are you?"

"A whore? Maybe," she said. "But I'm not interested in anyone's emotions except my own."

Cold, abrupt… alluring. "And that's why you win every time," he said. "Because with a body like yours and that tempting little mouth there isn't a guy around who would stop calling as long as you're offering to suck his dick."

Her short, sharp inhale was joined by her manicured fingers touching the swell of her breast. The expression of feigned shock on her face made him sure he was about to be chastised for his language. But her eyes flicked up just a fraction before she took her ass off her seat and slowly bent over the table.

"Mr. Orion," she murmured as she inched closer and closer to him. He couldn't back off, he had to match her stare even if the way her eyes began to smolder was actually making his dick forget about her breasts, despite them coming closer. Tilting her head, she got so close that her breath warmed his lips. "You think my mouth is tempting?" Her voice lowered to little more than a vibration. "How dare you."

His lips opened, preparing to accept hers, then he heard a ding, and she was gone, sitting back down, pulling her phone from her purse, dismissing him without so much as a glance.

Shit.

What was he supposed to do? Get up and move onto the next one? What the fuck? She'd screwed his head so bad that he couldn't even remember what number came after thirteen.

But when a guy appeared at his shoulder, Oak had no choice except to get up. Snatching for his beer, he quickly shuffled along and planted himself in the next chair. He wasn't even sure how the hell he was going to hold a conversation… didn't even know what a conversation was anymore.

He hadn't even managed to look at the woman sitting opposite him when he heard the lilt of the sweetest, most innocent giggle coming from the table he'd just vacated. Who the hell was that?

"Are you my Prince Charming?" the naïve murmur of an almost childlike voice drifted to his ears.

"Is that what you're looking for, honey? A knight in shining armor?" a male voice asked.

Slowly standing to peek over the top of the separating screen, Oak was surprised to see Thirteen there, sitting back, chewing on her lower lip as she twisted her hips back and forth in the seat, making her whole body sway in an innocent arc.

Tugging on a length of hair that hung over her breast, she twirled it around a crooked finger while blinking wide eyes that suggested butter wouldn't melt in her mouth.

Her new date looked so pleased with himself as he turned to look the other way to check out the competition of who'd be next with this girl.

Oak was too stunned by Thirteen's quick personality change to be surprised when she lifted her eyes to his that were still peeking over the top of the screen, proving she'd felt him watching.

Yeah, Oak had been caught looking, but what the fuck?

Thirteen winked at him and her lips slanted in a brief saucy smile that vanished as soon as her current date turned back to her.

Oak dropped into his chair and grabbed for his beer, obsessed with just one thought.

What the fuck?

TWO

THIRTEEN LEFT AS SOON as the last guy left her table.

Oak knew it because he'd come up short when he sought her out as all the participants returned to the bar. That was the portion of the evening when the daters were supposed to fill out their comment cards, stating who they'd like to see again and who rated highly and not.

MatchMate took negative feedback as well as positive and added it to members' private notes, so that if they ever requested counselling or help from a dating advisor, they had a starting point established.

Thirteen made no notes and didn't wait to hear who wanted to see her again. Oak checked after, almost every single one of the men wanted a follow-up date with her. But she'd never be linked to any of them if her profile didn't state an interest.

Five days after the speed-dating event, he saw Miss. Thirteen again, standing at the bar waiting for a drink during a Friday night mixer.

"So, who are you tonight?" Oak asked as he approached.

She turned around and lost her blinking innocence as soon as she recognized him. The number on her chest stated that she was thirteen again. Odd, usually people had different numbers at every event; that was why everyone had a membership card, so their details could be taken and noted down to correspond to their new number each time they attended an event.

"My skirt isn't short enough for me to be sexy siren tonight," Thirteen said, scanning the room behind him. "So it's a tossup between simpering bimbo and bitter spinster." She took a breath that suggested she was fed-up. "I'll decide after I've had my first drink."

"Seems you don't stick to just one style," he said, sinking onto the stool next to where she was standing. She was shorter than he was, much shorter than he'd thought and it felt wrong to be sparring with her when his physical size dominated hers, not that she seemed to notice.

"I like to mix it up if the night starts to get stale," she said.

"I'll try not to be insulted that your night got stale after our date," he said, resting an elbow on the bar.

Grinning when the bartender came over with her drink, Thirteen hissed in a breath of satisfaction. "If I don't get a bite tonight, I'm coming back for you, sweetheart," she said to the bartender who smiled and winked at her. "Don't leave without me."

"The Harley out back is mine."

"Oh," she said, sipping her drink and pouting. She leaned toward the bartender who was lowering to her level and admiring her cleavage while he was at it. "I've always been a sucker for a motorcycle. What time do you get off? Or are you going to leave that to my discretion? You get a break, right?"

"Yeah, at—"

Oak twisted to glare at the bartender. "Customers need drinks, Sy."

"Yes, sir," Sy said, clearing his throat and disappearing to the other end of the bar.

Thirteen huffed and tipped more alcohol into her mouth. "Oh great, you're one of those guys."

"Those guys?"

Spinning to pin her displeasure on him, Thirteen wasn't feeling so flirtatious anymore. "The ones who decide that since they haven't tasted pussy in a while no one else should be allowed the pleasure. You're clam-jamming."

Ducking toward her, he couldn't believe that she was accusing him of… "I'm what?"

Exhaling, she twisted to look at the clock above the buffet and took another drink from her martini glass. "Do you want me to suck your dick? Huh? Will that make you feel better and get you out of whatever funk you're in? Let me guess, you've got a birthday coming up? Typical guy, you're getting older, need to feel desired. Whatever. There's a janitor's closet between the restroom doors, just—"

"A janitor's closet?" he asked. The last time he'd spoken to her he'd told himself not to display any kind of shock at what she said, he didn't want to be spitting beer everywhere again. But Oak couldn't contain his astonishment. "You have sex with guys in the janitor's closet?"

She lifted a quick, straight finger. "Ah, I didn't say I'd have sex with you, I said I'd suck you off." Easing back, she looked him down and then up. He'd never felt so objectified. "Nope."

"Nope what?" he asked, watching her turn back toward the bar to pick up her glass again.

"I've changed my mind."

What had happened in the space of ten seconds that made her go from, *"I'll suck you off in the janitor's closet" to "no, not interested"*?

"Why?" he asked, then cursed himself for asking because it didn't matter.

Oak hadn't intended to sneak away into any closet with her. If they were going to hook up, he'd take her upstairs to one of the hotel rooms on the second floor. Wait, no, he wasn't going to take her anywhere, he wasn't going to have sex with her… of any sort.

"I like MatchMate," she said, leaning over the bar to check out the bartender's ass without any kind of modesty or shame. "I like being a member." At least she liked something about him. "And you said you'd never stop calling if I sucked your dick, so… yeah. If I did that, I'd have to quit MatchMate 'cause you'd be calling and calling and calling…"

Her ass was rising and falling as she lifted her weight onto her forearms to get a better look over the bar, probably at the bartender's ass. She was too short to keep her feet on the floor as she did it, so she just bobbed there, distracting his sanity and making him wonder why she'd been so adamant about not having sex when clearly she had the rhythm down.

That wouldn't be a bad pace to start her at, slowly, gentle, tease her, torment her a little, let her think she was going to go insane waiting for him to get down to it for real. Yeah, that would put her sweet little ass in its place and that was what she needed, a guy with a strong hand and a stronger will than hers. She was a challenge and would be every single day.

"How can I call you when I don't even know your name?" he muttered.

Her ass stopped bouncing and slid downward as she found her feet and twisted toward him. "You're telling me you didn't check out every woman at that speed-dating thing before you went?" she said, without concealing her suspicion. "You have access to all the membership records."

"Yeah," he said, turning to rest his forearms on the bar. She hunched with him and their upper arms met. Damn, she was warm, and he'd never hated his shirt more. It didn't matter that the cotton between them was thin; somehow it still felt like too much. "But checking up on my dates wouldn't be sporting, would it? And it's not the true MatchMate experience."

"Is that what this is about? Having the true MatchMate experience as part of your midlife crisis?"

Tightening his fist around his bottle, Oak wondered if Thirteen had conspired with his sister to rile him. "I'm thirty-three."

"Huh," she said, and although he didn't look at her, he felt her looking at him. "Shame. Forty's my minimum."

Spinning around, she was about to flounce off, so he grabbed her arm to hold her at the bar. "You can't be more than twenty-six," he said.

Members did get to set preferences on the mate they were interested in finding, such as an age range, but usually they kept the parameters as wide as they could.

"Twenty-eight," she said and grinned as she leaned in. "I have daddy issues."

His hand slid from her arm as she walked away toward the buffet. It didn't take long for the first guy to move in on her and Oak saw several others watch her progress with interest. Thirteen was the kind of woman who should be snapped up quickly, even with her apparent aversion to finding love. She couldn't have been a member for long and probably wouldn't be.

"Isn't this fun?"

Turning, Oak saw Taylor jumping up onto the stool beside him. "Do you want a drink?" he asked, trying his best to ignore the files she had in her arms.

"No," she said. "I'm here for your autograph, not to distract you from finding true love."

True love had never seemed further away.

Members were invited to their preferred locations, and they could note more than one. Some liked places closer to their work; others liked the MatchMate spots near their home. But they could pick any; some people wanted to put distance between them and their dates. They were also entitled to mix it up and could request invitation to any MatchMate get-together or buy tickets for special events anywhere.

His number one preferred locale was right here. Trouble was, this establishment was their flagship site and part of the MatchMate corporate offices. So he worked right upstairs, giving his sister this chance to descend on him in his social time. Not that he felt particularly social right now.

"Gimme," he said, taking the folders from her and stacking them on the bar before he opened the top one. "Did you bring a pen?" Taylor's hand slid onto his face and when she drew him around to look at her, there was concern written all over her expression. "I'm fine."

"No, you're not," she said. "What's wrong?"

"Dating makes me hate myself," he admitted. "Always has. I really suck at it."

She smiled, a warm, reassuring smile, and brushed her thumb back and forth on his cheek. "No, you don't. You're just out of practice. You'll find your groove."

"It's not that," he said and tried to look at the folder, but she strengthened her hand and wouldn't let him.

His sister's concern hadn't gone anywhere. "Then what?"

"I'm great at the flirting and I love a challenge,

you know I do, but…" He growled. "I hate the bullshit. Why can't a guy just say to a girl, 'Hey, you're hot, you're interesting, let's do this.' Why can't that be enough?"

"So what?" Taylor asked, a smile flirting with her lips. "You want to skip the fun part and jump straight into marriage?"

Lowering to her eye level, he wanted her to know that he wasn't playing. "I don't have time for the fun part, Tay."

"Everyone has time for the fun part," she said. "I was only kidding about your age; you've got plenty of time. You're a guy… You can have kids in your seventies if it takes that long to find someone to love. If you have to wait until you're fifty or a hundred to find it, wait as long as it takes."

"Just forty apparently," he muttered, pissed at himself for wanting a woman who seemed to be the epitome of bullshit.

"Aren't you tired of dancing with me and Mom at all these stupid parties we go to? Wouldn't it be nice to put your arms around a woman you feel something non-familial for? All the crap about kids aside, you need someone, Oak. Someone to talk to when you go home at night. Someone to share your worries and your dreams. You've taken care of me and Mom for long enough, we're sick of seeing you throwing yourself on the pyre of self-sacrifice, doing everything you can to make sure we have good lives while yours passes you by. It's time, Oak. You're done. We don't need you every minute of the day anymore. We're all grown up."

Taylor included their mother in that statement because for a long time after their father died the woman was a shadow of herself. It was tough. Tougher for him because he had to hold his mother up while helping to raise his sister, completing his college work, and starting MatchMate.

His mom faced some dark times, darker than Taylor could ever imagine, but he'd done whatever it took to get them through and he was proud of his family because they'd come out of the tragedy stronger and closer.

There were so many things for him to consider, the business, his full schedule, his family. How could any woman put up with his hours and his need to prioritize his family over everything else in his life? And he'd have to make compromises for whatever his woman's priorities were and if they clashed with his…

Then she wouldn't be the woman for him.

Oak gained a new respect for the members of MatchMate. Dating was difficult. Sometimes there was chemistry, but that didn't mean a relationship would work. And there were certainly matches made by the system that didn't produce marriages, what was the secret?

Turning around, he saw Thirteen was there by the buffet, nibbling on a shrimp, one small bite at a time as her interested eyes were flicking up and down from the food to the guy talking in front of her. She wasn't interested. She looked it, but she wasn't listening, he knew it.

Letting a smile slide to his lips, he exhaled. "What do you need me to sign?"

"Oh," Taylor said with sudden joy. "I hear a sense of purpose, brother. Do we have a live one?"

Taking his focus to the files, he yanked the pen from Taylor's hand and began to sign. "Love or not, I'll get my cock sucked, so nothing really to lose, right?"

"Ew, Oak," she said. "TMI."

"Says the girl who talks about our mom's sex life in the boardroom."

"Yeah, if she hadn't told me about sex stuff it would've fallen to you and I'd still think babies came from the stork. Mom is mom, she doesn't mind girl talk. You're you and… ew. You don't have a penis."

Taylor made him smile; she'd always managed it, even in the bleakest of times. "Yet you want me to have kids, how does that work?"

"You know what I mean. You're my big brother, I don't think of you…"

"Not talking?" he asked. When he was done, Oak slapped the last folder closed, gave her back her pen, and kissed her cheek. "I love you, Tay."

"Course you do," she said and grinned. "I'm the only good thing in your life… Change that for me, will you? Please?"

It might only be temporary, but he planned to. With that decision made, he sought out Thirteen and planned to interrupt her conversation and hopefully, her life.

***

EVIE DEWAR HADN'T WORN brown for years. Though tan was a variety of brown, right? She'd worn tan. Beige, was that brown? It might be classified as a brown tone… depending on the depth of it.

What the hell was an earth-tones party anyway? Who ever heard of one of those? Sure, black tie, she got that, but earth tones? Who looked good in blah green? Tipping her head the other way, she took her final bite of shrimp and picked up a napkin from the table beside her to wipe her fingers.

Lime-green, she could rock lime-green—she had a lime-green bikini. Smiling, Evie tried to imagine how that would go across if she showed up for a formal function in a neon bikini. Though black tie meant formal, maybe earth tones was more relaxed.

"Excuse me, there's been a mistake."

Last she'd seen him, Oakley Orion had been at the bar with a blonde who seemed to like touching him. But here he was, striding over to her and… this buffet guy… wearing a stern expression.

"A mistake?" the guy asked.

Oakley took her arm and pulled her aside. "Yes, we have reason to believe that this woman is not who she appears to be."

Shrugging at the buffet guy, Evie let herself be dragged away. "I thought you didn't know who I was," she hissed. "How can I not be who I appear to be when you don't know who I am?" He led her over to the distressed-leather armchairs near the front window. "Do you think lime-green is an earth tone?"

"What?" he asked as he pushed her down into one of the high-back chairs set on either side of a low circular table. "I don't think so."

"Hmm," she said. Damn, what was she going to wear now? Beige was her least favorite color ever. There was a brown dress in the back of her closet, but it had a plunge neckline, like a serious plunge neckline. "Have you ever heard of an earth-tones party?"

He smiled as he sat down and waved at the bartender. Okay, good, alcohol. But that was such a man thing to do, *let's steal the woman and liquor her up.'* She should refuse to drink on principle… but she wouldn't.

"Why do you always do that?" he asked when he looked at her again.

"What?" she asked. "What do I do?"

"You take control," he said. "I just dragged you over here, you have no idea why, and you don't even blink, you just jump straight into steering."

She'd have thought the why was obvious. "Are you threatened by confident women?" she asked, pushing out her lips in a mocking pout. "Oh, Mr. Orion, I'm sure your penis isn't that tiny. Most men greatly overexaggerate—"

He laughed. "And then you do that. You say something shocking that you think will make me capitulate. Don't worry, I'm sure it works with plenty of guys and I commend you for trying." Their eyes met. He peered closer, lowering his volume. "I don't scare that easy. You talk about my tiny penis as much as you like."

The female server who approached with their drinks slowed.

Evie couldn't contain her grin but did wrinkle her nose as she waved her pinkie at the blushing youngster. "We give him points for admitting his shortcomings," she said, beckoning the woman over. Taking the drinks from the tray, she put Oakley's on the table and sipped from her own. "You remind your friend behind the bar not to break my heart."

The server glanced at Oakley before turning the tray under her arm and scurrying away. "Can't wait for the memo I'll get about that on Monday," he muttered.

Sipping her drink, Evie crossed her legs. "Oh, you have to admit, that was funny… and I'm sure your blonde at the bar will set everyone straight."

"My blonde at the bar?" he asked, glancing over at the bar with his hand half-way to his beer bottle. "I haven't touched that server."

Evie tutted. "The blonde with the files who loved touching you."

It took a second, but clarity came with a smile. "Taylor?" he asked and picked up his drink. "No, actually, I think she'll kind of enjoy the office having a laugh at my expense."

"Oh, then I like her already. And what a great way to scare off the competition; just let everyone think you're sexually inadequate and you'll never screw around on her."

Something odd crossed his face as he pushed

back in the seat. "I'm not sleeping with Taylor," he said.

"Why not? She's hot. I'd do her."

That amused him into a half smile. "She'll be pleased to hear that."

"Is she gay?" Evie asked, happily sitting up straighter to enhance her interest. "Lucky me." Letting her purse drop from under her arm to the chair, she popped it open. "Can I have her number?"

"You want to sleep with Taylor?" he asked, really seeming to enjoy this. "You know, what? I should give you her number. It would serve her right to be pestered by you."

"I don't pester," Evie said. "And whether we sleep together or not, you won't be invited to the party."

"I'm okay with that," he said, bobbing his head before he drank more beer.

Hmm, no flirting about a threesome or seeing some girl-on-girl action. Okay. Time to figure this guy out.

Tipping her head, Evie focused on his bottle. "Men like you don't usually drink beer."

He raised his brows, signaling interest. "What do men like me usually drink?"

"Bourbon," she said. "Expensive Scotch… Daddy drinks."

Angling his bottle, he licked the beer from his lips as he considered it. "You want me to drink a Daddy drink? Would that do it for you?"

Her nose scrunched for half a heartbeat. "It doesn't sound right when you say it… maybe in ten years."

Taking her time to sip from her own glass, she glanced over her shoulder at the clock.

"Why do you look at the clock so much?"

"Because I time my interactions," she said and then stopped to regroup.

What? Had she just been that honest?

"Ah," he said. "I'm on a countdown."

"Yep," she said. "So if you have something profound to say, you should say it now."

"Don't you ever get tired of being someone else all the time?"

"Who says I'm being somebody else?"

"You played the confident sasspot with me, then moved onto the innocent babygirl with the next guy at the speed-dating. I bet if I asked any of them about you, they'd all tell me that you have a different personality."

Shaking her head, she sucked down more martini. "I only have five or six personalities, and they're all me."

That was enough to worry him into a frown. "You have split personalities?"

She should say yes just to scare him away, but instead she laughed. "Don't we all? Come on, Mr. Orion, we're all different people depending on our audience. You're not the same guy with your blonde as you are in the boardroom, are you?"

"The blonde is usually in the boardroom," he said. "And she's usually busting my chops."

"Foreplay," she said, dismissing him with a lift of her glass.

His eyes slipped to the side and his expression contorted. "Uh, no, definitely not that."

"Sure, it is. Arguing is the best form of foreplay."

"Is it?" he asked, flaring with interest. "You'd like a fractious relationship?"

Ha, not a chance. Admiring the light playing on the surface of her drink, she leaned back. "I don't want any kind of relationship, Mr. Orion."

"Oak," he said. "Everyone just calls me Oak." Whatever, why should she care? She didn't. "And what should I call you?"

Pushing her shoulder into the chair, she thrust her right boob forward to show him the sticker on it. "I'm number thirteen."

"You were number thirteen at the speed-dating too," he said.

Nodding, she enjoyed another mouthful of alcohol. "No one ever wants to be thirteen, so I give the guy on the door taking our cards a break, and I ask for it… Puts a lot of guys off too. I'm unlucky."

Intrigue narrowed his eyes. "What kind of person joins a dating agency but wants to put guys off?"

"The kind of person who likes open bars, free food, and desperate cock," she said, raising her glass to him again. "Now, Oak, I think we've exceeded our six minutes."

Leaving her chair, Evie was going to go back to the buffet, but he lunged forward and caught her wrist, stopping her in her tracks. "What's your name?"

"None of your business," she said.

"What do you do? Honestly?"

Sucking in a breath, she acted like she was considering the truth, then smiled. "That's none of your business either."

"You'll talk about sex with me, offer to suck me off, but you won't give me your name."

"I retracted that offer," she said. "And what do names have to do with orgasms? I could be Priscilla, or Nancy, or Jane Doe… whatever the hell the guy wants to call me, what does it matter?" Snatching her hand away from him, she bent to put her face near his. "If it makes him happy to call me Mommy, or spank me like a naughty schoolgirl, why should I limit his pleasure? Isn't that the point, Mr. Orion? Aren't we all here to maximize our pleasure?"

"You are a whore," he said, but she didn't know if he meant it or was trying to shock her, giving her a dose of her own medicine.

Either way, it didn't matter; she wasn't going to give him the response he wanted. Instead, she smiled and inhaled a sharp pant that might mimic a woman surrendering to passion. "Thank you, Oak… That's the nicest thing you've ever said to me."

Turning her back on him, she swayed her hips as she moved toward the buffet table. Inhaling, she circled her lips and blew out her breath slowly.

Evie. Keep it together. She hoped he didn't notice the rise of her shoulders or the erratic thrum of her pulse.

Of all the men she could find herself attracted to, after all this time, why did it have to be that one?

THREE

EVIE DID THE SMARTEST thing she could and switched her routine. Going to the Tuesday night speed-dating on the other side of town was the best way to ensure she never saw Oakley Orion again.

There had been something so shrewd about the way he looked at her, and the way he spoke, as if he knew her, and had a right to talk to her in a familiar way.

No. She couldn't tolerate that.

The bell rang out and she sat back to pull her phone from her purse to make her notes. The guy who sat down next didn't say anything... and she kept her head down. Maybe he'd stay quiet for the whole six minutes. Good. Finally, she'd get a break.

"Seems pointless to rate the guys when you don't stick around at the end to fill out your comments card."

Oh. Great.

Forcing herself to smile, Evie looked up and considered the man opposite her before she sighed out his name. "Oak."

"Hey, Thirteen... or can I call you Evie?"

Ah, she circled her lips. "Somebody's been naughty," she said. "Does the handsome, rich CEO want to be punished? You want Mommy to spank you?"

"My mom never spanked me."

"Then I guess there's nothing weird about you enjoying it then, is there?" she asked and folded her arms on the table. "Should we do it here, in front of all these people? Think we'd go over our six minutes?"

"Depends how good you are at it," he said.

"Oh, I'm good," she said, straightening her spine. "What a shame I'm not interested in being your media patsy."

Ha, she liked that look, he was surprised. "My media patsy?"

"Sure," she said. "I saw the article online this week. You're on a quest for love and trust the only way to find it is through MatchMate." Waving her hand at him, she scowled. "You're not looking for love, Oak. So, it's a marketing play."

Grinning, he got closer. "I guess you know about business, Ms. Freelance Personnel Consultant. You majored in psychology. No wonder you know how to play every guy who sits opposite you. People are what you do all day."

Pressing her fingertips to her lips, she did her best Marilyn Monroe gasp. "Not all day, Mr. Orion, a girl has to eat. She can't exist on a diet of spunk alone."

"She can if her guy eats right."

Damn her for enjoying that joke, but the smile that burst to her lips was genuine and as if he knew that, Oak returned the expression with equal sincerity.

Fuck.

Dropping her attention, Evie tried to pull it together, but when her eyes rose to his, they were looking right through her. "Has it been six minutes?"

"Not yet," he said. "I've still got time."

She should never have told him about timing her interactions; Evie was still beating herself up about making the confession. Honesty was against all her rules.

"What are you doing away over here on this side of town anyway?" she asked. "All the classy chicks are uptown."

"You never showed at the event last night. So I checked, you changed your dates… and your location," he said and seemed to enjoy smirking at her. "Are you avoiding me, Miss Dewar?"

"I don't know," she said. "Are you stalking me?"

"Stalking? No."

"Good, because it's against MatchMate rules and I would *really* hate to have to report you."

He laughed. "I think there are few things in life you'd enjoy more than reporting me to my own management team."

Actually, now that he mentioned it; that could be a lot of fun. Nothing would ever come of it, except her possibly losing her membership, but it might be fun all the same.

"Then I think you better come up with a damn good reason for coming here tonight that doesn't involve stalking… and do it fast, because we're running out of time."

"I came to offer you a job."

A job? What the hell? She was here to date not to solicit work. "I told you, Oak. I would be an awful media patsy… imagine me on the morning shows, what the hell would I say? And you know, I'd never be discreet. I don't know how to be. I'd spend all day talking about your tiny penis and how you love to call me Mommy as I spank you for being naughty."

God, he had the most amazing grin. His whole face came alive with the emotions he didn't even try to hide. Oakley was the complete opposite of her in so many ways; he was open, so free with his answers and his emotions. None of which was on her agenda.

"Which is exactly why I'll never put you in front of a camera," he said. "Come to the office tomorrow at nine and we'll talk."

"What is it you want me to do for you? I'm a whore, I'm not a hooker," she said, folding her arms and wondering why the hell he'd gotten it into his head that she would want to see him every day. "Freelance personnel consultant does not mean prostitute, just in case the Urban Dictionary somehow gave you the wrong impression of what I do."

"No wrong impression," he said. The bell sounded, making him rise from his chair. Oak leaned over the table to mutter, "Switch it on, honey, the next guy's got a monster cock, he was talking about it at the bar before we started."

As he leaned back, he winked at her and then disappeared to the next table. Her date came around the screen and the scrawny guy couldn't top more than five foot. With sweat stains under his arms and a sheen on his forehead, Evie wasn't sure she wanted to shake his hand, but when he noticed her breasts she took a breath.

Well if he was going to be polite, she should return the favor.

***

IF OAKLEY ORION wanted to play her, she was going to do exactly the same thing in return.

Showing up at his office, Evie had expected to be told the whole thing was a big joke. But there was a guest pass waiting for her. So she held her purse strap high on her shoulder as she hooked the pass onto the lapel of her trench coat.

Going all the way to the top floor, she was

directed to an office at the back of the room. Glass-fronted, and elevated above the bullpen below, Evie grinned, she couldn't have set this up better if she'd had full run of the place.

Sitting at the bottom of the stairs to the office, she smiled and winked or blew kisses at every man who looked her way. Yep, the shocking red lipstick always got attention. When she heard footsteps, she turned to see a bunch of people leaving the glass office above and hurrying down the stairs next to her seat.

One of the men stopped at the bottom and offered her his hand. "Ian Blundell," he said. "Oak said you can go on up."

"Of course he did," Evie said and picked up her purse before taking her time to ascend the stairs.

Going into Oak's office, she closed the door and moved into the center to stand with her feet apart. "Evie," he said after he looked up from whatever he was writing.

"Shh," she mouthed without actually making a sound as she lifted her straight finger to her lips, though she didn't actually touch them, she didn't want to smudge her lipstick onto her finger.

This was going to be fun.

Bending at the waist, she put her purse on the edge of the desk and then straightened. Narrowing her eyes on his, she slowly pulled the knot from the belt of her trench coat. After she pulled it free, she held the edges of her coat and let her tongue run the width of her upper lip before she winked once and let the coat slide from her shoulders.

Stiletto thigh-highs, garter-belts, and a push-up bra, yep, she'd relocated his shock zone.

Good.

But she wasn't done. Reaching to the top of her head, Evie pulled the clasp from her hair, letting it cascade down around her breasts. While Oak was still sitting there with his mouth open, she straightened one leg in front of the other and took a step toward the desk to dip her hand into her purse.

Pulling out her flogger, she let the strands of leather run through her fingers and lowered her chin toward her chest. "Has someone been a naughty boy?"

"Evie," he said on a quiet exhale.

"You can call me Mommy."

Leaping up from his chair, Oak ran away from his desk. Bypassing her, he rushed to the window and pulled the blind cord, plunging them into almost darkness. But she didn't mind that. Turning around, she was pleased to see how frazzled he looked. With one hand on his hip, the other went through his hair.

Strutting toward him, she tossed the flogger against her shoulder, letting the strands run down toward her cleavage. "Evie," he said again.

"Doesn't look so tiny to me," she said, eyeing the impressive erection in his slacks. "Let's find out."

Grabbing his belt buckle, she was thrilled when he snatched her upper arms and thrust her back. "No, Evie, honey. This… this isn't what…"

Pointing the flogger at him, she made sure he knew the rules. "I do this and that's it, Oak. Don't call me. Don't show up at events I'm at. I'll avoid you. You avoid me. And don't cancel my membership—that wouldn't be sporting."

He'd said looking her up wouldn't be sporting, but he'd done that. Still, what choice did she have? If he was going to chase her all over and make up excuses about bogus jobs just to screw with her then she had to put a period at the end of this and finish it. Especially since…

She hadn't been this attracted to a man in a long time. Evie had thought she could keep a check on her hormones and had always managed to, until damn Oakley Orion showed up with that smile.

Taking the handle of the flogger to her teeth, she bit it gently and scrunched her eyes as she sank to her knees in front of him.

"Why the hell are your blinds shut? Oh my God!"

Peeking around Oakley's leg, Evie saw the blonde from the bar standing just inside his office.

Grinning, she took the flogger from her teeth. "You want to join us?" Evie asked. "We haven't started yet."

"Oh my God!" The blonde said and glared at Oakley who dashed away from her to close the door behind the unimpressed newcomer. "This is not what I meant when I told you to find love!"

"Tay," Oakley said. "This isn't... it's not what it..."

"She's in her underwear, Oak," the blonde said, what had Oakley called her in the bar? Taylor? "She's on her knees! She's holding a whip!"

Evie held it up. "It's a flogger," she said. "I have a paddle too. Two actually... and a tickler, and a crop... maybe I didn't bring the crop..."

Shuffling on her knees toward the desk, she was going for her purse when Oakley swore.

"Please get off your knees, Evie," he panted.

"Evie?" Taylor asked, blinking at him. "This is the personnel consultant you want to hire? This is her?"

"Yes," Oakley said. "She's usually..." He exhaled and squeezed his eyes closed. "Dressed."

"You can't be serious," Taylor said. "She can't work here."

"I can if he takes his pants off," Evie said, slapping the flogger on her thigh.

"Evie," Oakley said, opening his hands to her as

he approached. "I didn't bring you here to have sex."

"Because I said I wouldn't have sex with you," she said. When he got within reach, Evie leaned forward to slide her hands up his thighs to cup his groin with both hands. "I never teased you. I was honest."

"Please don't do that," he groaned, grabbing her hands to pull them from his body. "My sister is in the damn room."

Clarity made her gasp and for some reason, Evie was filled with glee. Using Oak's grip on her hands, she pulled herself to her feet and urged him aside to go to Taylor. "You're his sister."

"Yes," Taylor said, keeping her eyes averted. "His baby sister. His very traumatized baby sister."

Twisting, Evie snapped her fingers at Oakley and pointed at the coat that was on the floor. He swiped it up and came over to help her put it on. When she'd tied the belt again, Taylor relaxed, and Evie smiled as she offered a hand.

"Evie Dewar." Taylor just looked at her hand. "You probably don't want to shake my hand." Taylor shook her head. "Because I was just touching your brother's—"

"Ahh!" Taylor said, thrusting her hands over her ears and looking past Evie at Oakley with panic and disgust all over her face. "I have to…" Dropping one hand, Taylor backed away, fumbling behind her for the handle. "I have to go throw up."

Spinning around, the blonde ran from the room, slamming the door behind her. Yes. This couldn't be going any better. Her satisfaction was probably written on her face as she turned to sigh at Oakley.

"I'd still do her," Evie said and shrugged.

"I think that's… unlikely to happen."

Oakley returned to his desk and Evie felt the world sink back onto its axis, exactly where she wanted it. "Oh well," she said, heading for her purse to drop the flogger back inside. "I guess my work here is done. Your sister is traumatized, your boner is gone, and your employees think you're a stud. I'd say I'm doing okay for nine a.m."

Zipping her purse again, she spun around. "What do you bill out at?" he asked.

Geez, this guy didn't get it. She wasn't a hooker. Not even close. It was a fucking game. He was supposed to freak out. He was supposed to tell her to get lost. Supposed to be disgusted and freaked and want to be as far away as possible.

"A hundred an hour. A grand for a twelve-hour day. Five grand for the week." Those were her actual top-tier rates, and she waited for him to ask for her sexual limits before she'd slap him down hard.

"How long does it take you to do what you do?"

Turning back to him, she wasn't sure what it was he wanted. With one elbow on the arm of his chair, he had a curled finger on his lower lip and seemed to be examining her.

"Do what I do?" she asked. "You're asking how long it takes me to get a guy off?"

"No," he said. "I'm asking how long it takes you to do what you're trained to do… You analyze personnel efficiency, right? Look for weak spots, flaws, make recommendations on who to hire, who to fire. You are a personnel consultant… aren't you?"

"Yes," she said.

Why the hell would he want to hire her after… this?

"Good," he said. "And how long does it take you to come up with your recommendations?"

"It depends on what you want," she said, returning to the desk. "I can tell you where you're going wrong in three or four weeks. I can tell you how to fix those issues in six to eight. Full service would take a minimum of twelve weeks, sometimes as much as twenty-four depending on access and foundation efficiency… You have approximately five hundred employees on site, right?" He nodded. "Two weeks to analyze existing data, another three or four weeks to conduct interviews, I could give you a grassroots plan in eight weeks. But it would be basic."

Shaking his head, he ran his finger back and forth on his lip. "I'll give you fourteen weeks and I want the works. Everything. And I want exclusivity."

Blowing out a laugh, she shook her head. "I don't do exclusive."

"Problem with commitment?"

"Huge problem," she admitted. It was only when she met his eyes that she remembered who she was talking to and tried to clear her smile. "I have regular customers and hire for several companies in the state on a regular basis… I have a job in Atlanta beginning in four months. I'm already analyzing the data they're trickling out to me… A sure sign they're hiding something from me, but hey… what you gonna do?"

His awareness grew acute. "You look happy about that."

She shrugged. "What's life without a challenge?"

"I know the appeal," he muttered. "I'll pay you a hundred grand on the proviso of exclusivity and you travel with us."

So he knew what she was up to at all times? Probably. But a hundred grand wasn't to be sniffed at, she had to be smart, that was much more than she'd usually be paid.

Drawing in a breath, she sat in the chair at his desk and crossed her legs. "Twelve weeks, exclusivity, a hundred grand. I'll need external access to your servers and I get full access to staff, records, meetings, everything."

"Member records?" he asked.

Squinting, she shook her head. "I don't give a damn about your members, unless they work for you, even then it's only their personnel records I need to see."

"Okay," he said and sat up.

"But I should warn you before we make any deals."

"What?" he asked. "There's a sex clause in your contract? I have to sell my sister to you?"

Yeah, she deserved that. "In ninety percent of cases, my final recommendations will include a salary cut for the top-tier earners, well… CEOs, really… you."

"Ninety percent of cases?" he asked.

"You don't have to adopt any of my recommendations. As long as you pay me my money, I don't give a damn if you take my suggestions or not. Though it would affect the chances of us working together in the future. It's about respect and I don't like wasting my time."

"What kind of cut?"

Closing her coat over her thighs, she answered, "Depends. I won't know that until I see your records. It can be anywhere from one percent to eighty percent. Though, the eighty percent tends to be more applicable to year-end bonuses dependent on disparity. I believe the lowest earners should be treated as being of equal value to the company as its highest earners. I do strict ratio analysis. My formulas are proprietary, but my final report and presentation will be balanced and transparent."

As she waited for his reaction, she hoped he wasn't one of the CEOs who kicked her out simply because she suggested they may be subject to scrutiny or compromise. Oak said nothing for a minute, maybe two, and then he smiled.

"You're a completely different woman when

you're talking about your work."

Dubious, she elevated her chin. "Is that what this was, Oak? Some kind of test?" Cursing herself, she grumbled. "Damn it, I knew you were playing me."

Surging to her feet, she grabbed her purse and headed for the door. What the fuck was she going to do now? Trust. It was the one thing not to be given out for free. She knew that! Where was her head?

Oak dashed past her, getting between her and the door before she could reach for it. "No game," he said. "Completely legit." Offering her his hand, she eyed it. "A hundred thousand dollars, Miss Dewar."

A hundred thousand dollars. What the hell? Sliding her hand into his, they shook. "You screw me over, Oakley Orion, and I'll make sure the whole world knows it and no number of media patsy's will save your reputation."

"I hear you, Thirteen," he said. "I promise, no screwing."

And as his lips twisted into a smile, she conceded and followed. "I can still go to MatchMate events though, right?"

"Yes," he said. "What do you need to get started?"

"From you? Nothing," she said. "I'm going to find your IT department and then I'm going to my office."

"IT?" he asked. "Oh, you need external access to the servers? Sure, we can get you setup with your own security credentials." Moving past her toward the desk, he was on a mission. "I'll need to call them to authorize—"

"Don't call anyone," she said, and he stopped to look at her. "I don't need your help."

"You think you can just stroll into IT and get full, unfettered access to all our systems without any authority?"

"I have Thelma and Louise," she said. Sticking out her chest, she put her hands to her hips. "They have fun getting what they want or they'll die trying."

"You named your breasts?" he asked, and his snigger had the weird effect of relaxing her.

In this low light, there was something familiar about this moment though there shouldn't be.

"Want me to name your penis?"

"Wouldn't you have to see it first?"

Oh, he knew nothing. "Hmm," she said, narrowing one eye as she considered the possibilities. "Pavlov."

"Pavlov?" he asked, folding his arms. "Why—"

"Because as soon as he hears a bell he gets up and moves on to drool over the next pussy," she said, in reference to their speed-dating. "Every pussy attending those events with your dick would've submitted if you'd demanded it."

What was she doing? This wasn't the time to be flirting. She had a hundred grand to earn and working hard was something she prided herself on. So, reaching for the door handle, Evie was ready to get to it.

"Every pussy?" he asked, making her pause. "Your pussy was at those events too."

Glancing over her shoulder, she looked at him through her hair. "Yes, it was… Now excuse me, I have to go home."

"Home? I thought you said you were going to your office."

"Home. Office. All the same," she said. "Efficiency is my game, Mr. Orion, it wouldn't be efficient to pay rent twice, would it?"

Oak headed over to open the blinds, filling the room with light. "We can set you up in an office."

"In two weeks you'll have to, I'll work on-site

then," she said. "For the first two weeks I do records analysis at my home office where there are no distractions. Fifteen minutes an employee. I guarantee by the end of it, I'll know everyone in this building. After two weeks, the interviews begin… I'll start working from here then."

Something about this room was making her grow anxious. It had just come on suddenly, but it was a sign she only had a few minutes before she had to get out of here.

"You interview everyone?"

"Nope," she said, seeking the door handle. "Only those at the top of the pile and those at the bottom. Records analysis always reveals a few certainties."

"Certainties?"

"I value loyalty and efficiency, I assign high values to each in my analysis equations," she said and as he went back to his desk, Oak frowned like he didn't get it. "If you have a janitor who works hard and has been with you for years, why should we question his position? He does the job, a job that needs to be done, and he does it well."

"So everything comes down to the math? You plug in your numbers for every person and—"

"No," she said. "That's why I do my interviews. There have been a number of occasions when I've tossed the math out the window… especially if he's cute." Oak's head came up quickly and she laughed. "I'm kidding. I promise, sex will not factor into any of my decisions… no matter how often you throw yourself at me."

Opening the door, she was ready to go when he spoke. "Thirteen," he said, drawing her attention. "You've got a killer body."

Curling one foot behind the other, she curtsied. "Thank you… but I know that."

"Of course you do," he said and grinned at her again. Why wouldn't he break eye contact? More to the point, why wouldn't she? "Oh." Remembering something, he bounced out of his chair, grabbing a pen and a card from the desk. Scribbling on the card as he crossed to her, he clicked the pen and put it in his pocket as he presented her the card. "My personal cell is on there if you need… anything."

He'd laced that last word with innuendo on purpose. He was starting to learn it was fun to play her at her own game. Damn, he was a quick study, and a good one. Pulling his jacket aside, she snatched his pen from his inside pocket and grabbed his hand to scrawl her number on the back of it.

"You send me one dick pic, Oakley, and I will report you to the MatchMate emergency complaints line. I have them on speed dial," she said, glaring at him as she finished writing.

He was grinning when she let her stern eyes drift up to his. Why did he enjoy her so much? He wasn't supposed to, he should be offended, but he looked so… happy.

Pulling his hand upward, she pressed her lips to the back, leaving an imprint of her shocking red lipstick directly above her number. Then with a wink, she pocketed his pen, turned and left.

FOUR

TWO WEEKS LATER, Evie was given an office on the top floor, in the corridor on the way to the boardrooms, where she would be heading in just a few minutes.

Ian Blundell was a sweetheart who was so accommodating. Anything she even hinted at needing, he made sure she got in quick time. After going through the employee records, Evie knew who everyone was, though she'd still to meet every individual in person. But this was just the start of her journey with MatchMate; she had plenty of time.

They were coming to the end of the workday, meaning she'd be heading out after this conference. Evie had only attended a few meetings here over the last couple of weeks. She liked to ease people into seeing her around, so she always made the effort to get involved with the business of her client. If people recognized her, they were more relaxed about talking to her, and honesty was vital to her doing a good job.

Evie was hoping this last-minute meeting wouldn't take long. It was Monday, it was late, and everyone would be ready to be done with the day, her included. She was still typing when someone darkened her doorway. Without breaking her pace, she didn't acknowledge her guest because she was determined to finish her thought. Evie didn't want to come back to her computer after the meeting. Once she was done, she'd shut down the machine and be out of her office in record time.

She had a MatchMate date tonight.

"Can I walk you to the meeting?"

Oak.

Concealing her smile, Evie kept typing until she'd finished her sentence, and only then did she let her eyes flick to his. "Want to carry my books too?"

"If you're bringing books, sure. But we keep most things on computer and your laptop's lighter so…"

"Maybe I want to test your strength," she said, saving her document, then closing down the program to scan her emails. "I like a guy with a bit of muscle."

"I go to the gym three or four times a week," he said. "Run every morning."

"Stamina's important," she said. "But not as important as drool-worthy abs. How could we ever go to the beach together if you didn't have a six-pack? What an embarrassment."

His laugh made her smile. "See a lot of people you know at the beach?"

"Depends on which beach," she said, firing off a quick response to an email before closing down her machine and leaving her chair. "How long do we think this meeting will take?"

He backed out of the doorway and seemed surprised when she looped her arm through his, but he *had* offered to escort her after all. "No more than an hour," he said. "It's just a catch-up. We usually have these meetings in the mornings, but things keep coming up and getting in the way. It's overdue, but everyone will want out of here."

"That's what I hoped," she said, and he opened the double doors at the end of the hallway that led to the boardroom reception, though it was deserted now.

"Why? Are you desperate to get out of here? Have you got a hot date?"

Her mouth reacted automatically, and she clasped her hands at the small of her back as she strolled through the door he was holding. "Actually… yes, I do."

Evie wasn't sure which boardroom they were going to, a couple still had lights on and the blinds were closed, so she couldn't see if there was anyone inside. Oakley wasn't much help, it took him more than a few seconds to release the door and come after her.

"Who?"

"I don't know," she said, trying to see where on the door she would find a number. "It's downstairs… I tell you, working here is going to do wonders for my sex life. I don't even have to go home, I can change right here in the building. And you have beds on the premises too. You know, I was never sure how you came up with the idea for MatchMate, now I get it, it makes so much sense."

Laughter rose in one conference room and she smiled as she strode across the hallway. When she went inside there were already half a dozen people present.

Ian stood up and went to pull out a chair for her opposite Kody. "Do you want coffee? Something to eat?"

Evie perked up. "You have food?" she asked, sitting as he pushed in her chair.

"No," Ian said, faltering as he moved away. "But we can order something if—"

"No," she said. "Let's just do this."

"We're just waiting for my dearest brother,"

Taylor said, taking the seat to the left of the head of the table while Ian sat opposite.

Evie turned her focus to the door. Where was he? "He was right behind—"

Oak came in and she stopped. "Everyone here?" he asked, closing the door like he'd already done a mental headcount and didn't need an answer. "Okay, what's first?"

"Convention in Washington," Ian said.

"Oh, I love Seattle," Evie said, though her reaction wasn't needed.

"Good, because you're coming," Oak said. Why did he seem pissed off? His face was all scrunched and he wasn't looking at anyone, just sitting there twisting his chair back and forth. "We're all going. This weekend, right? We leave Thursday."

That would give her enough time to do some interviews. She could take paperwork with her and interview anyone who was going to the event while they were there. Evie considered arguing, but why should she? It was a free trip to Washington and she needed a little R&R.

They raced through another couple of items on the agenda. Evie was feeling good, this was going well, at this rate she'd have time to shower in the employee changing room before her date and probably even blow-dry her hair.

She praised herself for having the foresight to pack a bag before coming to work. She hadn't been kidding when she said working here was going to do wonders for her social life. Okay, so out there in the hallway she'd said sex life, but Oak didn't need to know the truth about that.

"Evie?" Ian asked. Everyone, except Oak, looked at her. "Anything to report? Any issues? Any support you need?"

"Nope," she said. "I'm good." She was used to working alone and it was too early in the game to start tipping her hand. "I'm still in the honeymoon period."

"The honeymoon period?" Taylor asked.

"It's a process," Evie said. "When I start somewhere, the first couple of weeks everyone's nice as pie. The next two weeks, people go above and beyond, they go out of their way to be accommodating and helpful. Then there are two weeks of paranoia, two more of gossiping and bitching, and the last month is pure hostility."

"You won't get that here," Oak said. His finger was curled over his mouth, so his words were quiet, and he was looking at the floor somewhere behind Ian, but he was trying to be nice all the same. "If anyone is rude or at all hostile, come see me."

"It's okay," Evie said, glancing at everyone who was looking at her. "I'm used to it and I understand their point of view, I'm a stranger who was brought in to judge them. I'd feel the same way… And we all know that I can handle people whether they like me or not."

"I like you," Taylor said.

It was so nice to see the blonde by the head of the table grinning at her. "Thank you, Taylor, I like you too," Evie said, sharing a smile with her.

"You terrify me most of the time," Taylor said. "And you're the most confident person I've ever met in my life. But you're… invigorating."

"Thank you! I think you're very sweet, and sincere, and absolutely gorgeous," Evie said, then when she saw Oak's glare, she flattened her lips. "In a completely non-sexual way." Oak's eyes fell again, and Evie winked at Taylor. "But I'd still totally do you."

Taylor blushed as everyone around the table laughed. Everyone except Oak. Something was bugging his ass and that made it bug hers. She wanted to call him out, but it wouldn't be professional to do that here in front of these people.

"Last item," Ian said and nodded at Kody.

The marketing guy seemed more nervous than usual as he opened the binder in front of him. "Okay, I have the final three candidates," Kody said and took out three plastic folders, each containing a few pages. "If you could rank them in order of preference, we can approach the first woman tomorrow."

Kody was seated opposite her. Evie glanced down at the folders and saw a MatchMate profile page on top. "Oh," she said, drumming her hands on the table. "Is this for the patsy? Let me see!"

"We're not calling her a patsy," Kody said. "She's—"

"Right, right, the marketing strategy, fake Oak lover, whatever," Evie said, rolling her eyes. "Let me see!" Lunging over the table, she took the three profiles from Kody and laid them out flat. "Taylor, come down here and we'll pick one."

Taylor laughed as she left her seat, but Oak grabbed his sister's arm to stall her. "This isn't a fucking game."

"That's exactly what it is," Evie said, skim-reading each of the profiles. "You're going to play with this woman and ultimately, she's going to get hurt."

When she glanced up, Evie noticed that no one was smiling, even Taylor looked dejected. "Why will she get hurt?" Taylor asked.

"Oak's not going to fall in love with her," Evie said and couldn't believe that these people appeared to be clueless. "You're picking a woman who has signed up to find love. She wants love. Wants to get married and have kids and find her Prince Charming. As soon as you ask her to do this, she'll say yes, fake or not, because she'll expect it to be a fairytale. She'll think that as soon as she spends time with Oak and they start talking and flirting and dating, that he'll fall for her."

"Why will she think that?" Ian asked. "We'll make sure she knows it's not real."

"Wow," Evie said aloud, sinking back in her chair. "You people don't understand what you do at all. She'll think that because it's what they all think every time they go on a date. Every time they show up to a mixer. Every time they go to your speed-dating sessions or the coaching sessions on dating, and your conventions. Every time they show up to anything. Every time they pay their membership they think, *This is going to be the one.'* They think the next date will be it. The next month's membership will be their last… You don't get that these women are vulnerable, they want love."

"You don't," Oak said. "You're a member and you don't want love."

She dismissed him with a wave. "I am the exception," Evie said. "You said it yourself, how many women join dating agencies and want to put guys off? I'll answer that for you now, the minority, the teeniest, tiniest minority. And those who don't want love will usually only pay a month or two and then find a new hobby. These women." Looking at each of the smiling headshots, she felt bad for each of them. "They've been members for over a year. Women who pay for membership to a dating agency for over a year… they want love… bad."

"Oh God, she's right," Taylor said, putting her hand on Oak's shoulder. "I was so fixated on you falling in love with them that I never stopped to think about what would happen when they fall in love with you!"

"They won't fall in love with me," Oak said.

"Yes, they will," Evie said and even though everyone else at the table looked at her, she kept her focus on Oak whose stern eyes were at the top of their sockets. His chin was turned down. He supported his head with a hand, his elbow propped on the arm of his chair. "Take it from someone who knows… They will fall in love with you." Slowly, his head rose, and she realized she'd have to do some fancy footwork to explain. "You're patient, you're smart, you're decent. You have a regular income, a good relationship with your family. The only cons in your column are your long hours and traveling for work, but trust me, these women will be desperate enough that they won't even factor those in."

"So, we don't do it," Taylor said, lowering herself into her chair.

The intensity of Oak's attention was making Evie itch, but she was too bull-headed to break eye contact first. "No, you should do it," she said. "Go with Lana first, she's in finance and will make a good asset to MatchMate, if she should join the company."

"If they should fall in love, you mean," Ian said.

Oak's eyes dropped, and Evie turned to stack the profiles into her suggested order before pushing them back to Kody. "Hope springs eternal, right?" she said, grinning at the marketing boy before she pushed away from the table. "And if we're all done, I have to go get laid. Excuse me."

***

THE TIME SHE TOOK to shower and do her hair turned out to be therapeutic; it gave Evie the chance to think about what she'd said and why she'd said it. How could she be so sure that a woman would fall in love with Oakley Orion? And why did she feel so bad for the woman who'd have her heart broken by him?

It wasn't until Evie was zipping her dress that she looked into the mirror and saw the answer staring her in the face. Her eyes were moist, her mouth straight, her whole demeanor was flat. She felt bad for the woman because she *was* the woman. Except, she'd never given him a chance, never let herself feel for him.

But it was the possibility she mourned.

There was chemistry between her and Oak. If she was any other woman, she'd be desperate to explore it. That she never would broke her heart. Evie would never know what it would be to love Oakley Orion. But she'd never know what it would be to love any man.

With ten weeks left on her contract, she didn't know how she'd be able to stay away from him without making her attraction to him more obvious. But she'd find a way, she had to.

Oak knew she was attracted to him, he must know it. There had been too many times when they'd shared a smile or held eye contact for a little too long. She couldn't be the only one who felt the spark.

It didn't matter. Evie couldn't be with him. She just had to find some way to get him out of her system and get over it. Making that decision was easier than figuring out how she'd go about it.

FIVE

YEAH, HE WAS A DICK, but he'd get over it.

Evie might not be so quick to forgive him, but so what? Oak felt better. When she'd said she had a date it was like a slap in the face. He'd felt sick and angry and… jealous. What else was he supposed to do except sabotage it? Especially after what she'd said in that meeting.

Why was she so sure that some random woman would fall in love with him? It was the way she'd said it that hooked his interest. *'From someone who knows.'* If that meant what he thought it meant, she wasn't going to be going on any more MatchMate dates, certainly not one-on-ones.

Leaving the building through the backdoor, Oak pressed the button on his key fob to unlock his car that was parked in the closest spot in executive parking.

"I don't have a ride."

Evie's voice startled him, and when he turned around to see her leaning against the wall near the door he'd just come out, he couldn't tell if she was pissed or playing. "Thought you had a date."

"He cancelled," she said, pushing away from the wall to strut toward him. Those goddamn hips. He'd dreamt about those goddamn hips and the way she moved them with that sway every time she walked. "Turns out, he called the bar about ten minutes after our meeting upstairs finished."

"That's funny," he said, staying stock-still when she walked right into his personal space. "What a prick leaving it so late to cut out on you."

"Hmm," she said, her eyes so narrow they almost cut him. "I don't think he's the only prick in my life tonight."

"No?" he asked, playing it innocent, but he was actually happy that she suspected him of sabotaging her.

It was true, and he didn't like secrets. He'd happily admit that he'd canceled the date for her.

"Oh, Oak," she said like she knew something he didn't, and although it made him edgy, he kind of liked it too.

Plucking his key from his hand, she sidestepped and curved that sweet body around his to sashay toward the car. Without even asking his permission, she opened the door and slid into the passenger side.

Okay, he'd have offered to take her home anyway, and he shouldn't have expected Evie to be anything less than direct. It was good to know that even when she was pissed at him for doing something he shouldn't have done, she still trusted him.

Heading for the car, he got in quickly and put his hand out for the key. But she didn't give it to him. Instead, she bent over his lap, deliberately sliding her breasts across his thighs as she elevated her ass.

Oh fuck.

Yeah, she trusted him, but she was going to get payback. It took her thirty seconds to find the slot for the key and even once she did, she stayed there, draped over him. Tossing her hair, she turned to glare up at him, her head right there in his lap.

It didn't even matter that she was pissed, all his dick sensed was proximity to her tits and to her mouth; he was ready for action. Holding his hands up like he was surrendering, Oak had to keep them away from her, far away from her. He'd never allowed himself to touch her like he wanted to and if he started here, now... Hell, he didn't even know what would happen.

"You're going to make it up to me," she purred, and he found himself nodding though he didn't have a goddamn clue what she meant. "GPS?"

Bending a wrist, he pointed at the center console. She sat up, not enough that her hair left his lap, but enough that he could think about finding a fucking gear. Wait... where the hell was the gear shift?

Shit. How was he supposed to drive when her hair was trailing over his thigh like that and her scent... Whatever fucking perfume she'd used mixed with her potent natural pheromones and in the tight confines of this car, he couldn't make his eyes focus past it.

After she punched something into the GPS, his car spouted out instructions and Evie finally sat up to fasten her seatbelt.

Right. Okay. Take the lady home. He could do this.

Oak found the gear and got the car moving. They'd been driving for five minutes and she hadn't said anything. She was just sitting there with her arms and legs crossed, her upturned nose pointed at her side window.

"So, you like Washington?" he asked, that's what she'd said in the meeting and given that they were stuck together for the duration of this journey, he figured he'd give getting to know her better a shot.

"Don't talk to me."

Okay. That was going to make getting to know her harder. "We go to Washington a couple of times a year," he said. "We travel all over the US and all over the world. We should talk about you sticking with us, after your contract is—"

"I told you not to talk to me."

"Evie, look, I'm sorry, okay? But I checked out that guy's profile and he wasn't your type. You'd have eaten him up. He wouldn't have been a challenge for you. You need a challenge."

"Don't. Talk. To. Me."

Why had she waited for him to exit the building and gotten into his car if she didn't want to talk? Maybe this was some kind of punishment. Maybe playing silent cab driver would be his role in her life while she had him in the doghouse.

But after another couple of blocks, he couldn't stay quiet anymore. "You're a great match with MatchMate. Everybody at the company loves you. We're lacking real management in the HR team; you should consider staying with the company full-time—"

"I'm freelance," she said.

Good, they were negotiating. "And you could stay freelance," he said. "We'll take you on as a contractor. You'd still be self-employed, and we could factor in time for you to take on other jobs as and when you needed them."

"No thanks."

"No? You haven't heard my terms yet, we pay well and—"

"I don't do commitment."

In any area of her life. Yeah, she'd said that before, but he figured if she tried it, she might like it. Evie was more suited to routine than she admitted, even her work was structured, and a dynamic company like MatchMate was perfect for her.

"There are opportunities for you to work all over. You don't have to stay in head-office fifty-two weeks a year. We could allow you to work from home too and—"

"Oak," she said, casting her frosty eyes to him.

"Yeah?"

"Don't talk to me."

Her attention went back to her window and he tightened his grip on the wheel. Damn. She was so infuriating. And beautiful. And vibrant. And vivacious, and… Recognizing the building on the corner, his thoughts stopped. Looking one way and then the other, he glanced down at the GPS as it told him his destination was on the right.

"This is my building," he said.

"Yep."

He pulled into the parking garage and into his space. "What are we doing in my building? Do you live in my building?"

Of all the things he'd done, memorizing her address hadn't been one of them. But he'd like to think he'd have recognized his building address even if he'd just glanced over it on her records when he was checking out her name and occupation. She could've moved recently. But into his building? That would be a hell of a coincidence.

"Nope," she said, unfastening her seatbelt and climbing out of the vehicle.

Oak was racing to catch up to her and almost forgot to lock the car, but he caught her just as she stepped into the elevator and selected his floor. Okay, she'd said that she would know everything about every employee; he guessed that meant learning his address too.

"Ev—"

"Nope," she said.

Lifting a finger to silence him and watched the numbers above the door light up until they got to his floor.

When the doors opened, she paced forward and went straight to his apartment. Stepping aside, she gestured at it and waited, patiently, while he fumbled with his keys and unlocked the door.

No woman had ever made him feel as out of control as she did. He had no idea what the hell was going on or what the fuck was in her head. Oak was literally chasing after her, following orders, doing as he was told, and waiting for scraps. But damn, he loved it, she was incredible and now, for some reason known only to her, she was striding into his apartment.

The long space of his living room had the kitchen laid out to the left with a dining and den area beyond.

He closed the door and flicked on the light. "Do you want a drink? I think I have Martini in—"

"Where's the bedroom?" she called over her shoulder as she strode away from the door and past the kitchen.

"Uh, straight ahead, but uh…"

She wasn't even waiting, she kept walking, stepping out of one shoe and then the other. Oh, fuck, was she here for…

But she'd said that she wasn't going to sleep with him.

Picking up the hem of her loose skirt, she reached underneath and two seconds later, her panties slid down her legs. She plucked them off to drop them onto the floor just before she pushed open his bedroom door.

Okay. They were doing this.

Hurrying forward, he pulled off his jacket and tie. He was struggling to free his cufflinks when he crossed into the bedroom to see her high on her knees in the middle of the bed.

"Sit down," she said, pointing at the headboard.

"Evie," he said, climbing onto the bed.

Oak reached for her waist, but she shuffled aside and pointed at the headboard. "I told you not to talk to me, Oak. If you say one more word, I'm out of here. Now, sit."

Either this was going to be the hottest experience of his life or he was going to learn a hard lesson. But she was here, in his bed, no show, no audience or bell signaling that their time was up. Just a man and a woman who shared an intense sexual connection.

Crawling to the headboard, he sat down, propping himself against it as he started to think of all the things he wanted to do to her. If she wanted to take control, he'd let her. He didn't want to be spanked, but he'd be happy to turn her over his knee if that's what she wanted.

Gathering her skirt, she straddled his knees and produced a condom from her cleavage. Wow, had that been there the whole time? While he'd been clueless, she'd known exactly where they were going and how this night was going to end. One of the best things about his Evie was her conviction; he'd never have to worry about her doing anything she didn't want to do.

She unbuckled his belt, then tugged at his waistband. Answering her unspoken request, he lifted his ass to let her pull his pants down, but she didn't pull them all the way off, just lowered them enough that she could grab hold of his dick. With a tight fist, she tugged on him, but the motion seemed more mechanical than instinctive.

Something was wrong here.

But his dick didn't care that her brows were tight and that she wouldn't look at him. It reacted for her as it always did and as soon as he was hard, she slid the condom on. Still, she hadn't looked at him.

"Evi—"

"Don't talk to me," she said, something firmer about her voice this time but was that… was she nervous? No. Not Evie. He'd just got through telling himself that she was assured.

Crawling higher on his legs, she held him in her firm fist and lowered herself onto him. Holy fuck. She closed her eyes and let out a long breath that flooded his face and made his dick throb inside the tightness that he was struggling to fit into. She wasn't wet, she was soft, but there was serious resistance to her body accepting his and her sharp inhales sounded pained, not pleasured at all.

But he could do something about that. Leaning in, he tried to kiss her neck, but she planted a hand on his forehead and thrust it back, thumping it on the headboard. "No."

"No?" he asked but got no response to the question.

So, she didn't want neck kissing, okay, he had other ideas. Sliding his hands onto her waist, he intended to pull down her dress, to kiss her breasts, to make love with her.

Instead, she grabbed his wrists and pushed them against the headboard. "Don't touch me," she gasped in a whisper, her eyes shut tight.

She was still pushing down onto him and although it was dark, he saw moonlight reflect on a streak of moisture as it slid down her face.

"Evie," he said, hit with the searing burn of panic.

"Shh," she said, "don't… don't talk to me."

Gritting her teeth, she swore at herself and thrust her hips down onto his, and when she cried out, all he heard was agony. No, this wasn't right. He wasn't doing this. No fucking way. But when her eyes opened and met his, there was a determination in them that stunned him.

But the connection didn't last, she covered his eyes with her hand and began to rise and fall on him. Her pace got faster as her natural juice began to seep around their joining.

"Yes," she whispered, and her head landed on his, her hand still over his eyes between them.

Her body was loosening around his; her breathing was getting more frantic. Pleasure bled into her moans and his body reacted. It was impossible not to feel the need for release with her bouncing on him like this.

She felt good, snug as a vise around his dick that wanted to make its home inside this woman who was proving to be far more complex than he'd thought. She was no whore. Not that he'd ever really thought that she was, but she wasn't as sexually experienced as she'd implied. She sure wasn't screwing a different guy every night, unless this was how she did it with all of them, but he doubted it.

Oak tried again to touch her, but she pushed his hand away from her body. A few seconds later, she squeezed him within her and let her nails curl into his shoulder. There was no big shout, no exclamation of joy or screaming of his name.

The pulse of her body around his and the friction of their rhythm forced his pelvis up. He hissed out her name and came in the woman he'd been dreaming about fucking since the moment they met.

She stayed on top of him for half a beat. She didn't relax or let her hand leave his eyes, not until she rose higher on her knees and freed him from inside her. Climbing from his lap, Evie didn't even sit on the edge of the bed, she was on her feet and on her way to the door before he'd even blinked the room into focus.

"Evie," he called, but she walked out of the

bedroom.

If she thought it was going to be that easy, she was mistaken. Leaping off the bed, Oak trashed the condom and darted after her. Hauling his pants up with one hand, he managed to close the button as he crossed into the living room where he found her wriggling back into her panties.

"Where are you going?" he asked.

"We're never going to talk about this again," she said, fixing her skirt and tossing her hair out of her face. "Not with anyone else, not with each other. Never. It's done."

"Done," he said, stumbling forward a few steps. "I don't even know what just happened. What was that?"

She picked up her shoes. "It was what you wanted," she said, heading for the door. "You've had me. Now you can get over it. We both can."

Get over it? How could he get over it when it had been so… he didn't even know what it was, but it was far from typical and far from what he'd expected it would be.

"Evie," he said when she pulled open his front door.

"Enough, Oak!" she snapped and made eye contact with him for the first time since before she'd covered his eyes in bed. The pain, the misery, the devastation behind that angry gaze took his breath. "No more, Oak. You understand me? No more. I'm done with you."

Backing out of the apartment, she slammed the door, and left him gaping into the ether. Who the hell was that woman and what had she done with his Evie? Where was the sexy siren? Hell, he'd have taken the simpering bimbo or the bitter spinster over seeing that incredible woman in so much pain.

Enough? No. Who the hell did she think she was

kidding? He was just getting started and he wouldn't stop until he took down every single bastard who'd ever hurt her.

SIX

OAK FOUND EVIE in the breakroom the following morning and when she glanced up from the coffee machine, she smiled.

Good.

That was a good start.

"You know, this doesn't look like one of those big fancy coffee machines," she said, taking her cup from under the spout. "But it makes really good coffee. Was it expensive?"

The coffee machine? "You want to talk about the coffee machine? Really? That's what you want to talk about this morning?"

"I don't want to have a conversation about it," she said, rolling her eyes. "A yes or no would've sufficed… I like your coffee machine, so sue me. I was making small talk."

Something he had no interest in having with her. Striding past the couches, he didn't even consider if he was too close or if his height would intimidate her. But she didn't look up from stirring her sweetener into her drink.

"Evie. We have to talk about—"

The breakroom door opened. Evie glanced up and grinned. "Taylor," she said, walking right past him to go to his sister who'd just come in. "Do you know how much the coffee machine cost? Your brother seems to think it's some sort of corporate secret."

"Uh, no," Taylor said. "But I can find out."

Evie put an arm through Taylor's. "That's a good response. You could learn a lot from your sister, Oakley. She's much more polite than you are." Checking out Taylor's outfit, Evie sighed. "Orange. I never thought about orange. Quick vote, do we think this gorgeous color that Taylor is wearing is an earth tone?"

"I think it is," Taylor said.

Oak shrugged, what the fuck did he know about colors and why was she always asking about earth tones? What the hell was an earth tone anyway?

Tapping her stirrer on her lip, Evie stepped back. "You're only a couple of inches shorter than me, it could work, can I borrow this dress?"

"Sure you can," Taylor said. "But your boobs are bigger than mine."

How could they be standing there talking about clothes like this was any other morning? Taylor had an excuse, she didn't know what had happened last night. Evie was pissing him off.

"I'll strap them," Evie said. "I won't stretch it, I promise. And I have plenty of push-up bras, if I have to lift the girls a little higher and show more cleavage, I don't mind."

"Or you could just buy your own dress," Oak said.

Evie considered the dress again with a frown. "I could, but the color is just perfect. Where did you get it?"

"I can't remember," Taylor said, turning around

to fumble with the back of the dress. "Read the label."

"Oh," Evie said.

Leading Taylor toward him, she shoved her coffee into his hands then pulled the zip of Taylor's dress down. Taylor just laughed, but Oak turned his back. If they were going to start stripping each other, he was going to walk out… Except he had to talk to Evie.

"Does the label help?" Taylor asked.

"It's not one I recognize, but I'll look it up," Evie said and reached around him to take her mug back. "Thanks, Taylor, honey… Oh, and I have back-to-back interviews today and tomorrow, so I can't do lunch, I'm sorry."

"That's okay," Taylor said, and when Oak turned around again, he was pleased to see his sister was zipped in her dress. "We'll do it in Washington."

Walking backward toward the door, Evie crossed her heart. "I promise," she said.

"Evie," he said, hoping she'd acknowledge that they had to talk.

Instead, she scowled in a mocking pout. "You laughed at my coffee machine question, you get no lunch."

She left the room with her coffee, leaving the door swinging, wafting air to fuel the fire of his frustration.

Taylor laughed. "I love her." He couldn't say he felt the same right now, but when his sister prodded him, Oak had to take his concentration from the door. "What's wrong with you? You could be nicer to her, you know."

"Nicer?"

How the hell was he supposed to do that short of signing over his corporation? She'd ridden his cock last night and disappeared from his apartment like she'd done him a favor when all she'd done was leave him with questions.

"Yes," Taylor said, setting about making her own coffee. "You were in a bad mood at the meeting last night and this morning you look like someone peed in your coffee, what's the matter with you?"

"Nothing," he said. Taylor paid too much attention to his mood.

His sister had told him that he spent too much time worrying about her, maybe he should be saying the same to her.

"Whatever it is, don't take it out on Evie, she's just doing her job. You hired her. If you don't like the way she's doing it, talk to her, but be polite about it. I know I was surprised when you hired her, but I get it now, she's good, and if she can help the company then I think it's a good idea to have her around for a while."

For a while, but how long a while? As Taylor made her drink, Oak returned his focus to the door. He wanted to know more, wanted to know why Evie had left his place so quickly, why he hadn't been allowed to touch her… why she looked so hurt when she closed the front door.

It made no sense to him how she could be acting so normally this morning without an ounce of awkwardness or upset. She hadn't missed a beat. It was like she had amnesia and had literally forgotten about everything that happened between them last night.

He hadn't forgotten, and he would make her talk to him… somehow…

***

EVERY TIME OAK went toward Evie's office, she had someone in for an interview.

As infuriating as it was, he had to take his hat off to how hard she was working. As the day progressed, he got annoyed with himself for his attitude that morning. He'd expected her to talk to him and hadn't thought that she'd just glaze over what had happened.

But it wasn't her fault that he felt so frustrated and helpless. Oak had to know why she'd acted the way she had and to let her know that it was okay to be vulnerable. If something had happened to her, or if someone had hurt her, he wanted to be there for her, to help, to support her.

Storming into the breakroom and demanding she reveal all probably wasn't the best way to ease her in to sharing her secrets with him.

Evie worked overtime, interviewing until late on the Tuesday and then she left the office when he was distracted. It probably wasn't deliberate that she waited until he was busy to sneak out... probably.

Oak resigned himself to talking to her on the Wednesday. A bit of time might relax them both, help to give them a bit of perspective and make her more receptive to talking.

He had a whole strategy for approaching her. He was going to be gentle and let her play her games and put up her front as much as she wanted. But he would keep telling her that he wanted to support her. Remind her that she could be honest. That he wouldn't judge her if she was soft and not as confident as she portrayed.

Trouble was, she was in meetings all day Wednesday.

Oak understood her need to do as many interviews as she could before they went away, but he really wanted to talk to her as soon as possible.

An afternoon meeting took Oak out of the office. On his return, he got out of a cab in front of MatchMate and his phone rang. Instead of going inside and maybe losing the call in the elevator, he took it on the sidewalk.

Oak didn't notice them going into the building, but when he turned around he saw Evie inside.

Through the glazed front of the bar, he had a diagonal view through the internal bar doors toward the front reception desk of the hotel. Evie was there with a guy; a tall guy, older than her, older than him, with salt and pepper hair and broad shoulders. They spoke to the receptionist for a second, the woman typed something, took a credit card from the guy and then handed over a key.

Wait a goddamn minute, a key?

Evie said thank you and then slid her hand down the guy's arm to link her fingers between his. The couple moved away from the reception desk and headed for the stairs on the other side of the lobby. Those stairs only went one place, to the hotel rooms.

The guy went first. Leading Evie up the first flight of stairs, he paused to say something to her and Evie threw back her head and laughed, stroking the guy's arm in a gesture too familiar for Oak to be comfortable with.

What the hell?

For the longest time, Oak stood dumbstruck. Shouting from the other end of the phone line snapped him out of his daze, but he didn't say anything. Hanging up the call, he put the phone in his pocket and strode up the sidewalk and into his hotel. His fucking hotel! His fucking business and his fucking woman…

Oak didn't even bother talking to the receptionist. Going to the stairs, he took them two at a time and got to the floor full of bedrooms in quick time. But what the hell was he going to do? He didn't know what room they were in and even if he did, what was he going to do? Bust in there and say…

He'd been played.

The whole innocent, hurt kitten act was just that,

an act. Why did he expect anything else? Evie played every guy she ever met and probably figured that with his need to be responsible he'd like a vulnerable woman crawling all over him. Or it was supposed to put him off. She'd pretended to be weak and inexperienced because she thought he wanted the aggressive sex siren and anything less would quash his interest.

Damn it.

Hell.

Damn it.

She was good.

A feminine laugh drifted down the hallway; he fell back against the wall. Evie would just love it if he made an ass of himself by storming in to interrupt her afternoon delight. Yeah, she was on his time. He was paying for her to do this with the chump in bed with her. It was the middle of the goddamn afternoon! Who couldn't contain themselves for the couple of hours it would take to get to the end of the working day? It didn't matter. She was happy, having fun, and so was the guy under her right now.

Wondering what this guy was getting, Oak wished he'd seen the sex kitten instead of the broken babe, maybe it would hurt less if he thought she was just a ho moving on to the next guy.

What a jerk. He'd really believed it. He'd really believed that she'd been affected by being with him, that giving herself to him was significant in her life.

Driving a hand through his hair, he pushed away from the wall and headed back down the stairs. Let her and her sugar daddy have their tryst, his conscience was clear. Evie wanted to use him and lose him; that was just fine by him.

Fan-fucking-tastic.

***

BUT OAK'S MOOD didn't lighten. It was supposed to. Oak was supposed to just get over it. Evie was seeing a bunch of guys, so what? She'd made that clear to him on the night they first met. Being with her had changed his opinion, but he should've known better. She played games and he'd walked right into her trap.

It was sort of low that she'd played him like she had. So he'd cancelled her date? That didn't mean she should act like some kind of wounded bunny rabbit who needed his protection. Goddamn her.

Flying out to Washington had been a hassle; it always was when they travelled in a group. By the time they checked into the hotel, everyone's nerves were frayed.

But even after spending hours on a cramped plane, the MatchMate crew were due to have dinner as a group. It helped that they hadn't all been seated together on the flight, and he'd been doing his best to avoid Evie since witnessing her sneaking off with her fuck buddy.

The only contact they'd had was when he saw her struggling to pull her suitcase from the baggage claim carousel. He'd gone over to help her pull it off, but as soon as she started her chat, he turned and walked away, he didn't even want to look at her.

Yeah, it was harsh. They hadn't made promises and she had told him they wouldn't talk about their encounter again. So that was it. One night. Not even a night. One… union. He'd been inside her, but—shaking his head, Oak cursed himself for still thinking about it.

He had to have dinner with her and the rest of the MatchMate staff who were on the trip. He couldn't be thinking about his feelings, or his anger, not right now.

Just as he went into the hotel restaurant, he scanned the room and saw the table with the MatchMate banner. Good. That was easy enough to find.

The hotel was filled with staff from different dating agencies. The convention was in the adjoining conference center and from tomorrow it would be filled with booths and anyone eager to learn about the world of commercial dating and those in search of love, of course.

But as he started toward the table laid for him and his colleagues, he noticed someone across the room. Oak didn't even know what had made him spot her, but when he did a double take and saw that Evie was at a corner table alone, he stopped walking.

What was she doing sitting over there when she was here on MatchMate's dime? He guessed that it didn't really matter where she ate, he'd be paying for it all the same. Yet, he found his feet moving again, not in the direction of his colleagues, but towards Evie.

He didn't see her notice him, maybe she hadn't and it was just coincidence that she closed the notebook she'd been writing in and stood up when he was a couple of feet away.

"What are you doing over here?" he asked.

To her credit, she did look surprised, but, as always, she covered. "I just finished eating."

"You just… you finished eating?"

Nodding, she drew the strap of her purse over her shoulder. "I recommend the salmon."

"You were supposed to eat with us," he said. "With MatchMate. What? We're not good enough for you now?"

Her eyes seemed cooler than usual, though she kept her tone jovial. "I was hungry. I didn't think anyone would mind if I ate early," she said. "It's not a big deal."

"It's rude."

She laughed. "Really? It's rude that I was hungry?"

"You're here with us, as part of our party, and you're going to stand us up."

"Would you like me to sit and watch you eat, honey?" she asked, slanting toward him. "Do you have a food fetish, boss?"

Sneering, his patience reached its limit. "Oh, stop it, would you?" he snapped in a hiss. "You said we were through, right? So why the hell are you flirting with me?"

"I thought it might make you feel better about eating without me," she said, sliding her notebook into her purse.

It infuriated him that she could hold herself so far away from any kind of emotion. "No, it's fine, you should eat alone. It's appropriate for someone who shuns real emotion to be by themselves. Saves the rest of us the trouble of being polite."

"Yes," she said and was nodding, appearing bored as she sought something out. "Is there a clock in here?"

"Fuck your six minutes, Evie. I'll be out of here in thirty seconds."

"Good. You better go and bond with your precious buddies and explain to them what a bitch I am for having an appetite."

"You're a goddamn adult, you can wait an hour."

She laughed, a single unimpressed snort. "Why should I? To assuage your ego?" Accentuating her cleavage, she slid into her pouting bimbo persona. "Oh, I'm so sorry I displease you, Mr. Orion, whatever can I do to make it up to you?" Leaning back, she curled her fingers around the strap of her purse and smirked at him. "Are you kidding me? I was hungry, I ate. Why should I sit with you and your buddies anyway? I'm here to take your company apart, right? You think they're all going to love me after my final presentation? No way. I'm not here to make friends, I'm here to do the job you hired me to do so you could get into my panties. You achieved your goal! Congratulations! I'm so sorry I didn't fall madly in love with you, Oakley. You just don't do it for me, okay? Big deal! Move on. Grow up and get fucking over it!"

Taking a step back, he couldn't believe how far he'd considered going for this woman. When he looked her up and down, all he felt was angry disappointment. "You know I believed there was depth, that there was a reason for the facades you put up, but now I see the truth. You're not deep. You're just a fucking bitch."

"And you get a gold medal for finally figuring that out," she said.

The bite of her vicious stare probably matched the ice in his. Good. They needed this. Turning around, he marched away from her. Sixty-four days was a long fucking time, but that was how many days were left on her contract and he'd be counting down every single one, he couldn't get her out of his life fast enough.

SEVEN

FROM THE MINUTE Evie walked into his hotel suite the next afternoon, Oak was ready for her to leave. It felt so fake. She sat there laughing and joking with his staff, people he trusted and cared about. People she had no respect for. He didn't get it. After what they'd said to each other in the dining room last night, how could she just sit there today like nothing had happened?

The group came up with their strategy for the next few days and everyone was dispersing to go off and do their designated jobs.

"Evie, wait a minute," he said just as she was about to reach the door.

Evie stopped walking and although her back was to him, he was sure she'd rolled her eyes. Kody had looked at her and smiled, a sure sign that Oak had just been mocked. The guy didn't know that Evie's bed was equivalent to the viper's nest... yet.

Taylor lingered for half a second, asking Evie a question with her gaze rather than directing it at him. Why had his sister latched onto this callous woman with such ease? Was she that bad a judge of character? Maybe it was in their blood.

Kody was on his own, if he wanted to leap into Evie's web, then Oak would stay the hell out of it. Taylor was a different matter. He'd be talking to his sister, telling her to stay far away from the bitch before her goodness was infected with Evie's evil.

The door to his suite closed, sealing them in alone. "There's no point," Evie said without turning.

"No point in what?"

Spinning around, she hugged her notepad to her chest and narrowed her severe gaze on him. "In apologizing. I don't care. Really, Oakley, you'll apologize, I'll yawn, you'll get pissed off and we'll fight again. Let's just do our best to get through this."

Wow, she was something else and he didn't even try to contain the laugh that burst from him. "I'm not going to apologize to you," he said. "Are you insane? You're a goddamn bitch. I don't give a damn. You apologize to people you care about to save relationships that mean something to you. This means nothing."

Her lips stayed together as she blinked, and he thought he might have shocked her. Good, it was about time someone stood up to her. She'd gotten away with her bullshit for too long.

"Good," she said. He saw the quiver in her throat when she swallowed. "Thank fuck for that. So, what?"

"What?"

"Why did you tell me to wait behind after class? Want me to suck your dick? Hmm?" she asked, striding closer to him at a slow pace, putting one foot directly in front of the other. "Hoping for a replay? Does your cock miss my pussy?"

She wanted to tempt him, but his rage was too powerful to be conquered even by the offer of her body. "No chance. Why would I want a replay?"

"Hmm," she said and managed to spin on the spot to take a step away from him.

"You were shit." That made her stop mid-strut. Good. Ha. She was exactly what she'd said on that first night, a whore who played with men's emotions and he'd been dumb enough to fall for it. He'd let his emotions get involved. Well, that was his mistake, but it didn't mean he would be taken down without fighting back. "Yeah, honey, you were the worst fucking lay I've ever had. You know what I should do? Extend your membership a year or two for free. Yeah, go on, ride every MatchMate cock I've got on the books. You need the practice."

Her shoulders hitched up a fraction and he heard her blow out a breath. Finally, had someone gotten through?

"You know what I love about men?" she asked, her voice so hard and deep that he felt the icicles of her anger pierce his skin. Turning to face him, she pinned her wrath on him. He'd never seen a person so furious, yet she was so cold and detached; a demon capable of being entirely separate from the power of the emotion scorching her insides. "Absolutely nothing. Every one of you is exactly the same. You care only about what women can do for you. You care about what's in it for you. You care about your pleasure. About your needs. About your wants. It's me. Me. Me. All the fucking time. Men want to take and the only thing they give is pain."

"Pain?" he snapped. "You're the bitch who laid out the rules. You took what you wanted and spat me out when you were done. And two days later you were on to the next guy!"

"The next guy?" she asked, her ire was still there but a flicker of curiosity flashed in her eyes.

"In the hotel, the guy, you got a room, in the middle of the afternoon, on my fucking time. Time I was paying you for!"

Closing her lips, she took in a breath through her nose; negative emotion sparkled around her. "Yes," she said, her voice flat. "That's exactly what I was doing. I was fucking him in your hotel. On your time. Does that make you my pimp? Do you want a cut? Is that why you're so hurt?"

"Hurt? Fuck hurt," he said, watching her grind her teeth. "I'm pissed I fell for it. I'm pissed that you use my agency as a brothel! I'm pissed that you switch it on and off like you're incapable of feeling anything."

"Why would you care whether I can feel if you don't feel anything?"

"No," he said, taking a long step toward her. "Don't turn this on to me. Don't think you can grab for control of this conversation and make it about me. This is about you! You are the fake here! You conned me and now you're conning my fucking sister!"

"Taylor? I would never hurt Taylor."

For a split second, she was soft; that crack made him retreat for a breath. But, damnit, no! This was what she did, she made him believe that she could be a real person and then he fell for it and… fuck her. Fuck hurt. Fuck everything.

"I think you should go back to HQ," he said, watching the shell close around her again.

She spoke fast, super-fast. "I can email my reports to you, pro-rate my invoice for work completed and be out of your life permanently within twelve hours."

He nodded once and she reciprocated.

Charging away, she was at the door before he stepped back, confused by how quickly she'd flicked off her emotion.

That fast change made Oak wonder if he hadn't just given her exactly what she wanted. "Evie," he said when she touched the door handle.

"You know," she said, leaving the door to march a few steps nearer again. "You never once stopped to wonder why I want to stay the hell away from men like you, did you?" Wow, that was anger, real anger, the kind that reddened her face and… shit… were those tears in her eyes? "You didn't think that it was weird how I constantly pushed away every man who tried to get near me? Did you ever see me kiss another guy? Did you? Did you ever see me touch one? *Actually* touch one, did you, Oakley? Did you?"

"No," he said, feeling about two inches tall.

She built up more fury. "Not that it's your business, but Noel is my therapist. He's the guy you saw me take a room with, and…" She exhaled a laugh. "He's a fucking MatchMate employee! I went to him in private practice and he told me about MatchMate because he does work for you guys on the side! And why would I need MatchMate? Why would a therapist suggest I take a membership with a dating agency with a reputation for providing a safe, secure environment? I'll tell you, Mr. Orion, it's because I haven't had sex for more than four years! Yeah, you heard me, you bastard! That's why I was shit in bed! That's why I wasn't good enough for you! I haven't had sex since before the night I came home early to find my sister being dismembered by the boyfriend she worshipped! Yeah," she said, sneering at his shock.

"Evie—"

"That's fucking right, a half-hour earlier and I might have saved her life! The real kicker? Half an hour later and I might have saved mine! He kept me in that room with her for eight hours! Eight hours of being beaten by him and watching my sister rot! Watching him taunt and demean her! So, you tell me I'd ever hurt Taylor! You tell me that I would ever harm a hair on her beautiful, perfect, innocent head! I fucking dare you to say it again, you fuck! My sister was already dead, and I still put my body between hers and his! I begged him not to touch her! Begged him! I'd have done anything to protect her! Anything! So, fuck you! Fuck your company! Fuck your job! Fuck love! Fuck relationships! Fuck men! Fuck you, Oakley Orion! Fuck you!"

He didn't even know how to start processing what she was saying. But he moved toward her as she screamed at him, tears streaking her face.

When he reached her, he touched her arm, but she recoiled. "Evie," he whispered.

"Fuck you," she said, but her voice was weakening. "Fuck you, Oakley Orion."

"Okay," he murmured, nodding.

He took her arm again, this time she didn't pull away, she let him draw her close, into his arms.

When he had her, she sagged, her whole body lost all its rigidity and he swept her up into his embrace as she wailed and sobbed against him.

Damn.

This woman.

How could one person live through something so horrific?

He'd find out everything, but not now. What she needed was for him to hold her, to comfort her and support her.

Oakley turned his anger on himself, he'd almost let her walk out of here. He'd almost lost her.

If he had trusted his instinct, he'd never have said those horrible things. But he'd make it up to her, because she'd given him something precious. She'd given him the truth and shown him who she was, and it only made him care for her more.

***

EVIE HAD CRIED until there was nothing left.

For so long she'd tried to keep all the anger bottled up inside. Something about Oakley had made it explode out. Embarrassed and exhausted, she kept her face buried in his chest long after the tears stopped.

Swallowing, she knew she couldn't stay here forever. Her heart was still thumping, and her skin was trembling from the residual adrenaline that was making her feel cold, but she had to get it together.

Drawing in a shaky breath, Evie blew it out and concentrated on trying to keep the next one even. "I should go," she whispered, pushing on his chest, but she only put an inch between them.

Somehow, she'd ended up with her legs over his lap, nestled between his body and the back of the couch.

"No," he said, stroking her hair. "You're not going anywhere."

"You don't have to take care of me, Oak. You want me gone. I'll go. I just… I shouldn't have lost it like that."

"I think you should have," he said, his index finger curving around from behind her head to hook her hair behind her ear. "I think it was probably overdue. You needed to get that out."

Evie couldn't argue against that, but she didn't really have the energy to argue at all. "Yeah, well, it's out now so…"

Pushing on him again, she tried to get him to move away, but he didn't, though he did let one arm fall to her thighs to keep them over his.

"Don't push me away, Sweet," he said. His voice had changed pitch, it was more aware now than it had been while he was soothing her. "Look at me."

Oh, shit. She didn't want to do that. With her eyes probably bloodshot and swollen, she'd have makeup on her cheeks making her look soft and vulnerable. Evie didn't want him to start thinking she was delicate, but her nerves were so stretched she didn't have the ability to sass him.

"Oak—"

"Look at me, Evie. Please." Something in his plea made her chin rise until her eyes found his. "You're not going anywhere." His hand drifted across her cheek. "And neither am I."

"Oakley," she said, capturing his hand. "Please don't start thinking I'm vulnerable and soft a—"

"I always knew you were," he said. "I just let myself forget it when you hurt me."

"I… I hurt you?"

He nodded. "My pride was hurt and then I saw you with that guy and I… I got jealous… I'm sorry I lashed out, Sweet."

This felt like bonding and the truth was, it terrified her. "I don't know how to… there are so many things that you don't understand. I'm not… I'm not like you think."

"I can't wait to find out," he said and slipped his hand from hers to touch her face again.

Something about the delicate feel of those strong fingers made her eyes close and her head relax toward them. Wouldn't it be nice not to be alone anymore? If she could just let herself be open and honest with someone, with Oak, her whole life would change. But how could she ever trust him? She couldn't trust.

Although she felt his body move, Evie didn't think that much about it until his lips met hers. Oh, a kiss. It was wonderful and slow and thorough. He didn't push her, didn't ask more of her than she could give. His warm lips moved over hers, pushing and relenting in unison with exactly what she needed.

It had been so long, but she couldn't remember a kiss ever feeling like this. Maybe it had. Or maybe this was something special. Right now, she was so tired and full of need that she didn't want to fight. She was so tired of fighting.

Opening her mouth, Evie tried to remember how to beckon him forth, but he sensed her need and let his tongue slide against hers. Oh, he was so warm and slick. He tasted like comfort and safety. It was an illusion, she knew it was, but Oakley made her feel secure. And in this minute, nothing could take away this sensation of belonging.

Lying in his arms, she let herself coast. It was day time, light flooded the room; there was nothing to fear.

Sliding a hand to his shoulder, she let it float to his neck and she pulled him harder against her. This body could protect her. If he cared about her, Oakley could be the fantasy. The man who'd stand beside her through anything.

The dream would never come true and she'd worked hard to come to terms with that.

Maybe in time, when she was herself again, back to normal, then she could think about opening herself to a relationship. But it wasn't time. She wasn't ready.

But, God, she wanted to be ready because she wanted Oak.

Her natural response to the kiss of a man she desired flourished. "Oakley," she whispered.

Squeezing her other hand between them, she kept one hand on his neck as she rubbed her palm against the erection in his slacks. And while she licked her swollen lips, she sought his gaze, keeping him close enough that their noses bumped.

"Evie," he murmured and there was such a strength of need in his tone that she smiled.

"Show me," she said. "What should it have been?"

"You're vulnerable and I don't want—"

Pulling him back to her kiss, she pressed hard,

asking for more. Sliding a hand over his, she guided it to her breast.

"Please, Oak," she panted, "show me… slowly."

He squeezed her breast and it felt so good to have him take control that for a second, she just let him touch her. But he must have sensed her lack of response because he stalled, so she made herself move.

Linking their fingers, she pushed him back, and he let her move him away this time. Yes, he was being respectful and probably giving her room to back out if she wanted to, but she didn't want to.

All his show of respect did was spur her need.

EIGHT

TAKING HIM OFF THE COUCH, Evie led him around the furniture and up the single stair into the bedroom in the back corner of the suite. Once they were inside, she unzipped her dress and let it fall to the floor.

Facing him, she started to unbutton his shirt. "We can stop," Oakley said, brushing his fingers over and through her hair as she went to work unfastening his pants. "Any time you want. Anything makes you uncomfortable and we can stop."

Unhooking her bra, she let it drop and then shimmied out of her panties before sliding onto his bed and seating herself in the middle. "I'm shit at this, remember? Stop making me take the lead."

Gritting his teeth, he lunged onto the bed and gathered her beneath him. "I'm sorry I said that, Sweet." He kissed her. "So sorry."

"I know," she said. Basking in the fantasy, Evie let her hand move onto his face and up into his hair. "You were right, I am a bitch. I deserved everything that you threw at me. I thought that if… that if I could have sex with you that my feelings… my attraction to you would go away."

Shaking his head, he kissed her again. "We don't want it to go away," he said, kissing her neck and down to her breasts. "Let's see what we can do about making it stronger."

Skimming his lips down the center of her body, he opened her legs and kissed her clit. Oh, that had never felt like that. His tongue moved over her quickly, slowly, tasting and circling her. He made her pant and writhe until she was driving her fingers into his hair, screaming his name.

Oh, shit.

Orgasm.

Yes. Oh, fuck.

Evie had convinced herself she didn't need it. Hadn't wanted to even touch herself for so long. But Oak made her forget everything. Absolutely everything.

While she was still bucking, and trying to find oxygen, he rose over her to flatten his body on hers. "Okay, Sweet?" he asked. "Want to stop?"

Seizing his face, she kissed him hard. Thrusting her tongue into his mouth, she only felt stronger when she tasted herself on this incredible man who was taking care of her needs before his own. Her legs opened around him, letting her enjoy the experience of him grinding his hips downwards. The thick pulse of his cock stimulated her aching clit.

"Oh, Oak, I…"

"Come, Sweet," he said, kissing her jaw and her earlobe then her neck.

Evie arched up and cried out again. "Fuck," she hissed and threw a hand over her eyes.

"No," he said, and pulled her hand down to make her look at him. "Stay with me, Sweet." Had he sensed her emotions bubbling beneath the surface?

"Want me to get a condom? Do you want me inside you? If you don't, I—"

Shaking her head, she was dismayed when his pelvis started to withdraw. "No," she screamed and grabbed for his hips. Winding her legs around him, Evie was determined to keep him near. "I'm on the pill… if you don't believe me, get a rubber, but I… for my cycle, it keeps me regular, I… if you want to go bareback—"

"Sweet," he said, kissing her. He was smiling at her. She didn't know how he was together enough to be smiling. Evie couldn't control her face, couldn't control her voice, or her body; this whole afternoon was turning into a clusterfuck. "You keep surprising me."

Next time when his hips moved, she let him have enough room to push himself into her. Groaning out, her whole body shook as he slid home. "Oh, fuck, Oak… I… I can't…"

"Yes, you can," he said, "just look at me."

Swallowing, she dropped her eyes to his and the look of smoldering desire he fixated on her made her shiver. "Fuck me," she whispered.

He shook his head and kissed her, sliding an arm under her shoulders. "Make love to me. Say it for me, Sweet."

His dick was inside her, all the way in there, fat and hard making her squirm and quake and shiver, yet he was just lying there on top of her, waiting. "Make love to me, Oakley Orion."

He'd given her so much today. He'd never know the gratitude she had for his patience and his understanding. Evie had been so afraid to tell anyone the truth that she kept herself closed off from everyone. But when Oak's hips began to move, she forgot about what he'd done for her and focused only on what he was doing now.

It felt amazing. Incredible. The thick length of

him occupying her and withdrawing, wringing her juices from deep inside her as her body responded to her need and his demand. Filling her only to tease her with emptiness, he worked slow at first, so slow she thought she'd go insane with the pace.

But as she clung to him and tried to hurry him on, he kept his rhythm steady. Only when she was wracked with a frenzy of want did he start to go faster and faster. The sensation of the easy friction built a pressure in her belly that shot down through her clit.

She clenched around him and cried out again. "Oh! Oakley, I... Oak! Oh! Oh!"

As her body spasmed around his, Oak clenched his teeth and hissed, the impact of his hips hit her hard and then he went still. Blinking at him, Evie dropped a hand to her breast as he grinned at her.

A second later, he rolled away onto his back, though his legs stayed twined with hers. "That," he sighed. "Is how it should've gone. Fuck, Sweet, can you say epic?"

For a good minute, neither of them said anything.

Evie straightened her loose arm, moving it from her breast onto his torso. Oak picked it up to link their fingers and raised it to his mouth.

"Oak," she said. "What do we do now?"

"Now," he said, straightening each of her fingers in turn, he kept his lips against the back of her hand. "I make a commitment."

The natural reaction of her body was to tense. He must have sensed it because he laughed and turned onto his side to press a hand onto her belly. "Oak—"

"Listen to what I said, *I* make a commitment. I'm not asking you for one. I'm going to commit myself to you."

"Why would you do that?" she asked.

As much as Evie knew she should get up and run away fast, she was beginning to understand that something in her had wanted to tell him the truth. She could've walked away cursing him and gone back to her life. But she hadn't, she'd opened up to him.

"Because I want to be with you," he said, sliding his hand up and down her body.

Dropping the back of her hand to her forehead, Evie sighed and admired the man who was admiring her. "You don't know who I am," she said. "I… I'm not trying to push you away, this afternoon has been…" Why couldn't he understand this wasn't as simple as good sex? That didn't solve everything. "Shit, Oak, you don't know who the fuck I am."

"I look forward to finding out," he said and kissed her, but she grabbed his shoulder and pushed him back.

"No, you don't. I'm fucked up. Seriously fucked up. It's been four years and… I still have nightmares. I still sleep with the light on. I booby-trap my apartment… I'm a crazy person."

Caressing her face, he didn't seem to be put off. "If you are, I want you to be my crazy person. I know you don't like commitment, so I'm not asking you to commit to me. I don't want to talk about the future. I just want to be with you today… and tomorrow… We'll take this one day at a time."

Why was he being so patient and understanding? "We wouldn't be able to spend nights together… I sleep with pepper spray and knives."

"Okay," he said. "I'm whatever you need me to be. If you want to let me in, I'll support whatever you need, even if it means sleeping with a machete under our pillows… But I'll wait, until you're ready to trust me and I'll take an inch at a time."

Her lips curled on their own. "I thought that was

my pussy's job."

He laughed and bowed to kiss her. "God, Evie, you're so amazing."

Teasing was instinct, it had been her defense mechanism for a long time. Being with Oak felt amazing, but it felt wrong that she should have happiness. His admiration was flattering, but misplaced. Like she'd said, he didn't really know her.

"How can you think that?" she asked. "I didn't save her. I wasn't there in time… I did nothing."

"How did you get out?"

Spreading her hand on his chest, she watched her fingers move over him. "One of the neighbors heard commotion, I think… Gemmell, he was Beth's boyfriend… her murderer… he was beating me for a while and… I pushed the floor lamp over when I fell, it smashed a window. The cops came about an hour later… But he ran off, after he… put a knife in me." Picking up Oak's hand, she pressed his fingertips to the scar on her ribs beneath her breast. "Think he thought I was dead… I was in the hospital for weeks."

"Sweet," he murmured, exuding sorrow. He pressed his hand to her scar. "I'm so sorry. I can't imagine—"

"No one can," she said. "But it's been four years, I've talked about it with Noel a lot. I can… I'm processing it."

"What about your parents? Do they support you?"

"I, uh…" Geez, this was tough. She couldn't make eye contact, but he didn't seem to be pushing her. "My dad died when I was a teenager and my mom, uh… She committed suicide the day after Gemmell was arrested."

"Fuck," he breathed out. "Sweet, how the hell did—"

"I had to testify," she said. "I had to, um… I had to get on with it, you know? She wrote me a letter, my mom…"

"What did it say?" he asked, his voice as soft as the hand he trailed over her body in comfort.

Here was the shame. When she blinked, a tear trickled out from the corner of her eye. "I never read it," she whispered and blinked her eyes to his. "How sad is that? I could never bring myself to…"

"Shh," he said, pulling her body to his again.

But Evie didn't want to cry, not again. It was nice being warm against him like this, skin-to-skin, her head tucked under his. He was so much bigger than her, and not just physically, but in confidence and sanity.

"Oak," she said, letting her lips touch him.

"Yeah, Sweet?"

"I'll hold you back."

Gathering her hair away from her face as he drew back, he smiled down at her. "You've already made me stronger."

"Breaking your dry spell or because I went all weak and girlie and made you feel like a macho man?"

"Both," he said, smacking a kiss to her forehead. "Evie, I've known that I wanted you since our first speed-date. I don't bail when things get tough."

"I need…"

Did she feel comfortable making demands? If she did, she was accepting his commitment. It didn't matter that he didn't want one from her, it was precious that he would offer her one.

He came over all serious. "What do you need?"

"I need time," she said. "To process this, I'm not… ready to be… a girlfriend. But, you're the first man I've felt anything for since before we lost Beth… and I don't take that for granted."

"Neither do I."

Evie didn't even realize she hadn't been looking at him until their eyes met again. "I wouldn't have told you the truth if I didn't trust you," she said, just figuring it out for herself. "But I'm going to say stupid things and act irrationally and… piss you off."

"This helps," he said, stroking her. "As long as you tell me what to expect, and help me to understand what you need, we'll get through it."

"But there might be times that… that I scare you."

This made him slide down a little to get closer. The intensity in his gaze grew. "Scare me? Sweet, do you think about… hurting yourself?"

"No," she said, digging her nails into him. "Not like that, I… I still have a lot of anger toward my mother for… what she did. I understand why she did it, but I would never…" Shaking her head, she tried to order her thoughts. "Noel's been my main support for years and… God, Oak, this is stupid, what the hell am I saying?" Pushing at him, she got away and shuffled to the side of the bed to look for her underwear. "Let's just forget this happened."

"Okay," he said.

Thank God, he was going to let her leave.

Picking up her panties, she pulled them on and then sought her bra. When she found his underwear, she tossed them back at him and followed them with his slacks.

"I can get a flight out tonight and—"

"You used MatchMate as a way to have safe social interactions," he said, still on the bed behind her.

She retrieved her dress from the floor. "Yes, and you have security on site and panic buttons in the rooms… not that I ever used the rooms. Noel thought it was a good idea for me to start interacting with people again. For a long time, I didn't leave the apartment. I had to for the trial and I did try to make myself go out, but… I narrowed my work to what I could do at home and was retreating into myself… I met Noel through the court. The defense wanted me to see a psychologist because they wanted to debunk my evidence. So the prosecution countered with Noel… I've been seeing him ever since."

Stepping into her dress, she wondered what had happened to the notepad she'd had earlier. It had to still be in the living room.

She saw Oak's feet first as he boosted himself off the bed. But he didn't stand up, he took her hand and drew her down to sit at his side. "You trust me, Evie. I love that about you."

Scooping her hair off her shoulder, he leaned in and kissed her. Gentle and slow, he held her head and angled her to breathe her tongue into his mouth.

A noise in the living room made them break away from each other.

A collection of voices filled the suite beyond the bedroom.

Grabbing his thigh, she turned to him. "Don't tell them, please."

"Never," he said. "Or you meant about us?"

"Us?" she asked. Seeking answers in his expression, she sagged and whimpered. "Shit, Oak, I don't have a clue what the hell we're doing, please, can we just keep this between us until we know what—"

"I'll get rid of them," he said, pushing her hair further back and kissing her quickly.

He got up and grabbed his shirt.

Whatever the debate was out in the living room, no one seemed to notice that the CEO wasn't present because they were too busy arguing with each other, giving Oak time to tuck his shirt back in.

Before he could retreat, Evie surged to her feet and ran her hands through his hair to smooth it, so he didn't look so just-fucked.

"Thank you, Sweet," he murmured and kissed the end of her nose before turning around and adopting his professional stance before he left the room.

Exhaling, she sank back down onto the side of the bed. What the hell had she done? Getting involved with the only man she'd cared about for years was a recipe for disaster. If he didn't put up with her eccentricities, he'd dump her, and she'd end up more bitter than she was pre-him.

She was just so tired. Tired of being alone all the time. Tired of feeling like no one could ever care about her. Tired of having no one to care about.

Something had happened between them, whether she chose to admit it or not.

Twisting around, she sought out the phone. Maybe her only ally could help her make sense of it, though she had a feeling he wasn't going to be happy about her giving in to impulse. All she could do was be honest, and hope that she'd find a way out of this, with or without Oakley at her side.

NINE

OAK HAD NEVER found it so difficult to switch on his professional mind. A beautiful woman who'd shared her body with him was in his bedroom. She'd ventured to take the first tentative steps of opening her trust to him. The only place in the world he wanted to be was lying with her in their warm sheets.

But it was clear from the rabble in his living room that he wasn't being given that option. "Hey, hey, what's the problem?" Oak asked Taylor, Ian, and Kody who were crowded together shouting over each other.

Ian took a step toward him. "Regent just announced that they're open to offers."

"Regent Dating are for sale?" Oak asked, glancing at each of them. "And we have different ideas on whether or not we should make a bid… Do we want Regent?"

Again, they all started to talk over each other and he couldn't pick one opinion out over the others.

All he wanted to do was get Evie in here; she'd make sense of this and help him figure out if it made sense to make a play for another company. Thinking for a second about whether or not it was weird he wanted her input on a decision about MatchMate's long-term future, he realized that instinct to include her was just another example of how sure he was about their relationship.

It might take her a while to start thinking about being with him on a permanent basis, but in time she would figure out that he wasn't going anywhere. That made MatchMate as much hers as it was his and Taylor's. Evie was their family now too.

Shaking off his urge to grin like a lovesick idiot, he held up his hands to silence his colleagues. "Okay, guys, enough. Look, if we're just getting this information, so is everyone else. We have time. There will be a bidding process and we have to find out what state Regent is in, why they're selling, and what they want. So, instead of screaming at each other, can we do this the same way we've done with every other business decision we've made for, well, ever? Put your thoughts down on paper, do some research, write a proposal, and we'll set a time for a meeting and have a proper debate."

"If we want them, we have to start courting them now," Ian said. "This weekend is the perfect chance for us to get close to their CEO and other key members who might make the decision on whose bid is successful."

Passion was never a bad thing, and Oak valued Ian's loyalty. Putting a hand to his friend's shoulder, he tried to calm his colleague's fraught nerves.

"We've known Charley and Ed a long time, we don't have to court them. But we can offer advice and friendship, we don't need to be in the game to be supportive."

Ian nodded. "I still think we should meet on this soon."

"We'll be in here for our usual briefing

tomorrow," Oak said. "We can toss ideas around then." Appeased, Ian gave his shoulder a slap. "Now, can we all get back to work?"

It was a bit rich for him to crack the whip when he'd been spending time in his bed with his woman rather than doing any work. But it was that woman who made him want these people out of here. Until they left, Evie was stuck in his bedroom.

Hmm… maybe that wasn't such a bad thing after all.

"We actually didn't come up here for that," Taylor said, grinning. His sister came over to shove Ian aside and grab his arms. She did an excited kind of scrunch thing with her face and her body. "Eee!"

"Taylor, what the—"

The knock on the suite door made the guys straighten up. Ian nodded at Kody who went toward the door. "Remember to be nice," Taylor hissed at him, smoothing a hand over his shirt. "You're creased. Damn. Way to make a good first impression, brother."

Good first impression? Taylor took his hand and began to cart him toward the door. Where were they going? Who were they greeting?

Kody opened the door and a tall blonde woman with refined features strode into the room.

"Oakley Orion," Taylor said, still pulling him forward. "Meet Lana Reading."

His sister pushed him forward toward the woman who smiled and offered her hand. "Hello," she said. "It's nice to meet you…. What should I call you?"

Taylor leaned in between them. "You can call him honey bunny, or pookie, or sexy love man… though that last one wouldn't be my preference."

Everyone, except him, laughed. "Tay," he chastised his sister before he shook Lana's hand. "Just call me Oak… But I'm sorry, Miss Reading, I didn't realize you were joining us here."

"Oh, it was sort of last minute," Lana said. "I have family in the area, so when Kody said you were traveling out here, I thought it might make sense for us to spend some time getting to know each other before… you know…"

Oh God, Lana blushed and she dropped her chin. Hmm, Evie was a smart girl. "I apologize if you went to any expense. But I don't think your…" Services? Could he use that word without making her sound like a hooker? "We've had a re-think on the strategy."

Lana's smile disappeared. Taylor stepped between them; Ian and Kody closed in too. "No, we haven't," Taylor said, smacking his arm. "Why would you say that? Lana came all the way out here. It took a lot of effort for us to organize this surprise for you."

"Well, I wish you hadn't," he said, lowering to whisper at his sister, though everyone was so close to him that there was no way this conversation was private. "We're here for business, not for… not talking."

Again, he was digging himself a hole because he'd been "not talking" with Evie not too long ago. But it was because of her that he couldn't build Lana's hopes up. It wasn't fair on either woman for him to spend time with them both. Lana was probably a wonderful woman, but she would never be his woman. It wasn't fair to let her think there was a chance she could be.

Evie wasn't as together as she portrayed. He'd just made a commitment to her and it was one he intended to honor. Being with her was going to be a rollercoaster, but somehow, he'd known that even before he'd known about her past. He wasn't going to give her any excuse to push him away and she could use Lana to do that.

"Not talking?" Lana asked.

Oak kept his attention on his unimpressed sister.

It was wrong that he felt hostile toward Lana, she'd done nothing wrong, and it was misplaced, he was really pissed at his sister and the guys.

"It's code for sex," Kody said.

Lana squawked. "I didn't… I wasn't expecting… oh my."

Taylor pinned her glare on Kody. "Good going," Taylor said. "Don't scare the poor girl."

The "poor girl" had to be older than Taylor, but it was nice that his sister was concerned for the woman who could probably take care of herself. Though at the first mention of sex, Lana seemed to waver, so maybe not.

Odd that he should think of Evie and her saucy little smile; she'd never shrink at any mention of sex. Yeah, he knew there was a reason for her need to project confidence, but it only made him more proud of her to know she was standing tall even when she was falling apart inside.

Frowning at each man in turn, Taylor reserved the worst of her displeasure for him. "I'm taking Lana," Taylor said, poking her nose in the air. "We're going to find Evie."

Taylor gestured Lana toward the door. "Evie?" Lana asked.

"Evie will fix this, she'll greet you properly," Taylor said and urged Lana forward. "And she'll tell my stupid brother to behave himself." Taylor opened the door then turned back to the trio of men. "All of you find something productive to do. Us ladies will see you at dinner and we expect all of you to act as perfect gentlemen." Kody got another shot of Taylor's scowl. "Which means no talking about sex!"

Ian raised his hand. "Uh, you might want to tell Evie that," he said like he was addressing the teacher.

But as Kody sniggered and Oak smiled, Taylor

just glared harder. "Evie is going to be pissed at all of you for scaring this woman and upsetting me." Taylor stood taller and found a grin. "I can't wait to see it."

Turning to flounce out the room with her new friend, Oak was glad to see his sister triumphant. "We'll give them a minute or two to get out of the corridor before we go back to work," Ian said out the corner of his mouth.

"Yeah," Kody said. Oak watched both men staring at the door his sister and Lana had just exited. "Except if we wait too long, we might meet Evie on her way up here to kick our asses."

Both Ian and Kody started for the door without saying anything else. Oak had to laugh at how quickly they ran out his room. It didn't matter that Ian technically hadn't done anything wrong, he didn't want to face Evie after Taylor claimed to have been upset.

He knew that his gorgeous, enigmatic Evie wouldn't be out there in the corridor because she was still tucked up in his bedroom. As he sank his hands into his pockets and began to saunter in that direction, he tried to think up any excuse he might be able to use to keep her there.

TEN

OPENING THE BEDROOM door, Oak stopped when he saw Evie sitting on the other side of the bed with her back to him and the phone to her ear.

"I know," she said into the handset that she was clutching with two hands. "Yes, I understand that... Yes..." Her voice was even, like she was listening to instructions. Then she exhaled. "I can't... Noel, I..." Okay, so she was talking to her therapist. Propping himself on the doorframe, Oak wondered if it was rude to listen in, maybe he should give her privacy. But he had to let her know that she was free to come out of the bedroom. "He won't want to." He? Oak wondered if he could be the he? Would she talk to her therapist about him? Probably, and he'd have to be okay with that. He was a new development in her life and one that he hoped she'd integrate fully. "I can't ask him... No, it's too soon... he won't—"

Stepping inside, Oak deliberately closed the door hard to startle her into turning around. "Thirteen?"

"Noel, I have to go," she said. "Yeah, he just

walked in… Okay… Bye." After replacing the phone on the hook, she got up. "Is the coast clear?"

"Noel?"

"That piss you off? I can cover the cost of the call if—"

"Don't get defensive." Leaving the door, he went to join her as she reached the end of the bed. "I don't mind… You told him about us?"

She nodded. "Before we left… I told him about the other night in your apartment," she said. "In our emergency session at the hotel. I didn't have time to leave the office to travel to him, so we met in the hotel and talked… He wasn't happy."

Shit. Oak needed the support of the therapist. He needed him on his side. If this Noel guy thought he was a bad idea, Oak would have to respect whatever was best for Evie's wellbeing, but that didn't mean he wouldn't seek a second opinion.

Catching a section of her hair between his first two fingers, he cast it back over her shoulder, hoping that she'd stop looking past him, which she seemed to do whenever they were talking about anything serious.

"Why wasn't he happy?"

Inhaling a breath, she looked so tired all of a sudden, making him realize what an emotional toll this was taking on her. "Because I'm not ready for sex… I skipped a whole bunch of steps."

Maybe they skipped a few, but they'd been on dates, and known each other more than a month. They weren't strangers and he cared about her. "Evie, Sweet, if you need to put the brakes on, I understand… But I figure that you're the best judge of what you're ready for."

It had been four years since she'd endured the trauma of losing her sister, and he didn't think he'd put pressure on her to get naked.

Growing suspicious, Oak wondered about this therapist who'd had her on his books for four years. As long as she still needed his services, Noel was getting paid.

Evie curled a hand around the side of his neck and pulled him down for a kiss. Was she looking for some more loving or about to break his heart?

"Should I get back to work or do you want me to return to HQ?"

"Work," he said, trying to take her into his arms, but she stepped back. He didn't want her to withdraw. "It's been a tough day for you, if you want some time off, we can—"

"No," she said. "I need to be… me."

So spending time with him had dredged up her trauma again. He'd have to tread carefully and find a balance between probing into her past to get to know her and embracing what she needed to be to get herself through the days while she worked to better herself.

"Do you want me to talk to Noel? About us?"

The offer seemed to startle her. "You would do that?"

Should he be afraid? "Sure," Oak said, but peered closer. "He's not going to bust my balls, is he?"

Still stunned, she blinked a bunch of times. "I have no idea."

To him, the offer wasn't all the way out there, and he had to explain his reasoning. "If the guy's important to you and you need him to help you with what you're going through then he's going to be a big part of my life too. I should have a relationship with the man, at least so he can be reassured that I'm not some sexual predator forcing you to go further than you're happy to."

"I don't think he's pissed at you," she said, moving in a step to touch his arm. "He's pissed at me."

"Are therapists supposed to get pissed at their patients?"

"We've known each other a long time," she said, intriguing him with the new slant of her mouth. "Haven't you learned that I'm not the easiest woman to get along with?"

The tilt of her chin and the thrust of her breasts distracted him from the point. Bending, he let his face hover above hers. "I'm learning that there are strategies to dealing with you."

"Hmm," she purred, angling her body so that her breasts pushed into him. She trailed a fingertip up his bicep. "I guess that's where you have an advantage over Noel."

"What's that?"

Blinking sultry eyes up at him, she caught her lower lip in her teeth. "There are strategies open to you that aren't open to any other man on the planet."

Damn. That was hot and… yep… he was hard. That was the first admission she'd made that was even close to acknowledging a relationship between them and he'd take it.

"You think our six minutes are up?" he asked.

She needed this. Needed him to tease her, to play with the confident sassy woman who got her through the tough times. Oak didn't know how he knew it, but he did read an appreciation behind the heat in her gaze, one that approved of him taking her lead.

"I haven't heard a bell, have you?"

"Thought Pavlov needed a bell before he started to drool," he said, tilting his head to bring his mouth closer to hers.

This was his woman, standing there with her head loose as she gazed up at him with those keen, tapered eyes.

"Want me to ring mine for you?" she murmured.

Dipping lower, he pulled up the front of her dress and pushed her panties aside to rub slow circles around her clit. "This one?"

"Mmm," she managed to say while gripping his upper arm tight. "Do you like my bell?"

Easing in, he kissed her slow. "I love your bell, Thirteen… She's the only one Pavlov hears."

"Will he drool for me, Oh?"

Brushing his lips up and down on hers, he nodded and asked, "Oh?"

"When I come," she panted as he let his fingertips quicken. "I… go from Oakley Orion to… to Oakley…" Curling her fist against his shoulder she brought it back to punch him lightly. "Damn." Her eyes closed. She whimpered, moving her hips against the press of his fingers on her clit. "That feels good, Oak."

"When you come…" he prompted, kissing her again.

"From Oakley, to Oak, to just… Oh!" Calling out the last word, he smiled and understood. "Thought I'd cut right to the finale."

Grabbing his shoulders, she bounced up into his arms and drove her tongue into his mouth. Oak lowered her to the bed, guiding her legs around him and loosening his own pants.

"Now, Sweet, you did say you weren't ready for this," he teased as he plunged his fingers into her pussy.

"Oh, fuck you," she said and thrust her hands to his shoulders to push him over.

Before Oak had even settled onto his back, she was climbing on top of him and sliding herself onto his dick. This was better than the last time she'd been on top. He wished that she was naked, but when he curled up and breathed against her throat, she moaned, and didn't push him away.

Kissing his way to the straps of her dress, he

pulled them down and she didn't object when he took both breasts in his hands and squeezed them together to sink his mouth into her cleavage.

Although her eyes were closed, and her head was back, Evie reached behind him and slapped his left thigh. "Bend this knee, Oh," she panted, and he did as she said.

She lay down, managing to direct her own left leg under his so she was scissored against him. Her mouth opened way before she let out the long, groan of pleasure that came from grinding herself down on him at this new angle. Hugging one arm around his crooked knee, she dug her teeth into it, then let her head bow to press her forehead against his kneecap.

Oak didn't know what to do with himself, he'd never seen a woman in such rapture. She rubbed back and forth, then rose and got into a fast rhythm before slowing to grind and ride, keeping him right on the cusp of orgasm once, twice.

"Fuck, Evie," he said, clenching his teeth to hiss when she pulled back again right before he went off.

She came though, more than once. He kept feeling the crush of her pussy around him, making him curse and crave his own release.

"Your cock is amazing," she said, hugging herself around his knee again, this time, she let her cheek rest on it as she blinked those blissed-out eyes at him through her amazing hair. Her hips were still moving, and her hand slid up under his shirt over his abs. "Let my pussy play with it."

Oak didn't remember saying anything in response, but she grinned and unhooked her bra to toss it away across the room. Grabbing his hand, she pulled him forward and he had to crunch up, but he only got a few inches when she yelped and slapped a hand onto his chest, grabbing his shirt in one sure fist.

"Oh," she screamed out and he felt that squeeze

around him again as her face fell to his knee.

Her hand opened and she began to bounce again, this time it was too much for him to hold back. She squeezed him on her last decent, and he grabbed her waist, thrusting up into her hard, filling her up with the seed she'd wrung from him.

But she wasn't disappointed by his orgasm, she grinned and let herself flop over him. "You know what I just realized?" she asked, but didn't move, she just kept her head there against his torso even as he drew her hair back from her damp forehead.

"What, Sweet?"

"This is your time too," she said with mischief in her tone. Turning her head, she rested her chin on him. "You're paying me to fuck you."

She didn't look offended, in fact, she looked… happy. He shrugged. "You're earning it. It's worth it."

Climbing up him, she tucked her forearms between their chests and rested her legs between his. "I might get used to being your whore, Mr. Orion."

"As long as you only ring your bell for me, I might be okay with that." He didn't think she was a whore, but there would be a lot of games between them, especially in the bedroom. He'd adapt to whatever she needed. Pushing up, she climbed off him and he was immediately disappointed. "We could spend the day right here."

But she was already seeking out her bra. "Change your pants, I just came over them about ten times," she said like it was no big deal. "You definitely need a shower."

Scooping up her bra, she put it on in record time, and then pulled up the straps of her dress, covering the fun times.

"I want to spend more time with Thelma and Louise," he said and loved that he made her grin, even if she did try to hide it from him.

"Well I can't leave them here for you," she said, "and I have a job to do."

"You're just going to leave me here? Spent and alone? I need my girls."

Pulling on her shoes, she did flash him a smile, then came over to drop one knee to the bed so she could lean over and kiss him quickly. "I'll bring them to dinner with me," she said, pushing his hair back from his forehead to press her lips against it.

The kiss was unexpected, quick, but… tender.

He just managed to graze his fingertips on the outside of her knee before she took it from the bed. She was so soft; her skin was like velvet. Closing his eyes, he tried not to get himself turned on again.

One thing was sure to kill that urge in him… he'd have to make a confession. "Thirteen, about dinner…"

"Uh huh?" she asked, stopping in the doorway. "You don't want me to come?"

Now he got the chance to play on her words and he flashed a smile. "I love it when you come."

"Oak," she said, angling her head left then right. "Tick, tock, what is it?"

Taylor had said something about organizing the surprise that made him wonder, "Did you know they invited Lana here?"

Evie gasped in a grin and rushed back to the bed. "She's here? Did you meet her? Is she wonderful?"

"Not as wonderful as you," he said, hoping to ensure that she knew where his priorities were.

"Oh, I know that," she said and threw herself down on the bed on her chest. He stretched his arm toward her and she turned her cheek against the inside of his forearm. "You want to invite her to join us?"

There were some games he wouldn't play. Rolling toward her, Oak stroked her cheek. "No, I don't.

I'm yours. Only yours… I tried to tell her that we didn't need her. Taylor got annoyed, said we'd talk about it at dinner. We'll send her home and—"

"No," she said, rising to move closer and rest a hand on his chest. "You need to do this. It's what's right for MatchMate."

Catching the fall of her hair on his wrist, he held it up, admiring the way it shone in the sunlight. "Yeah, but we—"

"You never intended to have sex with her," she said. "So I'm not getting in the way of anything. If you end up thinking she's your great love, I'll back off, but—"

"Evie," he snapped, pissed that she would think he'd toss her aside.

Making wide eye contact, she bowed lower, almost touching her nose to his. "Did you hear me say 'but'? Will you let me finish, please?" He conceded with a single nod. "But," she said, drawing out the word. "If we're going to be an us, then us needs to belong to us. I can't be the public face of anything, Oak. And if that's what you need—"

"I need you."

Snagging his lower lip in her teeth, she purred and rubbed her breasts on him. "Then you're going to make me happy by doing what's best for the company. You stick to the original plan and make your sister happy."

"My sister wants me to fall in love."

"Does she?" Evie murmured and dropped onto her side. Pinning his arm in place when she lay on him, she nestled against him, breathing in his ear before letting the tip of her tongue trace the outer shell. "Did she say with who?"

He shivered. Evie was the most naturally gifted sexual person he'd ever met. She was practiced in the art of feigning attraction and confidence and had studied psychology. His woman knew how to reach inside him to grab his balls and his heart in the same fucking handful.

Such a simple touch of that amazing tongue and his body reacted, then with those words that gave him permission to fall in love with her, she seduced his mind.

"Evie—"

Lunging over, he intended to scoop her body beneath his, but she laughed and dodged, rolling away to the edge of the bed in the same move, meaning all he grabbed was an armful of empty air.

"Don't lead Lana on," she said, wriggling that body as she ran her hands down her dress to straighten it out. "You make sure she knows this is a business arrangement. Be polite, be a gentleman. I don't doubt what you said about making a commitment to me. Protecting her heart, that's your priority… I don't want to get into a cat fight, I always win, and it makes me look like a bitch when they start bleeding and blubbing… and it plays havoc with my cuticles."

Propping his temple on his fist, he smiled. "You'd fight for me?"

Narrowing her eyes, she got suspicious. "Are you thinking about jello and bikinis?"

Scanning her figure, he made a show of adjusting his slacks. "Bikinis optional."

Cupping her breasts, she bowed toward him to give him a cleavage view. "I'll make you a deal. You don't play us off each other and I'll let you put jello anywhere you want."

Tempting as her cleavage was, he needed her to know he was serious. "I won't play anyone. I've never strung two women along at the same time. That's why I don't know if this is a good idea."

"You're not stringing two women along. She's

business and I'm…"

When she didn't finish, he leaned back to show her his raised brows. "What are you?"

But Evie was too good at saying only as much as she wanted to because she winked. "Not business." No, she was not. Heat began to build in the air again and he knew she felt it because she began to walk backward to the door. "I have work to do."

Scoffing, he teased by deriding himself, "Just tell that boss of yours where to get off."

Widening her curled lips, she tipped forward again and raised her chin to draw a line from her throat down into her cleavage. "How about right here, sir?"

"Come back to bed and we'll negotiate. I think I'll be able to raise you a few inches. That smart mouth looks like a good spot."

"Later, lover."

After drawing the tip of her tongue the width of her upper lip, she puckered her lips, and blew him a kiss. But as soon as she spun around, she stopped, just in the doorway. Taking his head from his fist, Oak worried something was wrong and when she turned back to look at him, there was a serious expression on her face, a hurt one… a fearful one.

"Evie?"

Her lips moved in silent words as she drew in a breath. "Taylor… I—"

He smiled. "It would be my honor to share my sister with you." When he thought about this statement, he squinted. She laughed. "Let's pretend I said that in a nicer way."

"Yeah, 'cause if you won't share Lana with me, we probably shouldn't jump straight into the sibling thing."

He shuddered. "Evie," he said, his grossed-out tone giving her the signal that he couldn't even joke about that.

With a quick salute, she took a step back. "You are a kind, sweet man, Oakley Orion. But don't you worry, I'll fuck that out of you fast."

And then she was gone. He heard her in the living room probably gathering her things and then the suite door opened and closed.

Falling onto his back, he covered his face with both hands.

Damn.

He had a girl.

He was committed.

When his arms spread wide on the bed, he was grinning. Thank fuck Evie Dewar had come into his life.

ELEVEN

DINNER WAS DELICIOUS.

Now they were enjoying the after-dinner entertainment.

The light and airy dining room they'd eaten in on the first night was upstairs in the lobby; it was a happy, open place. This dining room was in the basement, it was dark, and reserved for those in the hotel who had booths at the convention, so it was cramped. But there was space for a dancefloor and they were being looked after, so Evie couldn't complain.

The tables were long and narrow, only about two feet wide, enough for two plates and two glasses to face each other, but there was a set menu, so serving was quick and easy. They'd be in this room every night, at the same table, so Evie was confident she'd get used to it.

Everyone was facing the stage in front of the dancefloor where there was a guy doing a stand-up routine. He was good. Not hilarious, but earning a few laughs. He'd just moved onto doing magic tricks. Hmm, an interesting combination. Maybe it was his plan to screw them up on purpose, was he a comedian or a magician?

Evie was content. She was seated beside Taylor and opposite Oak who had Lana beside him. He hadn't been all that happy about his position, but he'd have to interact with his patsy eventually.

Evie and Oak were at the end of the table, which meant they could steal the occasional glance at each other whenever Taylor and Lana were occupied. It was weird to share such an intimate secret, but thrilling too.

Distracted by the sheen on Taylor's hair, Evie combed her fingers through it. Taylor didn't even glance all the way around, just turned her head enough to confirm that Evie was the one touching her before she went back to watching the comic.

Evie ran her fingers through the ends of Taylor's hair until the motion of Oak picking up his beer bottle made her glance in his direction, that was when she found him watching her. Why was he watching her and not the guy on stage who was being paid to entertain the room?

But when Evie recognized the source of that darkness formed by his hooded brow, she smiled.

Ah, so that's what he was thinking.

He wanted her.

Sliding her shoe off, Evie extended her leg to let her toe skim up the inside of his calf. One of the good things about such a narrow table was that with a slight slouch, she could stretch her toes out and press them to his cock in his slacks.

Oak's attention dropped, and he pulled his chair further in until his torso was against the edge of the table, covering what she was doing from anyone who walked by or looked, and giving her greater access to him.

The hand that wasn't clasping his beer bottle went under the table and he took hold of her foot, pushing her into him; his thickness grew and hardened. Oh, wow, he wasn't shy about rubbing her foot up and down against him.

Her own heart responded by speeding up. Evie licked her lips, keeping her eyes on his as she twisted away from Taylor's hair and laid all her attention on him, joining the first foot with the second.

"Unzip," she mouthed. The corner of his mouth tilted as he took another drink of his beer, using it as cover to shake his head. Pouting, she folded her arms, emphasizing her disappointment. "Please."

Moving her lips slowly, she felt how his dick pulsed as she massaged him. He liked her mouth and she liked to see him liking it.

The room erupted with applause and Evie did her best to be discreet about sliding her feet out of Oak's lap. Taylor and Lana straightened to face the table again.

"He was good," Lana said. "What did you think?"

"Underachiever with an inferiority complex who's desperate for his mommy's approval," Evie said, and took her eyes from the table to see those around her looking at her. "Oh, you weren't really asking? Uh, yeah, he was cute." Turning to a smiling Taylor, she combed her nails through her friend's blonde locks again. "You have very pretty hair." Picking it up, she pressed it to her nose. "It smells good too. What shampoo do you use?"

"Something the salon gives me."

Screwing up her face, Evie shook her head. "Chemicals? In your hair? No… I mix my own shampoo and conditioner. I'll give you some, it's good. Smell," Evie said, leaning to let Taylor smell her hair.

"Wow, that's really strong, what is it?"

"A bunch of stuff, all natural," Evie said and picked up Taylor's tresses again. "But yours is so shiny. Do you use shine spray?"

Taylor shook her head. "But look at yours, your hair is glossy and it bounces, it's so much nicer than mine. Oaky," she said, grabbing a length of Evie's hair and combing it through her own so their heads were touching. "Whose hair is shinier?"

Evie kept her expression serious, which wasn't easy given that Oak's was hilarious. With the top of his bottle in his lips and his arm resting over the back of Lana's chair, he froze like he'd just been asked the sixty-four-thousand-dollar question.

"What?" he asked.

"Whose hair is shinier? Mine or Evie's?" Taylor asked.

Evie loved this girl more and more every minute. Taylor adored her brother, his opinion was like gospel to her. "It's dark in here," he said.

Taylor huffed. "Are you telling me you've never noticed?"

"Your hair?" he asked. "No, Tay, I don't give a fuck about your hair."

Dropping their combined hair, Taylor stroked a hand from Evie's parting to her shoulder. "Evie's hair is so bouncy. I want bouncy hair."

"Do you want to know why your hair is fucked?" Oak asked, putting his bottle down to straighten up. "'Cause you go to that salon and spend thousands of dollars getting them to make it that fucking color." Picking up his hair on the top of his head, he tugged it. "See this... I'm your brother. Brown, dark fucking brown, that's what yours should look like."

Gasping, Evie turned to Taylor. "You're a brunette. Of course! You're a brunette!" Dropping her eyes to the table she thought about Taylor's natural color. "Is your pussy dark?"

"Oh my God!" Lana exclaimed.

Evie clamped both hands over her mouth, but

Taylor laughed. They weren't supposed to talk about sex. Well, the guys weren't supposed to, Taylor must view her as exempt. Good.

Cupping her hands around her own mouth, Taylor leaned in to seal them around Evie's ear. "I have it all waxed."

Taylor leaned back and when they made eye contact, Evie let her mouth open and she wrinkled her nose. "Really?" she mouthed. "Bare?" Taylor was blushing when she nodded. "Good for you," Evie said, picking up Taylor's hand in one hand and her wine glass in the other. "I go for the Hollywood myself, that's thinner than the Brazilian but thicker than the Playboy. Which do you prefer on a woman, Oh?"

"Suddenly I feel like I'm sitting at the wrong end of the table," Oak said, his eyes rising to the ceiling.

Evie finished her mouthful of wine and put her glass down again. "Oh, you're no stranger to a bit of manscaping," she said, but when his head tilted in time with his amused lips, she glanced at Lana. "Not that I know personally. But I can't imagine that a man as high maintenance as Mr. Orion here doesn't trim, you know?"

Lana was red in the face, but Evie guessed that might be her natural coloring. "He's… high maintenance?"

"Oh? God, yes," Evie nodded, keeping sincere eye contact. "You should see him in the morning when his bagel isn't waiting on his desk. Phew! He's in a funk *all* day. The rest of us are lucky to get out of the building with our jobs." Looking at Taylor, she noticed that the girl had barely touched her wine. "Would you like something else to drink?"

"I—"

Twisting in her chair, Evie arched her shoulders back and bowed to present her breasts as she batted her eyelashes at Oakley. "The house wine sucks."

He didn't even look at her breasts, but he did catch the waiter who was walking past. "Can we have a dirty martini and a cosmopolitan please?" he asked.

Evie couldn't believe he'd been so dumb as to forget to ask his own date. "Lana, what do you drink?" she said, doing Oak's job for him.

"Right, shit, yes, sorry, Lana?"

"Uh… Appletini," Lana said.

Evie was impressed. "Flirty," she said. The waiter took a step, but she leaned toward him and batted her eyelashes. "Will you bring him a Sam Adams, please? The strong one, whatever that is. Thank you, honey."

The waiter seemed to falter for a second, but smiled and disappeared. "Everyone set?" Oak asked, but she didn't respond.

"Okay," Evie said, taking a breath and lifting her shoulders. "Where were we? Hair. Right." Grinning, she leaned toward Oak and pretended to whisper. "See how I just deflected away from the whole carpet conversation?" Smoothing her hand out, she exhaled a whoosh. To his credit, he smiled, but he was shaking his head as he sat back. "Do you dye your hair, Lana?" Pointing to her head, Evie was explicit. "That hair."

"Uh…" Lana touched her hair and glanced at Oak.

"Oh, he doesn't care if you dye your hair," Taylor said. "Oak hasn't dyed his hair… ever… But he did get a girl's name shaved into it once."

Twisting away from the table, Oak was getting his grump on. "Taylor," he grumbled in warning.

"You did?" Evie asked, catching her chin on the heel of her hand. "Did it get you laid?"

"Nope," he said. "Got me a black eye. Her brother wasn't impressed."

Evie laughed in time with Taylor. Letting her eyes dance downward, she swung her finger at him.

"Wait, are we talking about the hair on your head or...?"

He just glared. "On my head."

"Your chances might have been better if it was down below," Evie said. "She'd have gone down there to look at it and..."

"Yeah, her brother would've loved that."

"All that event proves is that karma has foresight," Taylor said. "How many guys did you punch for talking to me?"

"Not as many as I hit for looking at you," he grumbled.

The waiter brought their drinks and Evie gave him the wine glasses to free up more space at the table. After he left they all shared a toast and relaxed. Then her clutch buzzed, and she popped it open to read the screen. It was her client for the Atlanta job she was doing after she was done with MatchMate.

"It's after hours, right?" Evie asked, lifting her eyes to Oak's.

"I guess," he said.

"You don't mind if I cheat on you then," she said, answering the call and surging to her feet. "Yes, Mr. Breen, it's late where you are, if this call is going to be inappropriate, you'll have to give me a minute to make myself alone."

"Miss Dewar, I wish to discuss the information we're sending to you tomorrow," Breen said down the phone.

"Hmm," she said, keeping her attention on Oakley. "It could go either way." Lowering the mouthpiece from her lips, she spoke to the table. "Excuse me, talk amongst yourselves. Take notes on the salacious stuff and I'll comment upon my return."

***

BREEN KNEW HOW TO TALK.

Everything he sent to her he prefaced with a phone call to explain and make excuses. Like she didn't already know that their company was in financial dire straits, and that their HR manager was responsible for the skimming operation that was putting them there.

Evie had departed the table to cross the width of the dining room. Descending the four stairs to the narrow corridor that led to the restrooms, she went past them to the end where the space opened out for the fire escapes and janitor's closets.

Pacing there, she did her best to listen and appease, but she was really just desperate to get back to the table; she'd been having fun and that was rare. Someone took her elbow and drew her sideways into the doorway of a closet, out of view of the rest of the corridor.

But she could smell Oak's cologne before he put her against the wall and ducked to kiss her neck, so Evie didn't have to panic, she could go with it.

"Well, yes, Mr. Breen," she said, stroking the back of Oak's head as he tasted her. "I will do my very best."

"This is… it's very important to us, Miss Dewar."

Oak's teeth grazed her collarbone and she gasped, digging her nails into the back of his head to scold him, but he wasn't dissuaded, in fact, his flat hand slid further down the wall as he lowered to kiss her breasts where they spilled over her neckline.

"It's very important to me too, Mr. Breen," she said, pushing her shoulders against the wall to arch into Oak's talented mouth.

He scooped a hand under her boob and plumped it into his mouth, the suction would probably leave a mark, but she wouldn't stop him, no way, not when he felt this good.

"And we do need your help."

"I know, sir," she said, her eyes drifting shut; her voice became a whisper. "I… I have to go. I'll call you when I receive the documents."

Snatching her phone from her ear before Breen could say anything else, Evie managed to hang it up though God knew how she did. Skimming her hands down Oak's back, she slipped her phone into his back pocket to free her palms for his chest.

"I'm sorry," she murmured, keeping her voice sultry, she slid her hands up over his shoulders into his hair. "Have we met?"

"Nope," he said, licking his way to her throat. "Saw you. Had to have you. Come to my room."

She loved that he played with her. Scrunching his hair, she opened her fingers. "Your hair is baby soft, but it's thick… you should be in conditioner commercials. Can I wash your hair with my shampoo?"

"If it gets you into my room, you can do whatever the hell you want." Rising, he planted his palms on the wall and kissed her mouth. "I need you, Thirteen."

"No, you don't," she said and inhaled when he pushed his groin against her belly and she felt the full, pulsing weight of him pressing into her abdomen. "Pavlov needs me."

Showing his straight white teeth in a grin, his gaze was almost feral. "Ring the bell, baby… Ring it for me."

Raising her eyes to the top corners of their sockets, she tapped a finger on her lip. "Hmm…" Growling, he swooped down to try kissing her, but she turned her hand against his mouth. "You're on a date with another woman, or did you forget?" His desire faded to panicked contrition, but she smiled. "I'm not angry, I'm saying you have to walk her back to her room… don't kiss her." He shook his head and she liked that he didn't take his mouth from her hand. "I like Lana, she seems demure… ladylike." Grinning, Evie caught his tie. "Not at all like me." She felt him inhale, but pushed her hand tighter against his mouth. "I'm going to my room now… alone… You won't let Taylor walk to her room alone, will you?" He shook his head behind her hand. Rising onto her tiptoes, she let her lips touch the back of her own hand. "You are the sexiest fucking man I have ever had the pleasure of inviting into my pussy… I'm going to let you kiss me now, and then you're going to let me walk away."

Making eye contact, she asked for agreement and only once he gave it did she let her hand slide away. It wasn't even off his chin before he'd stolen her mouth. She had to be clear on what was to happen, but she didn't want to fight with him.

When she'd said they couldn't spend the night together, she meant it. This wasn't the time to talk about her issues, she just wanted to be kissed by this man, the man who'd wormed his way into her consciousness.

Evie didn't know when it had happened, when she'd started to care about him, or when she'd started to want him to care about her. But as she wrapped her arms around Oak's neck, she pulled him close and gave him as much pleasure as he gave to her.

TWELVE

OAKLEY HAD WANTED Evie to come to his suite early and had deliberately left his own post to be here just in case she arrived before the others.

But it was only after Ian, Kody, and Lana had shown up and gotten drinks, that his door opened and Evie came in with a giggling Taylor. Seeing them together warmed him with a weird sense of pride.

They were bonding. More than that, they'd bonded. They cared about each other and that was important to him.

He'd never be able to be with a woman who didn't care about his family, and one thing Evie did for sure was care about Taylor; maybe more than she cared about him at this point.

The women exchanged whispers as they approached the seating area, but when Evie spotted him watching her, she widened her smile and narrowed her eyes.

Uh-oh.

Was she about to bite him for something or was

he going to have to start reciting baseball statistics in his mind?

"You look very handsome today, Mr. Orion," Evie said.

Glancing left and right, he waited for the other shoe to drop. "I saw you at breakfast, Thirteen," he said. Her and everyone else. He was getting tired of sharing her with every goddamn MatchMate employee who chose to sit with them… sometimes, that included Taylor. "Do I look different now?"

She waved a casual hand and he noticed a sheet of blue paper in it. "Maybe it's the light in here or something, but, wow, you are an extremely attractive man."

He couldn't hide the amusement that twisted his lips. Okay. Well if she wanted to come on over and show him just how attractive she found him in this room full of people, he wouldn't stop her. Except that fantasy was killed when Taylor laughed.

"She wants something," Taylor said.

"Hush," Evie hissed at her.

Taylor went over to the bar to the coffee pot on the end.

"Okay, Miss Dewar, what is it?" he asked, watching her clasp her hands at her lower back and twist left and right like an innocent schoolgirl.

"I have a thing… it's something you might have noticed about me," she said, batting those seductive eyelashes.

Oak let his gaze float down over her fuckable body. He'd noticed several things about her, most of which he wouldn't list in present company.

Sipping his coffee, he let her stew for a minute. "What thing?"

"I like dating events," she said, slowly, like she was confessing a shameful secret, though she did it in a loud voice.

"You want to go on a date?"

As her boss, he couldn't be annoyed about that. He couldn't even be annoyed as the owner of the dating agency she was a member of. As her guy…

"Several," she said, whipping out the blue sheet of paper from behind her back. She scampered to him and held up the flyer.

Damn. She smelled good. He couldn't even see her face because she was holding the flyer over it. But her body was within an inch of his, and the couch was right there behind him, if he just slid an arm around her back and—she shook the flyer. He cleared his throat and tried to focus.

Speed-dating.

It was a flyer for speed-dating.

When he took the piece of paper, she walked away to join Taylor at the coffee machine though she didn't pour herself anything. Good, if she was over there, he had a chance of remembering how to read English.

"This afternoon," he said. "In the convention center. You registered?"

"Yeah, she did," Taylor said. "I think it's a great idea. Everyone sits for an hour. Six minutes a date. After the hour, daters can decide whether to leave or not. It goes on all day, daters sitting and leaving every hour. There will be like three hundred simultaneous dates, it's very cool."

"You want to go on three hundred dates?" he asked, reading the details on the flyer over and over.

It was ridiculous for him to be this jealous about something that meant nothing. Evie wasn't going to fall in love with another guy in six minutes and they weren't even allowed to touch at these things, so she couldn't be felt up either.

"I'll gather useful intel for MatchMate, I

promise," she said.

"That's not your job," he said.

But she had an answer for his every objection. "I'll take Kody," she said. "If we sit on opposite sides of the arena, we'll gather twice as much data."

"I don't want to speed-date," Kody said.

"Does it really matter?" Taylor asked. "I'll do it."

"You will not," Oak said, pinning a scowl on his sister.

She was one woman he at least had some chance of controlling. He couldn't handle having both the women under his protection vulnerable at the same time.

"Why do you have a problem with Evie taking part?" Lana asked.

Shit. Why did he keep forgetting about her? But there she was, sitting on the other end of the couch, her legs crossed, her spine straight, yeah, she was ladylike, Evie was right about that. He lifted his eyes to his woman who was staring right at him.

"I don't," he said. "You want to go, you go."

"Thank you, sir," Evie said, playing up her pout as she came over to sit beside Lana on the couch.

"Now can we talk about Regent?" Ian asked.

"Yes," Oakley said, sinking down onto the couch.

Hell. Why had he done that? He'd sat here now, he couldn't move, but with Evie so close, he was mesmerized by her scent again. Right. No. Focus.

"We have to do it," Ian said, sitting on the opposite couch with Kody and Taylor. "It's an excellent opportunity to expand.

"I agree with Ian," Kody said. "We were talking about that. We're already the largest, but we can't allow any of our competitors to pick up Regent's market share."

Evie took her phone from her pocket and settled

against the back of the couch to start typing into it. Was she even listening? Did she care?

"We can put together a solid plan fast," Ian said. "I think we might be able to undercut the others. We have the personnel to make this a speedy takeover."

Confidence suggested optimism, but they had to be sensible not hasty. "Have you looked at Regent's books?" Oak asked, relaxing to rest his arms along the back of the couch. "Do we know why they're selling?"

"Personal reasons," Kody said.

Oak didn't like that and sneered. "That's a huge red flag."

"Charley's mother has been sick," Ian said. "We think they want to spend time with her before… you know."

Okay. If it was genuine personal reasons that was okay, but he'd want to verify that before he jumped to any conclusions or subscribed to gossip. Taylor wasn't saying anything, she was looking at Evie, who was still buried in her phone.

Bending his elbow, he rubbed the pad of his thumb against Evie's crown. "What do you think, Thirteen?"

Evie glanced at him, then over at Ian and Kody before returning to her phone. "Oh, me? I think it's an awful idea."

She said that like she was making passing comment on current events and not on a significant business decision that could alter the makeup of his company. "Mind filling us in on why?"

Again, she looked at everyone before moving her focus to her phone. "I'd rather not."

"Why?" he asked.

Shifting forward, she sat upright. "I can leave if you don't want me in the meeting."

"I want you in the meeting," he said. "I want

your opinion."

But her tight smile made him nervous. "Then it will cost you extra."

Rolling his eyes, he sighed. "Fine, bill me, now tell me what you think."

"Taylor knows what I think," Evie said, slouching into the back of the couch again, angled slightly more toward him. "She'll tell you for free."

"I think it's a bad idea too," Taylor said.

"Shit," Kody said, flopping back and folding his arms.

"Now, now, Kody, dear, don't have a fit," Evie said. "Oakley will listen to everyone's opinions and decide on what he thinks is best for the company."

"He listens to Taylor," Kody said. "And he likes your tits."

Thrusting them forward, Evie presented them for everyone. "Thank you… I don't think you're averse to them either."

She shimmied a bit and Oak felt another pang of jealousy. "Okay," he said, pulling her back into her seat. "Why is it a bad idea?"

"Because Regent doesn't fit with the MatchMate brand, though it's not different enough to be classified as a diversification. If you expand your brand too far you'll make it unwieldy and you'll lose your appeal, which is the personal and safe approach. Regent has had twelve reported cases of assaults on agency arranged dates in the last two years."

"We can quash that," Ian said. "We'll review their members and educate them on the MatchMate ideology."

"Perhaps," she said and lifted a shoulder. "But their regressive approach has left them in the Stone Age while other brands try to be forward thinking. They're bogged down in bureaucracy, they're not dynamic or adaptable. They're slow and stretched thin. Their personnel are inexperienced because they've suffered a cash flow issue over the last few years and can't afford to pay decent salaries. They have a vast number of under-utilized assets, but little cash on hand. They believed that recruiting a higher number of members and marketing themselves as the low-cost, high-class option would lead to increased gross profit, which it briefly did. But they had an IRS problem and have back taxes owing which severely impacts their bottom line. And, they spend a *huge* amount of money on ineffective marketing that does not provide a decent, or even acceptable, return on investment and attracts all the wrong kind of members."

"No one who is actually high-class is interested in low-cost," Taylor said.

Evie continued, "Their campaigns have drained what little equity they have, plunging them into the red while their high business rates owed in their city center locations and contractual obligations to vendors leaves them with a negative reputation in the business community as they continue to build up arrears with most of their creditors." She scanned everyone and shrugged. "In my opinion."

"You can't just—"

She cut Kody off by elevating her finger. "But, there is a light at the end of the tunnel. I would support you buying them, as is, if they dealt with lay-offs prior to finalizing the deal."

"Who would they lay off?" Ian asked.

Inhaling, she bobbed her head in a nod. "Absolutely everyone," she said. "Their only appeal is their fixed assets. If you could negotiate settlement figures with every creditor prior to sale of all fixed assets you might, *might* make a profit... but it would be marginal. The effort would be for sport rather than smart business. You have a relationship with the CEOs, talk to them, help them out with advice and personnel support… don't bail them out or you'll find yourself going down with someone else's ship."

Sitting back, she typed into her phone again. "How do you even know all of this?" Kody asked.

While still typing into her phone, she pushed her shoulders back to accentuate her breasts. "Have you met Thelma and Louise?" she muttered, still typing. "They have fun getting what they want or they'll die trying… I did research, Kody. When I heard Regent wanted to get out of the game, I talked to people to find out why."

God, he wanted to kiss her. It didn't even matter whether they bought Regent or not. It was her confidence that got him; that woman, that one right there, was his.

"I think we need to look at their books," Ian said. "To assess what their current position is. We can't make any assumptions."

"Agreed," Oak said. The guys actually looked surprised. Evie didn't flinch, and Taylor settled back wearing a grin as she crossed her legs. "We're going to go around the room and we're going to hash this out. I want to hear everything. Every voice. Every idea. Every opinion. Ian, go…"

Sitting back, he focused on his friend and listened to every word he had to say. It might take some time, but Oak would give everyone the respect of a chance to talk.

THIRTEEN

EVIE HAD HEARD EVERY word that everyone had said. So had Oakley. He was still listening even though almost everyone was on their feet. Taylor was talking to Lana about taking her to the convention center to show her around, but they were looking through the welcome pack right now. Ian was going to make some calls and get some figures. Kody was busy on his laptop doing his own research.

Oakley was writing an email on his phone.

Evie touched his arm. "Can I talk to you alone for a minute?" she asked, without hiding her request from anyone, though they were all too busy to care.

"Sure," Oak said and kept typing as he walked around the couch toward the bedroom.

He went inside, and she followed, closing the door behind them. Grabbing his phone, she threw it onto the bed and then pushed him against the wall, right next to the door. "Ev—"

Putting her finger to his lips, she winked and dropped to her knees. Opening his pants, she didn't even wait until the blood filled his cock before she took him into her mouth. Something about listening to him talk just did it for her.

Sitting beside him, so near to the man who'd said he had pledged himself to her, without being allowed to touch him, was enough of a tease. But listening to his patience. The way he'd questioned everyone like he was really listening, like he really cared… Oh, God, it got her hot.

"Shit," he hissed.

She let him hit the back of her throat and sucked harder. It had been a long time since she'd done this, but her need for him made her push so hard that the task became easy.

This was Oak who was scooping her hair from her jaw to hold it on the top of her head. He was hot and hard, throbbing against her tongue, treating her with the great girth that made it difficult for her to keep breathing even through her increased suck and extract motion.

"Oh," she said in a whisper.

Pushing her circled lips to the tip of his dick, she opened her eyes wide and lifted them to his.

Yes, she wanted that. Evie wanted him to look at her like that with those dazed eyes that fixated on her.

Opening wide, she pushed him as deep as he'd go and shook her head to take him even deeper; he swore again. She had to do this fast because she didn't want them to be interrupted, but damn, she wanted to take her time tormenting her man…

Her man? Was that what he was?

Pushing him into her cheek, Evie rubbed her thumb over his head from outside and smiled at him before taking him from her mouth and running his head from her chin down her throat to her cleavage and back up before sucking him again.

Concentrating on going as fast as she could, Evie

sucked, listening to him hiss and curse just before he spilled himself on her tongue.

The intense wash of satisfaction and power that surged through her made her proud of herself and proud of him.

Climbing to her feet, she tucked him away back into his pants. "Anything," he murmured, his body draped against the wall. "After that, you can have any damn thing you want. No Regent. Make all the decisions, I can't even care right now, that was so… Fuck, Sweet… I can't even remember words."

He tried to cup her face, but she ducked away from his hand, pushing it to his side then stepping in near again. "You want to know what I want for doing that?" He nodded, his head so loose, she knew he was still overcome. On her tiptoes, Evie got as close to his mouth as she could before she whispered, "Absolutely nothing." She smiled and patted his chest as she dropped to her heels. "Take a minute before you join us, Oh."

Leaving him there against the wall, she went back to the living room and took her place at the table. She still had some time before she was due at the speed-dating event that she was really looking forward to, and so while her man recovered, she'd do some work.

***

THIS WASN'T AS FUN as she'd thought it was going to be.

Evie actually found herself kind of paranoid and uncomfortable, but she tried not to let it show. This was a good exercise and some of the men were interesting, sort of.

The bell went, and she didn't even offer guy number nineteen a smile. Turning her phone over as she picked it up from the tabletop, Evie began to make notes.

She'd make this her last date. It had been her intention to stay for three hours, but two was proving to be as much as she could handle.

Dinner was in a couple of hours, she could go upstairs and take a shower before having a look at whatever Breen had sent to her.

"Get a lot of numbers today?"

Keeping her chin down, she forced herself to conceal her smile and to erase it before she looked up at the man seated opposite her. "Don't you look proud of yourself, sir."

Oak shrugged. "Paid your date ten grand to step aside."

Her pulse kicked. "You did not."

Though she'd prefer he'd done that than he'd been on nine dates before seating himself at her table.

"I did," he said, leaning back in his chair. He slid his ass to the front edge of his seat and drummed his hands on the table in a brief rhythm and he nodded at her phone. "What is it you're writing down in there after every date?"

"Oh, you know," she said, putting her phone face down on the table again and folding her hands over it. "Estimated cock size, predicted fetishes, clues about income, upbringing, insecurities, anything that might make it easier for me to seduce my date." His brow rose like he didn't really know whether or not to believe her. Picking up her phone again, she unlocked it and turned it to him. "See for yourself."

He only hesitated for a second before he took it and leaned forward to rest on a forearm. "Underestimated my dependence on MatchMate protocol," he read, his tone went from fed-up to surprised. His eyes flicked to hers, concern written all over them, but she smiled and nodded at the device again. "Can't relax. Don't feel safe. Too noisy. Not enough security presence… Wish Oak was here…" He sighed and put the phone down. "Baby…"

He tried to reach for her, but she picked her hands off the table in surrender. "Ah, you're not allowed to touch," she said and grinned. "It's okay. Not a big deal. It's something I started a long time ago. Noel encourages me to record my thoughts and feelings. I take notes about me. About how dates make me feel about myself. What did I like? What didn't I like? It's all about identifying my weaknesses and triggers, so I can concentrate my efforts on improving."

"If you feel unsafe, what are you doing here? You could've got up and walked away."

"No," she said, trying to make him understand. "I went through a phase where everything made me uncomfortable… Pushing through, making myself do difficult things is what's helped me to get to where I am. This is my second hour. I knew I hated it as soon as the first guy sat down, but I stayed, I did it." Pride made her smile and correct her posture. "Now I have positive emotions about my day because I'm proud of myself. I'm confident. If I'd scurried away and hidden in my room, I'd have been so angry at myself. I'd have felt like shit. Like a failure… and I hate failure."

"But, Sweet, if you wanted me here, you should've texted me or called."

"I knew you'd come," she said, letting her foot slide up his leg. "You can't stay away from me, Oh."

Watching his concern melt to an infatuated smile, she kept her demeanor cocky, but really wanted to sigh and return that look. Oak had been on her mind all day, he seemed to be on her mind a lot and when she lost herself in him she felt better about herself and her life.

"Doing my bit to ensure fidelity," he said. She tipped her head, hoping this was part of the flirt and not an accusation. "You're a valued MatchMate member; I wouldn't want you to be poached by another agency."

Opening her mouth in a silent, "Ah," she hooked her chin on the heel of her hand and rested her elbow on the table. "You might think about reducing my membership fee then. You know, MatchMate offers no incentive for loyal members. New members get all the great deals. Us old hags who are left on the shelf get gouged."

He didn't actually laugh, but he was close. "Old hags. Yes, Miss Dewar, unfortunately that is your official classification on your sealed membership records."

Sticking out her bottom lip, she feigned sorrow. "Oh, no," she whimpered. "What will become of me, Mr. Orion, if not even the best agency in the world can find a match for a lost cause like me?"

Bowing even closer, Oak took some time to admire her cleavage before he spoke. "Well, Miss Dewar, I maybe shouldn't tell you this, but there is a very exclusive position available to you."

Glancing away, she brought her ass off the chair when she looked back at him. "Mr. Orion, this position… it wouldn't happen to be on your cock, would it?"

It amazed her how serious he stayed. "Yes, Miss Dewar, an exclusive opportunity offered only to you."

Pretending to consider it, she sank into her chair again and folded her arms. "Does it come with other member benefits? Like reduced rates or preferred parking?"

With a slow nod, he remained studious. "Those options could be considered as part of the package. Though your fidelity to MatchMate would have to be assured."

"I don't do commitment," she heard herself saying.

But the words jarred. Did she…? Did she want

to do commitment with this man?

"Come up to my suite and we'll see if we can negotiate you into a position more comfortable for you."

"Oh, I'm perfectly comfortable on your cock, Mr. Orion," she said, enjoying the smolder that built in his gaze. "Unfortunately, current restrictions forbid me from making carnal appointments."

"Current restrictions?"

Lifting her hands to their environment, she reminded him where they were. "We're on a speed-date. We're not allowed to make dates outside the scope of this event… You should feel free to take note of my number and add it to your comment card."

Pushing her breast toward him, she let him look. If he'd paid off her date, Oak had no comment card; he wasn't supposed to be here. It didn't matter anyway, he knew she didn't stick around to fill in her own card because there was never anyone she wanted to see again… until him.

The buzzer sounded, indicating the end of the date and that was it, the end of her hour. Rising, she picked up her purse from the floor and dropped her phone inside. Oak stood after she did.

"You need to change that shirt," she said, sidestepping from her chair and prodding his chest with a single finger.

His chin fell to check out his apparel. "What's wrong with my shirt?"

Edging sideways around the table, Evie didn't slow as she murmured and let her eyes drift up to his as she squeezed past him. "Ding. Ding."

She couldn't make plans to meet him during their date, but technically, the date was over. To change his shirt, he'd have to go to his room, and she'd just rung the bell, so it was on.

FOURTEEN

SPENDING THE REST of the day in bed with Oak was a great plan, until it came to concentrating through dinner.

In these close quarters, Evie was sure she could smell herself on him, even though she knew they'd both taken showers. But Evie wasn't so worried about anyone suspecting what they'd done, she was more worried about herself and how enamored she was becoming with the man sitting opposite her.

It was becoming more and more difficult to maintain any distance. Sometimes she caught herself just staring at him and any time her thoughts drifted to anything in the future, she found herself including him in her ideas, like it was just a given that he'd be around.

Taylor had gone to take a call a while ago. Her phone had rung, and she'd run off wearing a grin. Evie hadn't thought anything of it at the time, but as she glanced at the vacant chair beside hers, she started to get worried.

Putting her napkin on her chair, Evie rose, and

bent over the table to cover Oak's hand with hers. "Sorry," she said to Lana for interrupting their conversation, then switched her concentration to Oak. "I'm going to check on Taylor. If we're not back in ten minutes, come find us."

He nodded. His brow dropping with concern, he turned his hand under hers, so they were palm to palm. "Is there a problem?"

Slapping a smile on her face, she didn't want to make him think anything was wrong because her panic wasn't usually justified. It was just her default to assume something awful would happen, and that's why Evie wanted to make sure back-up would follow… something she hadn't had when she walked in on Beth and Gemmell.

"No," she said. "You know how it is, guys drooling all over us babes; sometimes we need an out on hand… so if anyone asks you're my really jealous husband, okay?"

It was meant to be a joke and Lana laughed, but Oak's eyes flared. Shit. It probably wasn't smart to joke about being married when he'd only just brought up the idea of commitment yesterday. But Evie had admitted her commitment issues, several times, so he couldn't really think she meant that they'd ever get married? Could he?

Her thoughts about Oak and his opinion on what she'd said became insignificant when she didn't find Taylor in the hallway outside the restrooms. She'd watched Taylor coming this way, but Evie's back was to the hallway entrance, so Taylor could've departed again without her noticing.

Her terror level rose when she clocked the fire escape at the end of the hallway. Anyone could've come in here and grabbed Taylor.

Searching for security cameras as she raced

toward the restroom, she started to think about cops and if Oak would have the connections to get the FBI involved fast. There were two women in the restroom when she burst in and they both stepped back, but Evie didn't care if she was making an idiot of herself.

"Have you seen a blonde in here about—" The sound of sniffing stopped her and Evie zoned in on an end stall. "Tay?" Marching to the stall, she knocked on the door. "Honey, are you in there?"

The women behind her were whispering to each other as they departed the restroom, probably commenting on her crazy dramatics, but Evie didn't give a fig what anyone thought of her. The lock of the door slid back, and she stepped away to let it open.

When it opened, her heart clenched when she saw Taylor's tear-stained cheeks and red eyes. "Evie," she sniffed and lost control of her tears again.

"Oh, honey," Evie said, rushing forward to take her into her arms.

Taylor sobbed. Evie moved further into the stall to hold her tighter and close the door behind them. Whatever had caused Taylor's heart to break was contagious because she felt herself ache for the pain this innocent soul was enduring. Evie would hold her for as long as she needed comfort and then they'd come up with a plan to make everything all better again, no matter what it took.

***

EVIE WAS AWARE that she'd told Oak ten minutes, so she calmed Taylor, got part of the story, and then excused herself. She only intended to wave at Oak across the room to tell him that everything was okay.

But when she opened the restroom door, the first thing she saw was him there in the hallway, leaning against the opposite wall. She didn't know how long he'd been there, but just the fact that he was made her want to cry.

Sinking back against the doorframe of the restroom, she exhaled and closed her eyes. "Sweet?" he asked.

Blinking at him, she read the depth of his concern. "How long have you been standing there?"

"The whole time," he said. "A couple of women came out and told me about the crazy babe looking for a blonde. Figured it was you."

The whole time. That pair of women had left the restrooms seconds after she'd entered, which meant he had to have been on her tail.

Instinct made her rush the width of the corridor into his arms. "Oh," she sighed.

Cupping the back of her head, he pressed his mouth against her. "What's wrong? Is Taylor okay?"

"Yes," she said, squeezing herself closer. "I mean, no, she's not okay. But physically, she's safe."

"And that's what you were worried about, that something had happened to her physically? Sweet, if you're ever worried, you tell me. You're not alone. We're family. Tay and I care about you as much as you care about us."

Easing back, she touched his lips. "Please don't say anything mushy right now, I'm trying to hold onto my anger. I don't want to cry in public."

She appreciated him so much when he smiled after she did. He was good at that, reading what she needed and going with it, even though he probably had a bunch of questions. Losing the smile, she scowled and punched his arm.

"Hey!" he said, rubbing his arm. "Why did you do that?"

Bowing forward, she hissed. "Men. You can be

real bastards, you know that?" His whiplash was sort of funny to watch because although he tried to come up with something to say, he had nothing. "Taylor deserves better, way better."

Oak got angry immediately, like there wasn't even a full breath of time between him figuring out what she was saying and him reacting. "A guy hurt her? Who? Give me his fucking name."

Oh, shit, that was sexy. He was mad, protective, willing to spill the blood of the man who'd hurt his sister. But Evie would do horny later, they didn't have much time.

"Ethan is getting married."

"E…What?"

"At least you're as stunned as she was," she said, glancing over her shoulder.

Oak put an arm around her to move her closer to the wall, out of the way of a group who were passing to go into the restrooms. It brought their bodies closer together. When he nestled her against him like this, she could lose her reserve and let herself relax.

It made no sense to her because she hadn't trusted anyone, not since Beth. But she wanted to believe Oak would never hurt her or let her come to harm.

But right now wasn't about her, it was about Taylor. "That fucker," he snarled. "She broke up with him months ago."

"Yeah, well they were talking about getting back together. Taylor was… besotted. She talked about him like it was a done deal… she was even worried about how you'd accept him into the family after what went on between them."

"I… had no idea you two talked about that kind of thing."

"We've been having lunch together a lot," she said. "I had to make up some ground after the whole semi-naked in your office thing." That's why she called Taylor a few days into her contract, well that and because she wanted the woman to like her. In terms of time, Evie had spent more with Taylor than she had with Oak… before this trip anyway. "Hey, can we have sex in your office now?" It was nice to see one side of his mouth look so happy, but when swagger bled into his expression, she folded her arms and tipped up her chin. "Forget I asked; no sex at the office."

"Sex at the office is definitely on my agenda," he said like she hadn't made her last statement at all. "We just have to find a way to close the blinds more discreetly than last time."

True.

They'd just have to wait until everyone knew they were together. After that, discretion would be damned, and he better get used to her taking what she wanted wherever they were. Evie had no problem being forthright, not with Oak.

The more people who knew he belonged to her, the less chance she'd lose him to competition… And if guys knew she belonged to Oak, she'd have to worry about fewer approaching her…

Yes, she'd have to be open about their sexual relationship, and make sure the world knew there wasn't a man alive able to satisfy her like Oak, then she'd be safe. Everyone would stay away from her.

Slowly, her eyes closed. Resignation filled her with dread. "Shit," she exhaled.

"What?" Oak asked, lifting her chin with a finger. "Sweet, what's wrong?"

"Nothing," she said, pulling away from his finger. "I just had a stupid thought that I shouldn't have had… it's becoming a bad habit."

"A stupid thought about what?"

It was sweet that he looked so worried, but she

put a hand on his chest and straightened up. "Taylor wants to go upstairs to get drunk."

"Okay," he said. "You were thinking about—"

"No, forget my thoughts. This is a new conversation." The poor guy looked so confused, but she carried on. "I… I'll go to her room with her, we'll watch sad movies, drink, and talk shit about guys. So, I apologize in advance, but your gender is going to take a hit tonight."

He exhaled a smile. "I forgive you."

When he ducked to kiss her, she slid down the wall and for the first time, ever, she appealed to someone, non-medical for help. "I need you to listen to me. I need you to do something for me," she said. "It's important… Important like if you don't do it, we'll be through because I won't be able to trust you anymore."

"I'll do anything," he said. "What do you need?"

Swallowing, she tried to forget about the fact that she hadn't spent the night with anyone or without her traps since before Beth. "At midnight, come to Taylor's room."

"Okay."

"Don't just knock and walk away. You have to see both of us, okay? Both of us. Don't take the other one's word for anything. And if we don't answer the door, you find a way to talk the manager into letting you in, okay? You have to see both of us." It was impossible to express how important this was because it probably didn't make sense to him why she was so adamant about it. "I know I'm a crazy person and if you want to dump my ass after tonight, that's fine, but I—"

He skimmed a hand over her hair. "I'm always looking for excuses to see you, and you've just given me one. I'm grateful, not pissed."

"Both of us," she said, not letting him make this into something romantic. "You put eyes on both of us.

Check for pulses if you have to… if someone gets into the room and—"

"I understand, Sweet," he whispered. "I promise you'll both be protected. I won't take your safety for granted. I'll check on you both."

Somehow, his reassurance helped to dispel her anxiety. "Thank you, Oakley."

"But…"

Uh-oh, a but? Was he going to make an excuse and back out? "Oakley Orion—"

"Why don't you get drunk in the suite?" he said. She was so taken aback that she sealed her lips. "There's a bar in there, better to drink from full-sized bottles than crappy miniatures. You can spread out in the living room, I'll leave you both alone, then you can share the bedroom when you pass out. I'll stay sober and sleep on the couch, right outside the door in case you need anything or feel unsafe."

Could that work? She was fine with the drinking part, but she wasn't so wild about spending the night with Taylor. But the girl needed a friend and if she got upset, Evie didn't want to be clock watching or making her think that she was a burden.

"Okay," she said. "That might work." She stuck a stern finger into his chest. "But this is about what's best for Taylor, do you understand?"

"No sex," he said with a straight face.

She had some of the wind taken from her sails. "Exactly. No sex for you."

"For me?" he asked, wearing a mischievous grin. "For no one, I hope."

"Well, I will be sleeping with Taylor," she said, getting sly. "She's vulnerable and might need comfort." Cutting off the tease, she gasped. "Can you make sure the sheets are changed? This afternoon, we—"

"I called housekeeping before I came down to

dinner," he said, "I figured you'd want fresh sheets to soil tonight."

In mock offense, she let her mouth fall open. "How dare you! I will never spend the night with you, Mr. Orion, I thought I made that clear."

As teasing as it was, there was a thread of truth to that statement, but Oak seemed to miss it. "But you'll sleep with my sister?"

"Your sister is sweet as a button… You're nothing but carnal urges." When he swayed closer, she had to ease him back. "You keep them to yourself. I have to get back to my favorite girl." Pushing him aside, she took one step away from the wall, then swung back around to face him, holding up a finger like she had an afterthought when really this was the most important item on her agenda. "Oh, one more thing."

"Yes, Sweet?"

Shaking her head, the last thing she felt was sweet. Evie narrowed her eyes and glared so hard that he shrank. "Hurt him."

"What?"

"This Ethan fucker. I want him punished… I'm not telling you to go and kick his ass, nothing so direct. Everything we do should be indirect. Keep yourself half a step away so nothing can be pinned to us, but close enough that the next time you lay your eyes on this bastard, you can raise your glass and wink at him and he'll know not to fuck with your family ever again."

"Evie—"

"I'd do it myself, but I'm going to hold Taylor for a few days, she'll be my focus. I figure you might have the connections to hurt him hard and fast. I want him to lose… everything if possible. His job. His apartment. His car. I don't care if he loses the girl, might be best if he doesn't because I don't want him near Taylor, but I don't give a fuck if his heart is broken. And we'll make sure

Taylor is protected. Call his boss, or his boss' wife, his brother, anyone who can hurt this fucker. Call in a favor. I don't give a damn how you do it, Oakley. But you take him apart and know that I will always hold a grudge against this guy for as long as I live and as long as you're with me I'll demand that you hold one too. Taylor is too sweet, she'll forgive him, probably sooner than she should. In a few days, this Ethan guy will call her, she'll soften, maybe start to feel sorry for him, and then the excuses will start… When Taylor starts that, you don't take it, get angry, tell her you won't hear her making excuses for the bastard. You'll fight, and she'll hate you… your relationship will take a hit and you'll want to relent, don't.

"She'll come to me, and I'll make her see that you're right, but I'll do it nicer, softer, then she's going to come to you and apologize and that's when you hold her. She'll cry. She'll need your support. She'll ask you why it hurts so bad. She'll ask you to take that pain away and your heart will break. She'll need you to promise that Ethan will never hurt her again… and you will make her that promise, Oakley Orion, because you and me are going to make sure this fuck never lays a hand on Taylor again. We won't let him get back into her head. Do you understand me?" With his mouth open and his expression stunned, he managed a loose nod. Twisting a saucy smile to her lips, she angled her hips and drew a fingertip down his tie. "If you do this for me, and defend your sister with everything you have, I'm going to find it very difficult to keep my clothes on around you. It will be very… very hard."

Purring each word while she pouted, she parted her lips as she looked at his, thinking about how sweet his kiss would taste right now.

"Our family," he breathed out though it seemed to be a struggle.

"What?"

"You said he would never hurt my family again," he said. "You meant our family."

The bottom fell out of her stomach and her pout became a gape. "Oakley—"

"You had a whole plan… you found this out ten minutes ago and… you have a whole plan," he said like he was impressed and awed and…

"I care about Taylor. I'm not even sure I care if I'm overstepping the mark," she said. "I want to protect her. It's not my place to tell you how to handle your relationship with her. I just know how women like—"

"Your advice is precious to me," he said, opening his hand on her cheek. "I'll say exactly what you want me to say. The fighting part I can handle, I wouldn't listen to her excuses anyway, that's for damn sure. The guy can rot in hell."

"That's too good for him," she said and shivered when Oak smiled.

"Right. You're right." His caress was making her forget that they were in a public hallway and shouldn't be touching each other at all. It gave her such comfort that she relaxed into it, how could he make her feel so safe and cherished just by putting one hand on her face? "You just tell me what she needs to hear when she comes to me after, when she's upset. I want to say the right thing. To say what she needs to hear to make her feel better."

"I love you," she whispered and when his hand stopped stroking, she regained some of her wits. Shit, what did she just say? "Taylor… that's what Taylor needs you to say, all she needs you to say. She needs you to say, I love you."

"I love you," he murmured, looking right into her eyes as he smoothed his fingers over her cheek again. "I can handle saying that 'cause I mean it."

Had they just…? No. They hadn't. That was…

they weren't even talking about them.

"She's, uh…" Damn, Evie told herself to get it together. "Taylor is… she doesn't want to talk about it. She said she just wants to get hammered, so… we'll get drunk… and then we'll talk. Don't pressure her to talk to you tonight."

"No pressure," he said.

His hand was still tormenting her face and her hormones were clouding her sense, but she needed to focus on Taylor. Pulling his arm down, she pushed it to his side. "I'm going back into the restroom, you go back to the table and I'll maybe see you later."

He caught her arm when she retreated. "You're a good friend, Evie. Thank you for taking care of Tay."

Sliding her arm from his grip, she backed a step toward the restroom. "You work on making it difficult for me to keep my clothes on, Oh."

Winking at him, she turned away to go back into the restroom to retrieve Taylor. Evie would do whatever it took to comfort her friend and had confidence that Oak would relish the task she'd put to him.

FIFTEEN

OPENING HIS EYES from their sleep, Oak intended to stretch out like he did every morning. But he paused when he registered the press of a body laid out on his. Blinking down, he saw he had both arms around his slumbering Evie. Facing each other, they didn't have a lot of space on this couch, but it didn't matter, he was pleased of the excuse to hold her so close.

By the time he'd gotten back to the suite last night, both Evie and Taylor were in the bedroom, wearing his tee-shirts, hollering and laughing. It sounded like they were having the time of their lives, so he'd left them to it and gone to sleep on the couch.

Hours after that, he'd been woken up by Evie sitting on him. She wasn't making a move, he doubted she'd even been aware of him before she'd dropped onto the couch with a plan to put on her shoes. It just so happened his body was between her ass and the seat.

She'd apologized and tried to slip away, explaining that she was going to her room.

But that's when they'd met their dilemma.

Oak wanted to walk her to her room. Except Evie didn't want Taylor to be left alone. But, Oak hadn't wanted Evie going anywhere on her own so late when she was drunk and vulnerable.

His woman had still been drunk enough that when he suggested they cuddle until they came up with a solution, Evie hadn't put up much of a fight.

Maybe she'd known they'd fall asleep together and just needed the excuse to crawl into his arms, or maybe she was just too drunk to think about it too much. Either way, it worked out for him because he'd just woken in the sunlight with his woman pressed against him. He couldn't imagine a better way to start the day.

Smiling at her sleeping figure, he wondered if he'd get away with sliding his hand down—someone cleared their throat.

Turning his head, he found his unimpressed sister standing at the end of the couch, her arms folded and her foot tapping. "What do you think you're doing?" Taylor asked.

"Nothing," he said, his gruff voice still switching from asleep to awake.

"You took advantage of her," Taylor hissed.

"No!" he objected. "We're dressed." Pushing the blanket from his torso and Evie's, he couldn't reach to push it further. Though he was pretty pleased about that because his morning wood hadn't dropped yet. But he showed his sister that they were both wearing tee-shirts at least. "Nothing happened."

That had the advantage of being true, they hadn't even kissed… not on this couch… not last night anyway.

"Oh," Evie murmured and, fuck, her leg slid up over his thigh to curl around his hip.

Grinding herself close to him, she wasn't helping him get rid of his morning glory. The damn woman encouraged his dick even when she was unconscious.

"She's having a dream or something," Taylor said, waving her hands at her brother. "Move before she wakes up embarrassed."

Taylor obviously hadn't figured out that Evie's use of "Oh" was actually a reference to him. But for right now, that was okay with him. Oak had seen Evie turned on. He'd seen her happy, both real and faking it. He'd seen her sad, devastated, falling apart, and angry. Boy, had he seen her angry. But he'd never seen her embarrassed, not about sex.

Shifting a little to position himself on his back, Oak kept an arm around Evie and curled the other behind his head. "I don't think Evie gets embarrassed about sex stuff," he said.

This new position worked out for him because his girl's thigh was resting over his groin, giving him cover for anything going on beneath the blanket.

Taylor thrust her hands to her hips. "So that makes it okay for you to take advantage of her while she's unconscious? Oakley! I thought you were a better man than this!"

Disappointing Taylor hurt his heart, but Evie broke the fraught moment when she whined and stretched, opening her hand on his chest to close it again in a tight fist that scrunched his shirt. "I smell Oak," she murmured and turned her head up.

He only had one second to think about what he'd do if Evie tried to kiss him because Taylor spoke before his girl got the chance to make a move on him. "That's because you're lying on Oak."

Evie lifted her head, blinking dazed, sleepy eyes at him, then at Taylor, then back at him. "Oh shit," Evie sighed out, but let her head fall hard onto his chest. "Did I accidently fuck my boss again?"

Again? He hoped that was a joke. "He says nothing happened," Taylor said.

Turned out that the blanket wasn't great cover after all. Evie made no secret of what she was doing when she slid the sole of her foot up his thigh and drew one of her knees high to touch her crotch.

"Still wearing panties," she said and then picked up her fingers to look at them. "No spunk… we're good."

When his sister laughed, he breathed a mental sigh of relief. "You're outrageous, Evie," Taylor said.

It was amazing that his sister could laugh given what she'd learned about her ex last night. If Evie hadn't been here, he couldn't see how Tay could ever be laughing so soon after getting the news about Ethan.

"Due diligence," Evie said and stretched again.

"You'd probably have used a condom…" Taylor said. "I hope to God you would have used a condom."

"Then check the trash," Evie said. "And go fill that amazing Jacuzzi tub in Oak's bathroom, I want to wash your hair."

Taylor sighed and shook her head. "Let's not tell Lana about this."

His sister walked away, and the bedroom door closed a second later.

Oak was about to get up, but before he could, Evie slithered on top of him and touched her fingers to his lips. "Nothing happened?" she asked. "I'm wet, like happy to be hanging with Pavlov wet."

"You were dreaming and wriggling around." Opening his lips, he tasted her, grabbing for her wrist to suck her fingers into his mouth. "One thing happened, you spent the night with me, that happened," he said, recognizing the significance of the last few hours. "But that's not what Taylor meant."

"Yeah, well, don't get used to it," she said, boosting herself higher to find his mouth with hers.

Sliding her wrist out of his grip, she took hold of

his instead to guide his hand under the blanket and onto her ass.

His boner woke up again and no time later, his fingers were insinuating their way into her underwear. "Think we can be quick?"

Evie smiled, rubbing her lips on his. "With Taylor a door away? We didn't do anything last night and she was passed out sleeping, she'll walk back through that door any second and you want to have sex?"

"Would it be so bad?"

He got just a glimpse of her quick grin before she bit his chin and sat up. Letting one leg drape off the front of the couch as the other crooked between his hip and the backrest, she rocked her hips, grinding into him.

"If your sister walked out of the bedroom to see me riding you? Yeah, I think that might be bad."

Clutching for her hips, he hissed through gritted teeth. "Not the sex," he managed to force out the words. "Would it be so bad if she… knew about us?"

Evie stopped moving and breathed out before climbing off him to stand up. Rolling onto his side, Oak caught her ankle before she could walk away from him.

After glaring at his hand, she drew her eyes up to his. "You appear to be holding onto my ankle, Mr. Orion."

Shit. She was pissed… or was she playing? At this early hour of the day he wasn't perceptive enough to read her. But, damn, Evie didn't have that problem. Apparently, she was 'on' from the minute she opened her eyes.

"You're gorgeous," he said, trying a compliment. "I want to wake up with you every day… whatever it takes."

Compassion softened her, or maybe pity was a better description. There was an equal chance that it was guilt that caused her to look at him with such sympathy;

she'd told him they couldn't spend the night together, so he assumed she was going to tell him last night wouldn't be repeated any time soon.

Whatever it was, she cut him a break. "If Taylor knows we're a thing, we can't offer opposing support with the whole Ethan mess."

Keeping them a secret was for Taylor's benefit?

Loosening his hand, Oak sagged onto his back again. This woman just kept impressing him; worming her way deeper into his affections with every second that passed.

"Shit, Thirteen, are you trying to wreck me?" he asked.

Because she was damn close to doing it.

"No," she said and puckered her lips while a glint of mischief flickered in her eyes.

He was still wondering how he'd got such an amazing girl, when she bent at the waist, yanked the blanket down and pulled his dick from his shorts. "Fuck, Thirte—"

Kissing his head, she opened her mouth and sucked him in hard. But it was the long moan of pleasure that came from her throat that made him groan. Sinking a hand into her thigh gap, he yanked her ass in his direction and spanked her hard. Her mouth left his dick in a laugh and that sound of joy made his cock throb for her. Had he just made her happy? Did he make her happy?

Dropping onto her knees, Evie faced him and pulled the blanket over his lap again, but kept her hand underneath it. "I'll finish you later," she purred, rubbing her hand over his balls before she took his shaft and squeezed it tight.

"I'm just supposed to lie here all day and wait?"

When she laughed again, a burst of pride fueled his own happiness. He'd known she made him happy before, but being like this, so overwhelmed with joy at making her smile? Wow, he was a goner for sure.

"We're due at breakfast with everyone in a while… and we have a meeting in here tonight before your big date."

Oops, was he supposed to have made a reservation? Evie did have a habit of making him forget pertinent facts. "My big date?" he asked, amazed that they could be having a conversation while she jerked her tight fist up and down his solid dick. "Remind me, where are we going?"

"Not with me," she said, digging her nails into his arm. "You're going to dinner alone with Lana."

"Since when?" His sitting up forced her hand away from his dick and he put his feet on the floor on either side of her. "When the hell did I start getting left out of all the decisions?"

Taylor came out of the bedroom. It was Evie who had the presence of mind to bundle the blanket in his lap and lean back against the coffee table to make their position look less intimate. "You're right, that tub looks amazing," Taylor said then looked at him. "Uh-oh, what's wrong with your face? Did you touch Evie inappropriately? Bet she knows how to slap a guy down."

"Hard," Evie called out as Taylor made her way to the coffee machine.

Evie winked at him before climbing to her feet, putting her ass in his face. He wanted to bite her. To reach under his tee-shirt that was draped over her body, pull down those panties and bend her over.

Damn.

Why did Taylor have to be here this morning of all mornings?

Though the truth was, it was only because of Taylor that Evie was here at all.

Her ass came even closer. Whatever she wanted,

she'd get, he just didn't know what it was. Quickly putting his hand under the tee-shirt, he gave her ass a brief pat and then she was walking away toward Taylor.

"I'm getting in the tub after you, Tay," Evie said. "I only have the excuse to use it 'cause you're here."

The women whispered and laughed at the bar while they made coffee. Evie could use the tub any damn time she liked, he'd get an identical one installed at his place too if it meant she'd come over and get naked.

Thinking a few steps ahead, he wanted to know when they could start living together. He'd have to convince her to stay with MatchMate first… though he could be with her even if she wasn't a permanent employee. She was good at her job; it was no surprise that she was in demand.

Before either of those things, he'd have to talk her into being with him, getting her used to the language of being "together" of having a "boyfriend" of being in "love".

A smile warmed his lips. They'd said it last night, real or not, it felt real and he liked it. Oak hadn't thought about using those words with her because he'd assumed it was too soon. When he'd heard them from her lips, he'd known he wanted to hear them again.

Just like when she cast him in the role of jealous husband. She might not have meant it seriously in that moment, but just the notion sliding from her tongue was enough to plant the seed in his mind. Oak did want to be married, like he'd said to Taylor, he wanted to jump into a commitment as soon as he found a woman he wanted to be with and he'd never wanted to be with a woman as much as he wanted to be with Evie Dewar. Evie Orion… had a nice ring to it.

Of course, none of that would happen if he didn't first figure out a way to make spending the night together a regular thing.

"What are you smiling about, brother?" Taylor asked.

Lifting his head, he saw Evie on her way to him carrying a mug of coffee.

Bending at the waist, she played up those plump lips and tapered eyes. "Your morning coffee, sir," she said in her best vixen voice.

Taylor laughed again. "Don't play with him, Evie, Oak isn't a morning person," she said and began to head toward the bedroom, not that he noticed except out the corner of his eye. "I'm going to get in the tub. Oak, don't come in there, I'm leaving the door open for Evie, but I won't have clothes on."

After the bedroom door closed, Evie fell to her knees between his feet again. "Not a morning person?" Evie asked, pushing the blankets away. "Let's see if I can help wake you up."

He resented the mug in his hand when she took him into her mouth again. Shit. This woman was going to kill him. Yep, she was actually going to kill him.

SIXTEEN

THE DAY HADN'T GONE so bad. After Evie was done with Oak's dick, she'd gone to get her shampoo and other things she needed to pamper Taylor in the tub. She felt good about cheering Taylor up. And as she refilled the tub after Taylor's soak, the women talked some more about the Ethan situation.

Taylor had to go to her own room to get changed, so she'd left Evie in the tub. Just before her new friend departed the bathroom, Evie told her to make sure Oak knew she was naked in his tub. Taylor thought the warning was meant to keep him out, to protect her modesty. But Evie hadn't even lifted her head from the towel she was using as a pillow when she heard him sliding into the water with her a couple of minutes later.

The rest of the day was a blur of paperwork and meetings. They only had one more full day here tomorrow. After the farewell party the following night, they'd all have to pack and be ready to go back to HQ.

Evie had enjoyed having dinner with Taylor and the guys. Having their company actually made it easier to forget that Oak was on a date with Lana. A business date. That's all it was.

She was in her room brushing her teeth, getting ready for bed, when she heard the tapping on her door. Rinsing her mouth, she wiped it with the towel then went to peek through the peephole. It had to be close to midnight, no one should be here this late.

When she saw Oak, she smiled and rolled her eyes. Opening the door, she didn't say a word while she waited for an explanation. His first move was to duck and kiss her.

Pushing on his shoulder, she separated their mouths. "Is there a problem? Is it Taylor?" she asked.

"Pavlov," he said, scanning her figure.

Giving him points for honesty, she exhaled a smile. "Pavlov can wait until it's daylight."

She tried to close the door, but he moved forward a step. "Okay, I'm lying. It's not him, it's me."

Something about his demeanor made her examine him more closely. "Did something happen with Lana? Did you sleep with her?"

"What? Fuck, no! Thirteen! How could you—"

"You kissed her?" she said like she was making guesses on a game show. "You were attracted to her?" God, men and their… whatever. "Oakley, it's okay. I told you if—"

"This is nothing to do with Lana," he said. "We had a perfectly benign evening. There's nothing wrong with her. Nothing exciting about her either. I just… I miss you."

"We had sex in the tub this morning," she said. "After I blew you."

Hope widened his eyes. "Yes, see, I owe you… I gotta owe you a couple now. Let me come in and make it up to you."

"I thought this wasn't about Pavlov."

"It's not," he said, edging even closer. "It's about his Bell."

Reaching forward, he tried to slide his hand into the front of her shorts. He was persistent, but she intercepted him, threading her fingers through his to guide them away.

"Bell isn't ringing for you tonight," she said. "She might ring for me, but—"

He groaned, and his forehead fell against the doorframe with a thud. "You're torturing me."

No, she wasn't. Why was he so attractive? And so obstinate? He stayed there with his eyes closed and his forehead against the frame of her door and she wished things were different. Evie wished she could be like any other woman, that she could be the woman he deserved. Maybe this was a good time to explain to him how she never would be.

"I'm going to show you something," she said.

With their already linked fingers, she drew him into the room and let the door close at his back. He stayed behind her as she led him past the bathroom. She stopped just at the end of the short hallway and stepped over the tripwire she had setup. Leaving him on the other side of it, she crouched to twang it.

"I have a bunch of these set up in my apartment," she said, and twisted to look at the push pins she had spread on the carpet. "They're not meant to kill anyone, they're meant to slow them down, to surprise them and hopefully make them call out to warn me that they're there." Standing up, she linked her fingers back to back behind her. "I have trip wires that trigger strobes too; they're disorientating." Opening her arms, she showed him her outfit. "I sleep in shorts and tanks when it's warm. Sweats and hoodies when it's cold." Standing back, she nodded at the sneakers on the floor. "I have shoes at both sides of the bed and if it's a bad night, I sleep wearing them."

He hadn't stepped over the tripwire, but rested a shoulder on the wall. "Sweet—"

Pulling the blanket back on the bed, she showed that she had a wall of pillows on either side, making a trench in the middle. "I sleep flat between the pillows, so if someone comes in, they don't know if I'm alone or exactly where I am if they want to attack while I'm asleep." Driving her hands under the pillows, she started to pull out her weapons. "I have pepper spray, knives, daggers, rape alarms, screwdrivers… I used to have a hammer, but it scared me, I don't know why… I have a Taser at home… couldn't bring that on the flight though… I collect things wherever I am and use them… There's broken glass on the windowsills," she said, looking over her shoulder toward the window. Climbing off the other side of the bed, she went to the curtain and pulled it back to show the pressure sensors on the floor beneath them. "And I have alarms on all the window frames even though the windows don't open…" She pointed upward. "I hide cameras in the smoke detectors or the air conditioner. They transmit to my cell and I check them before I come into the room. I have four cell phones in this room, all programmed with speed-dial and speech recognition to dial 9-1-1 with the right command… and as soon as you leave this room I'll set up more alarms and traps behind the door… I hate doors." Nodding to the vent on the ceiling, she smiled. "I put glue seals around the vents and tape razor blades in the slats… You want to know why I went to dinner early the first night we were here? Because I have to set all this up while it's daylight. It has to be done before the night. It has to… and it takes a long time for me to put everything together and rig all the traps… I'm not the most dexterous person."

Sorrow welled in his intent expression. "Ev—"

"You want to know what's really sad though?" she asked, crawling over the bed to bypass the pins scattered on the floor at the end. Going to him, she stopped beside the corner he was leaning on. "She trusted him. He wasn't even a stranger. I do all this…" She turned to sweep her arm around at the room before she looked at him again. "As if it somehow protects me. But my sister wasn't killed by an intruder. He wasn't a psychopathic serial killer. She wasn't just in the wrong place at the wrong time. He wasn't satisfying a compulsion brought on by an illness. Do you want to know why he killed her?"

"Why?" Oak asked, but when he tried to touch her face, she swatted his hand away.

Angry, bitter, and unfulfilled, she whispered. "Because he could."

"Evie," he said and straightened up.

She shook her head. "That was what he said, that was his reason. The head doctors talked to him, dozens of them, none of them found anything wrong with him. He's never apologized. He shows no remorse. He did it because she trusted him… because she let him get close enough to hurt her… He didn't hate her."

"He didn't love her."

"No," she agreed. Her gaze drifted to the pins on the floor. "But can you imagine that moment… the moment when he had his hands around her throat… Beth knew what was happening. She knew her killer. She looked into his eyes as she took her last breath… That was the last thing she ever saw… She saw him enjoy it."

Oak put an arm around her shoulders and pulled her to him, kissing her hair. Evie didn't unfold her arms, her shoulder bumped his chest and she didn't fight him, but she didn't encourage him either.

Whenever she thought about Beth and that night it felt surreal. It was so long ago, but there were still so many things about that night, about what happened, that made no sense to her.

"You put him in jail," Oak said. "You don't have to be afraid of him anymore and wherever Beth is, she's looking down on you proud of what you did."

Gemmell's sentence was life, though he was still going through the various appeals processes. But it wasn't really him she feared. "Walking in… it took me a minute to realize what I was seeing," she said. "I… As soon as I realized Beth was… dead, I… I started to grieve, like that very first second, I tried to pick her up. I tried to… I didn't even realize it was him, I didn't even see him… I was surprised… taken off guard…"

"That's what you fear," he said, sliding his hand over her shoulder into her hair, around to the opposite side of her neck; all the time, keeping his mouth in her locks. "You fear being taken by surprise… that's the point of all this. You're trying to prepare for any possible eventuality."

"Yes," she said, knowing that was the point. Evie also prepared for fire and flood, and other types of emergency too. Though her compulsions and anxieties only flared at night for some reason. Twisting, she pushed him, pulling his hand away from her to put some space between them. "But it was the relationship I obsessed about for years… not even the sex, there was no sexual assault. I don't have sexual hang ups, it's the trust… the bond of their relationship…that's what caused me to keep seeing Noel, and to join MatchMate. She trusted him. My sister trusted the man who murdered her." It was impossible to convey how incredible and heartbreaking that truth was to her. So many people didn't get it. "Imagine the one person in your life who's supposed to love you and share your life with you… imagine that person being the one who turns on you. I mean… how does someone even tell who is going to turn like that? How can you tell if your trust in your lover… the man you love… how can you tell if that's misplaced? How do you know if you've gotten it wrong?" Something made her look at his hands and a slow urge made her pick them up. "Could these hands kill me?"

Shock shot through him. "No!" he said and tried to pull away, but she grabbed his wrists, digging her nails in deep as she gripped him tight. "Evie! Stop it! There's no goddamn way!"

Moving closer, she raised them to her neck, but he kept his hands in fists. "Hold me."

"No," he said, his stern eyes weren't angry, but his worry was severe. "I would never hurt you, Evie. I promise you, there's no way that—"

"Prove it," she said. "Put your hands around my throat."

The tilt of his head suggested pain, and it was intensified when his eyes tapered. "Sweet, I won't hurt you."

"What if I fall in love with you and then one day you decide you want to know what it's like?"

"Evie," he whispered in a pant. "I already love you and I would tear apart any person who thought about hurting you." Although she still had hold of them, he lifted his hands and let his fists graze her cheeks. "And I don't want to be in any world that doesn't have you in it."

"You can't leave Taylor," she said, panicked by the gravity of his statement; it reminded her of what her mother had done. "Promise me, Oak. You'd never hurt yourself? Would you? Not for me. Not for anyone."

"Sweet," he said, still stroking her; his fingers loosened a little. "I'm going to protect you with my life, and Taylor too… I won't ever leave you. I won't leave either of you… And I won't ever hurt you."

There was something safe about him. Probably some part of her that considered him the epitome of safe simply because he was the guy responsible for all the safety measures in place at MatchMate.

"I'm terrified of getting it wrong, Oak," she admitted in a single exhale.

Her eyes were warming. The last thing she wanted to do was cry in front of him again. Evie was supposed to be putting her life together. She'd been grieving for years, faced so many demons and conquered every one. But like she'd said to him at speed-dating, she had to force herself to do what was difficult even if it meant she was unsafe. It was the only way to take a positive from a negative, to give her fear productivity. She had to tell the truth even though the idea of being exposed made her heart beat in her throat.

"Don't ever fear me, Sweet," he said, skimming a hand up to brush the hair from her temple. "I'm not capable of hurting someone who's so precious to me."

"I can't commit myself to you… not while I'm this fucked up."

He smiled. "I'll wait. I'm sorry if I rushed you, but… I want to know this stuff. I want to help you. I want to be the guy you let in."

"It doesn't scare you?"

"It scares me that you think I might ever hurt you," he said. "But we'll take our time and you'll see…" As he scanned the room behind her, she didn't see any indication that he was repulsed or freaked, but he could be a good actor. "I don't want to take any of this away from you. I would like it if you trusted me to take care of you and protect you, but if this is what you need…" There wasn't a hint of hesitation when he made eye contact with her. "I'd sleep with an axe hanging an inch above my throat if it made you feel safer."

Her sinuses began to sting—it was so weird that

such a disturbing statement struck her as so romantic. "You would?"

"I'm not a threat to you," he said, finally opening his hands all the way to hold her face. "But if you need to treat me like one, I understand why… And I know you don't need any guy to take care of you financially, but… I have the means to provide you with anything you need, and if you want twenty-four-hour security guards around you, you'll get them, and they'll be the fucking best. My girl only gets the best. They'll be at your disposal a hundred percent. They'll take their orders from you and if you ever feel like I need to be put on my ass—"

"Why would you want to be with someone like me?" she asked. Oak was a catch, he could have an easy woman. "You could have a woman who'll stay home and bake cookies and squeeze out your kids… I'm so… complicated."

"I love you," he said.

Sighing, she resigned herself to it. "You're really saying that, aren't you?"

Grinning, he nodded and lowered to kiss her. "Yep, sorry, Thirteen, it's a sad, unavoidable truth. It's not a dream you're going to wake up from. I am actually your guy now. It's completely real."

"I'm going to a MatchMate coaching session on Saturday," she said. "Maybe they'll teach me the best way to let you down gently."

Teasing her lips with a kiss, he touched her tongue with his, only to withdraw. "I'll check the curriculum, make sure that's not on there."

"You know, you talk about me not needing a guy to look after me financially, but now that we're having sex, you should be waiving my MatchMate membership fees."

"I will have them take the debit from my account," he said, kissing one cheek then the other. He kissed the end of her nose, the bridge between her eyes, her forehead, then grazed his lips down her hairline to her temple.

"You're not getting laid, Oh."

His lips stopped on her cheek and he inched back to look at her. "I'm not?"

Smiling, she shook her head and gave his chest a shove. "Out."

Stepping over her tripwire, she shoved him another couple of times to get him to the door. "But I thought that maybe—"

"I know what you thought," she said, reaching around him to open the door. "Call my cell in thirteen minutes and I'll talk to you until you come."

"Phone sex?" he asked and tried to kiss her again, but she ducked. "Thirteen minutes?"

"Yes," she said, pushing him out the door. "Go, Oakley Orion."

Bending his knees, he made one last attempt. "I love you."

Laughing, she nodded while closing the door. "Uh huh, great. Thirteen minutes."

He was still there in the hallway, with his hands on opposite sides of the doorframe as she closed the door in his face and locked it. Resting back against it, Evie didn't know if she should laugh or curse. Maybe a bit of both.

Something about Oakley made her tell stories, ones she'd kept to herself for a long time. But there was something cathartic about confessing to him.

Oakley was either going to cure her… or kill her.

SEVENTEEN

OAK HADN'T SEEN enough of Evie over the last few days.

Somehow they'd managed to get to Wednesday and back to the office. Though how they'd managed it was another story. Returning back from Washington the previous day had been a cacophony of farce, but they'd made it and after a night of rest were back to the grind.

Catching up with work was frantic, he'd had constant calls, emails were piling up, and everyone needed a minute of his time.

Monday, the last day of the convention, had been all work. He'd hoped to see her at the farewell party, and well he had… on stage with Taylor. Turned out that karaoke was a feature of the last night. He'd been stunned to a stop when he first heard her singing. His woman's voice was incredible.

It had taken another few drinks before Taylor would get up with her, but they eventually sang a duet. Taylor had wanted to sing *Stand By Your Man*. When he'd vetoed the song and glared at his sister, Evie had leaned in to tell him in a sing-song voice that she was struggling to keep her clothes on.

Although he was getting better at playing to her vixen nature, it still surprised and aroused him.

Conversation had moved on to Evie's impressive vocal range, though she shrugged off the compliments and dragged Ian up to sing a duet from *Grease*, which led to Ian and Kody singing *Greased Lightning*, giving Evie the opportunity to pull Taylor onto the stage so they could offer backing and slither up and down the guys.

Yep, the MatchMate crew had been drunk and he'd loved it. At least, he had until Lana tried to take his hand. Lana didn't get on stage or sing, and she seemed to think their mutual refusal gave them some kind of bond.

Oak wouldn't get up to sing, no matter how much they tried to beg him, but someone had to stay semi-sober. He certainly wasn't trying to show any solidarity with the only other person left at the table.

After some whispering, Evie went to sing again, dedicating her song to him, and he'd held his breath expecting to hear *Ring My Bell* or something equally salacious. Instead she sang *Bitch*.

Yep, his woman had a sense of humor.

Yesterday, the journey home, had been about luggage and boarding passes. Someone lost a purse. Then they lost Kody altogether and the flight almost had to be delayed. It turned into a headfuck of a day when their flight was diverted because of a mechanical issue and they didn't get back to the city until after dark.

So getting to Wednesday had been a bit of a trial, but they'd made it. Though he still hadn't managed to see Evie and this day was starting to get away from him too. Before anything else got in his way, Oak left his own office to make a beeline for hers. He found Evie leaning over her desk, muttering a song and swaying like maybe she was thinking about the party.

Skirting the door, he closed it as quietly as he could and leaned against it for a second before creeping forward. Sliding one arm around her waist, he ducked to kiss the side of her neck. She increased her volume a fraction and didn't push him away or object, she actually turned into his arms, pulled herself close and started dancing with him as she sang.

Really? Wow, okay.

He didn't mind if she wanted to dance with him, though he'd prefer to do more of the smooching variety. Before he got the chance to make a move, her office door opened, and Taylor swung in.

"Oh, Evie," Taylor said and laughed. Evie kept singing and left him to go to Taylor. Taking the binder away from his sister to put it on the filer at the door, Evie wrapped both arms around Taylor and took his sister into a cheek-to-cheek number. "We had mimosas at lunch."

"Shh," Evie said, touching Taylor's lips. "You said it was a secret."

That explained Evie's mood and Taylor's glow. "You got drunk on company time?" he said, but sank down to sit against the edge of her desk wearing a smile.

Evie kissed Taylor's cheek. "I still love you, Tay, sweetie. But if you're going to tell anyone about drinking on company time, it shouldn't be the boss."

"Oak doesn't mind, as long as you're with me," Taylor said, running her fingers through Evie's hair. "And you're leaving early today anyway."

Evie took her arms from around Taylor and turned the watch on her wrist so she could read the time. "Shit, yes, I am, and I am going to be late."

"Are you coming over to mine tonight?" Taylor asked.

Evie halted her rushed journey to her desk,

thought for a second and spun, though she did it so fast that her heel caught and she lost her balance. Thank God someone wasn't drunk, because Oak's sober reflexes let him lunge over to catch her before she went down.

Both women seemed to think it was hilarious. They were snorting and laughing; Evie put a demure hand to her chest and tucked herself in close to him.

"Oh, Mr. Orion, my hero," Evie said, tossing her head back and making no attempt to take her weight. "Whatever would I do without you?"

Taylor was laughing so loud that people who walked past the office were peeking inside to see what was going on.

"I think I should drive both of you home," Oak said. They didn't just have a mimosa or two at lunch, they were hammered. "Tay, go get your purse."

"I don't want to go home!" Taylor whined and sagged. "Don't be a party pooper."

"Tay, it's three in the afternoon," he said. "Not really party time."

"Any time is party time," Evie said and after stroking his torso a couple of times, she did a double take. "Why am I still in your arms?" Although she asked the question, she didn't move away, instead she winked at Taylor. "I think he works out."

Taylor laughed again. "Ew! That's Oak! He's our brother."

"Right, our brother," Evie said and patted his chest before pushing away to stand on her own two feet again. "Go get your purse, Tay, honey, and lock your door so the creepy clerk can't jerk off on your chair again."

His sister blushed but giggled as she swept out of the office. Evie grabbed his tie and started for the door, pulling him with her. "Creepy clerk? Who's jerking off on her chair? What the hell is—"

"Shh," she said, closing the door and putting her back to it to pull him down for a kiss.

Okay, he'd argue with her about that in a minute.

"Taylor was upset, that's why we had a drink," she murmured, turning her face to push higher to deepen their next kiss. Although she was buzzed, she didn't quite seem as drunk as she had a second ago. "Ethan called her, said he was laid off and they lost the venue for the wedding..."

"You put me to work," he said, flattening his hands on the door because he didn't trust himself not to touch her like he wanted to; Taylor would be back any second. "His car's being repossessed this afternoon and he's going to lose his apartment deposit when his lease isn't renewed at the end of the month."

Preoccupied with his mouth, Evie's hands climbed higher up his tie. "Very difficult to keep my clothes on," she whispered and tugged him down to slide her tongue into his mouth.

They were a good team. He could take care of the practicalities while she nurtured Taylor who was oblivious to what was going on behind the scenes. "If you want to come over later—"

"Taylor wants me to do her hair," Evie said, and when her hands slid away from his tie, they snaked to loosen his fly.

"Oh, hey, honey," he said, pulling his hips back to zip up again. She tugged his tie and pressed her mouth to his even though he wasn't prepared for her kiss. "Taylor will be back any minute."

"I can't come over to yours later. You're meeting your future wife tonight," she said, rubbing her hands up his chest over his shoulders beneath his jacket.

"What the—shit, the mixer... Are you going?"

Her shoulders bobbed up, and she laughed. "Oh, baby... Lana, you're meeting Lana tonight."

"So you're staying home to do Taylor's hair?" he asked, kind of returning her kiss, but his eyes stayed open as he thought about tonight from her perspective. "Does it bother you to see her and me together?"

"It would bother me less if you let me touch your dick when I wanted to," she said, digging her nails into his shoulders. "Are you keeping it for her?"

Evie was still laughing. Her eyes stayed closed as she joined her mouth to his, but he took her chin and put some space between them to look at her. If she was tipsy, she might be honest.

"Are you worried about me falling for her?"

Searching his gaze for a second, she didn't say anything. "Can I get back to you on that?"

"Back to me—why?"

"I'm going to see Noel this afternoon," she said, looking at her watch again then easing him aside to go over to her desk.

Closing her laptop, she slid it into her leather briefcase, then bent to pick up her purse.

"Noel?" he asked. "Do you want me to come with you?"

Shaking her head, she picked up the coffee mug on her desk to gulp down what was left in it. "No," she said, putting the mug down. "I need a solo session."

"To talk about us?"

Smiling, she came over and put a hand on his chest. "Yes, my egotistical lover, to talk about us."

It might be arrogant of him, but Oak also felt it was important to acknowledge that he was a big development in her life and one that she'd use her therapist to help process. "But you will schedule a session for us to talk to him together, right? You're not going to let him break us up without giving me a chance to put my case to the guy."

"He told me not to have more sex with you and

how did that work out for you?" she asked and bounced up to kiss him quickly. "Noel knows I'm not easy to control."

She started for the door, but he caught her hand to take it to his lips for a kiss. "Do you want me to drive you over there?"

"I want you to take Taylor home. I want you to make her strong coffee and I want you to listen to her."

"Listen to her?" he asked. "You…" He figured it out. "She's making excuses for him?" Right on Evie's schedule. Sometimes he couldn't believe that she had her own issues, she seemed so together, so sane and level-headed and perceptive. Shit, the woman could read people, she just didn't trust herself. A sudden curiosity made him ask. "Did you like him?"

"Who?" she asked, straightening the strap of her laptop case on her arm.

"Gemmell." The surprise that made her look at him wasn't drunk or distracted. "If you don't want to—"

"No, I…" Oak didn't blame her for not expecting the question, and after she'd recovered from her surprise, she answered him without any anger. "I didn't like him, no. But I don't know if that was because of him or because of how Beth reacted to him. He didn't come across as controlling. Beth and I were living together so I saw Gemmell a lot, he seemed like a sane guy, I didn't see red flags, but her mood changed depending on his mood like… she was so in love that she… she became him."

Kissing her knuckles again, he felt his love for her grow. It made him want to hold her again, all night… always. "I love you."

He didn't even care that she got a look on her face like she was amused and humoring him whenever he said it. "I'll tell Noel you said so… now I have to go before Taylor comes back and asks where I'm going. Please, Oh…"

Releasing her hand, he let her fingers drift away from his as she backed to the door. Blowing him a kiss, she winked, and then she was gone.

EIGHTEEN

THE NEXT DAY, Evie had put her head around Oak's office door. She didn't even go in, just waited for him to take his eyes from the tablet on his desk.

"Friday work for you?" she asked. "Three o'clock?"

"I'll make it work," he said. "Where are we going?"

He didn't even care where they were going or what they were going to do. "Downstairs to one of your hotel rooms…"

Evie did usually go to Noel's office, but it didn't seem fair to take Oak so far away from MatchMate HQ when he had actual work to do. It also meant that if he wanted to leave the session early, he didn't have to hang around waiting for her to give her a ride back.

Evie didn't even know what would happen in the session or how long Noel expected Oak to be there and her therapist hadn't been forthcoming when she asked. Evie had a feeling that Noel was going to let Oak be the guide on that, not as any kind of test but because he found actions as telling as words.

"Which one?" he asked.

Tutting, she pretended to be disappointed. "You don't know? You can't be that in love with me if you don't know—"

"Thirteen," he said and when she grinned, he relaxed. "I'll be there."

And so there they were.

Noel had texted her to say when he arrived at room thirteen. Evie was halfway along the corridor to meet him when she felt someone behind her and turned to see Oak leap to the top of the stairs. He closed most of the gap between them while she was knocking and waiting for Noel to open the door.

When he did, she went inside. "Just wait a second," she said, holding the door as Noel went into the room. As soon as Oak was there to take the door from her, she left it and went to Noel. Pushing to her tiptoes, she kissed each of his cheeks. "This will look so bad if anyone catches us in here." She laughed and turned to present Oak. "Doctor Noel Brewer, meet Oakley Orion… the man who says he's in love with me."

"Yes, indeed," Noel said.

The two men shook hands.

Oak tried to thread his fingers through hers, but Evie took her hand away from his reach and shook her head.

"No, don't touch me," she murmured the instruction, but turned to use his hips to maneuver him onto the couch that was against the wall opposite the end of the bed.

This room contained a dressing screen meant for decoration and probably to give women cover to protect their modesty if they were in here on dates. When she and Noel had a session, they put the screen at the end of the bed to conceal the majority of the room.

In the sessions they had just the two of them, she and Noel would sit at opposite ends of the couch, but this time the couch was empty for her and Oak. Noel had brought the wicker chair out of the bathroom, and he was seated in that, facing them.

After Evie sat Oak at one end of the couch, she went to the other and sat down. "That's interesting, Evie, why did you do that?" Noel asked. "Why did you put space between you and Oakley?"

Growling at her serious therapist, she got irritable. "Don't do that, Noel," she said. "Don't start analyzing me, we haven't been in the room two minutes."

"It's about as interesting as you introducing Oakley as the man who claims to love you."

Groaning, she let her head fall back, but rolled it on the back of the couch to look at Oak. "This man hates me. The doctor thing is a complete sham."

Noel laughed. "Would you prefer me to analyze Oakley?"

"Yes," she said, cheering up. "If you say something about his behavior I'll feel much less picked on."

"Okay," Noel said, scrutinizing Oak for a second. "Strong handshake and he showed up, those are points in his favor."

Evie shouldn't let Noel rile her, but he knew her buttons. "Something judgmental about his behavior," she said. "Geez, Noel, you're not going to be nice to him just 'cause he signs your paychecks, are you?"

"Hey," Oak said. Suddenly, he relaxed and lit up. "I hadn't thought about it that way. Excellent." Resting one arm on the back of the couch and the other on the arm, he got comfortable. "I'm sort of your boss, Brewer."

Evie sneered. "You're kind of my boss too."

"And that has never stopped me from acting

inappropriately with you," Oak said. "So why shouldn't I take advantage of my position of authority with this guy too?"

Great. So he was chilled enough to make jokes. He might be meaning that he'd take advantage of Noel in a different, less salacious way, but Evie chose not to take his statement that way.

"Well I hope you enjoy having sex with Noel," she said and surged to her feet.

"Evie, sit down," Noel said. She didn't want to, she wanted to storm right out of there. Therapy had the power to make her more emotional than she ever liked to be. Sometimes it was fine, water off a duck's back, but bringing Oak was a big deal. "We're going to acknowledge it, just sit down and take a breath."

She could feel Oak looking back and forth between her and the therapist, he might be worried, he might be laughing. Evie didn't know which it was because she maintained eye contact with Noel until she calmed and then she dropped down into her seat.

"Acknowledge what?" Oakley asked.

Folding her arms, she looked toward the window even though the curtains were shut. "How significant this session is," Noel said. "She's never brought anyone to a session before, much less a man she's romantically involved with. And, Evie, do you realize what you did?"

His soothing voice made her turn because she didn't know what he was talking about. "What did I do?"

"You put Oakley between you and the door," Noel said. "You never do that. You never put yourself in a corner. Either you don't mind being cornered by him or you have an expectation that he would protect you in the event that someone was to come in here and threaten you, which do you think it is?"

"I'd protect Evie with my life," Oakley said.

Although he was vehement, she was focused on

her doctor again, trying to figure out why she'd done that and more, why she hadn't even noticed it.

"Oakley went exactly where you told him to go," Noel said. "He let you put him there."

"He's never been in therapy with me before, I was letting him know the procedure," she said, but the stilted words were absent; she was trying to figure out if there was significance behind the gesture.

"Oakley, is that why you let Evie direct you?"

"Maybe," Oakley said. "I usually go where she tells me to go… I do what I'm told."

Hissing, she scowled at him. "I don't tell you what to do."

"Okay," he said.

Her mouth opened. "Damnit, I do," she said, and he smiled, slouching even further into the couch. Kicking off her shoes, she twisted her whole body toward him, bringing up her knees under her. "Why do you let me do that?"

"Most of the time," Oak said. "Because I don't give a fuck."

"About me?"

He shrugged. "About whatever it is," he said. "If you bat your eyes at me and tell me to get you a drink, I'll get you a drink. Why wouldn't I?"

"And when she directs you somewhere?" Noel asked. "Like into that seat."

Oak seemed to think about it for a second. "I guess… I want to make her happy and…"

"And?" Noel prompted.

Oak's eyes slunk to hers. "I usually get a reward."

"A reward?" Noel asked.

"She kisses me or touches me."

"And that's your version of a reward?" Noel asked. "Physical gratification?"

"Sometimes." Oakley shrugged, but even after he

turned to Noel, Evie kept her attention on his profile. "But I guess it's not the physical act as much as it's the acknowledgement that there's a connection between us. When she touches me, she's giving me a sign that she wants to be near me. Sometimes it's a wink or she smiles at me in a certain way and it makes me feel like I'm…" Lifting his hands at the wrist, he took a second to find the word. "Important in her life, I guess, different to other people."

"That's very interesting," Noel said.

As the doctor examined the couple, she exhaled and folded her arms. "Ignore him, Oh, he does this. Now he'll just sit and look at us for a minute without saying anything… a minute I'm paying for by the way, doctor."

"I'll deduct it," Noel said, seemingly more interested in Oakley than her right now.

"Deduct a whole minute?" she asked. "Thanks very much."

Because her doctor was used to her sarcasm, Noel ignored it to ask, "Evie, do you have your—"

"Yes," she said, leaning forward to pull her notebook from the front pouch of her purse.

Handing it over to the doctor, she knew it would take a minute for him to read it.

"What's that?" Oak asked her.

"My notes, remember, like I showed you in my phone?" she said. "I transfer them into that notebook, expand where I want to, and Noel gets a quick overview of the week. We used to spend a lot of time rehashing unimportant stuff. Now he knows what was significant at a glance."

Oak became sort of reserved. "Are we in that?"

"Yes," she said.

"I mean are… *we* in that."

"Sex?" she asked. Enjoying how he seemed to be embarrassed, she straightened her legs toward him and leaned back against the couch arm as she folded her arms under her breasts. "Yes. But it's not a critique of your performance. I don't go into detail, I write quick notes. A sentence or two, Noel decides if we need to talk about anything that jumps out at him."

"We'll definitely be talking about sex at some point," Noel said.

Evie blinked when she saw she was under his scrutiny again. "What did I do this time?" she asked and when she saw that her feet were on Oak, she quickly bent her knees, pulling them to her chest.

But the contact didn't seem to be what the doctor had deemed significant. "You showed Oakley your notes?" Noel asked.

"At the speed-date thing on Saturday," she said. "I told you that... didn't I?"

Noel shook his head. "Have you spoken to each other today?"

"Morning briefing, that was it," she said. "We don't talk about sex in the morning briefing." Picking up her hand, she shielded her mouth on one side to whisper, "His sister sits in those meetings."

"We'd talk about it if Tay wasn't there?" Oak asked.

His hand landed on her toes, but she didn't pull away. Evie never knew what would be significant to the doctor, the action of pulling away or the inaction of not?

Turning her flat hand to herself, she addressed Oakley. "I talk to Taylor about sex all the time... From what she says, you're more uptight about it."

"Are you uptight about sex?" Noel asked. "Does talking about it upset you?"

"Upset me, no," Oakley said, and she wondered when he folded his arms if he was feeling uncomfortable. "I prefer not to think about my sister like... that."

"Why are we talking about Taylor?" Evie asked

and clapped her hands once. "Isn't this about me?"

She'd take Oak's frown, yep, she was okay with him being offended that Taylor was cut out of therapy. But Noel wasn't so reticent about his feelings.

"Evie," he said like a parent chastising a child.

"I've told you, I won't talk about Taylor," Evie said and let her eyes slink side to side implying she was being sly and saucy at the same time. "Want to talk about Oakley's cock?"

"No," both men said together.

Evie exhaled and looked at Noel again. If he was going to push her about this, she'd really prefer him to do it while Oakley wasn't in the room. But it was actually Oak who spoke.

"She's protective of Taylor," Oak said. "It humbles me how much she cares about her."

"Would you step aside for the sake of their friendship?" Noel asked.

Shoving to the edge of the couch, Evie felt a rush of rage. "Don't you fucking do that to him. He doesn't have to choose when he can have both of us."

"Can he?" Noel asked. "What happens when the siblings argue, Evie? Whose side are you going to take? I think we both know the answer to that one."

"I would always expect Evie to stand with Taylor," Oakley said.

Turning slowly, she couldn't believe that he was so clear and serious. "You would?"

"Of course I would," he said. "And I'd expect to grovel to make it up to both of you… I'm never going to ask you not to care about Taylor… I just want you to care about me too."

"I do care about you," she said, her heart breaking a little that she might not have made that clear. Sliding toward him, she picked up his hand. "I trusted you. I've told you the truth… I haven't told Taylor anything about Beth or Gemmell… I didn't show her how I live, my traps, my insecurities… Oak, I asked you to put your hands around my throat… I've given you so much of myself."

Brushing his fingers across her cheek, he used a gentle tone. "I know that. I told you I don't take your feelings for me for granted… I meant it when I said I wouldn't ask you for a commitment, but I want you to understand that I'm in this all the way… and sometimes I don't know if I'm doing the right thing when I'm honest with you about that."

"Are you?" Noel asked. "Are you in it all the way, Oakley? From how I understand it, you've had your fun with Evie, you've had sex with her… Shouldn't you start losing interest in the relationship now?"

"I've had sex with her," Oak said and the edge of anger in his voice made her wary, she didn't want him to be offended. Sometimes Noel was confrontational just to provoke a reaction, maybe she should've warned Oak about that. "That doesn't mean I'm done with her… And yes, I'm in it all the way. I love her."

"Because this is not going to be an easy relationship. It will never be an easy relationship," Noel said. "And if you care about Evie, you have to be aware that it will take time to build intimacy and trust… I'm, quite frankly, amazed by how much faith Evie has shown in you, about how vehemently she defends you, about what she shares with you about her past. Evie wants to love you, whether she knows it or not."

NINETEEN

HER THERAPIST SURE DIDN'T beat about the bush. Evie hadn't been convinced that bringing Oak here to her therapy session, to meet Noel, was a good idea… she still wasn't sure.

Oakley's hand scooped over her cheek even though she wasn't looking at him. "I want her to love me; I'm not going to pressure her into doing anything before she's ready. But, doctor, I will take her word for it if she says she is, I trust her and if she tells me she's ready for something or asks for it, I will give it to her. I will do it even if it's against your advice."

"I'll probably never be ready for anal sex," Evie said, but her joke didn't break the men's stare.

"She uses sexual humor to deflect when she's nervous or uncomfortable," Noel said.

"I know," Oakley said. "And she uses it to tell me she's done discussing a subject or expressing a particular emotion."

"Uh," she said, raising both hands to shoulder height. "I'm right here."

Oakley took her hand. "We're ignoring you, Sweet, because your doctor is trying to figure out if I'm for real or playing with you… Listen, doc." Sitting forward, Oakley kept her hand, letting it drape between his wide thighs as he rested an elbow on his knee. "You should be worried about Evie; you've known her a long time, and it's your job to help her make sense of developments like me. I want her to keep coming to you, for as long as she needs to. Just like I told her about the traps she sets and sleeping with the light on, it's all okay with me. I've never been to therapy in my life, but I offered to come here because I want to help Evie too… I love her. You can question that. You can tell her to dump me. You can tell her she's not ready and I'll tell you that I don't mind waiting until she is. Nothing is going to make me love her less. I want to be with her. Not just this week or next, but I want to build a life with her, a long one."

Noel waited a minute, assessing them both before he took a deep breath and eased back in his chair. "I'll be honest, I came to this session assuming that you didn't know what you were getting into or that Evie would guard herself. Your actions and reactions to each other, and things you've said… It's made me think… this could be a positive development for you, Evie."

She'd never needed Noel's approval, never needed anyone's approval for anything. But having it made this relationship take on a new significance.

"You think?" she asked, and clenched Oak's hand tighter. "He could kill me one day."

Noel countered. "Or he could father your children and give you the measure of stability you've always lacked."

"Now it's my turn to remind you both that I'm here," Oakley said, but he seemed relaxed again.

It was only when he kissed the back of her hand

that she thought about how they'd moved together, sitting so close there wasn't any light or air between them, their fingers locked together like they were… partners.

"Don't think that this won't be a lot of work," Noel said, warning them both. "Oakley, I'm going to ask you to join Evie for future sessions."

"Any time," he said without hesitating for a second, overwhelming her with his conviction.

"We'll have to set out a plan," Noel said. "Yes, Evie, you will likely drive a lot of the physical developments, and I don't just mean the sexual ones, but other physical factors. How comfortable are you with the idea of letting Oakley near your apartment?" She shook her head. "I didn't think so. Oakley, if Evie wants to come to—"

"I'll get her keys made for my place," Oakley said. "She's welcome any minute of the day."

"Good," Noel said. "You have to understand what this will mean for your life, Mr. Orion. Evie is going to be…"

"Difficult?" Oak asked. "Yeah, I already know that about her."

"No," Noel said. "Her trust in you may waver if you give her even the slightest excuse to doubt you."

"I wouldn't think about touching—"

"Evie's insecurities aren't rooted in sex," Noel said. "She may be completely comfortable and confident with you in sexual matters. Her issue is trust."

Oakley was intent as he pulled her closer. "I don't understand what—"

"Secrets will be significant to her," Noel said. "I'm not suggesting you can tell her every detail of every second of your day, but if something is happening in your life, or an event happens that may be brought up at another time, I'd suggest you make the effort to tell her about it. Especially if the matter is personal."

Self-conscious, Evie tried to play. "So, if he develops a burning rash he should—"

"No," Noel said, displaying the patience of a saint as he came up with an example. "If he's thinking about having a party for his sister to celebrate a birthday or a life event, how would you feel if he discussed that with someone else or made plans without telling you he'd even had the thought?"

It wasn't difficult to answer that question because she reacted just at the idea of it. "I would feel… pushed out, suspicious—"

"Doc, I would never—"

"That's my point," Noel said. "I'm not suggesting that there would be any reason for it. Perhaps you just hadn't seen Evie that day or something serendipitous happened that made you make a call to arrange something on the spot. It could be benign, perfectly innocent, but Evie's perception could—"

"I got you," Oakley said. "No parties without consulting Evie." He kissed her hand again. "The truth is that even in business decisions I find myself craving her input, so it won't be a problem."

Peeking at him, she was surprised again. Oak winked at her. "You should get used to talking to each other on the phone and exchanging emails," Noel said. "Both of you. Evie, you should keep taking your notes for these sessions, but you should also exchange those spur of the moment thoughts with Oakley when you feel comfortable enough to do so… You must help him understand what you're going through and how he can help."

"He told me that already," she said, thinking about the bed in his Washington hotel room.

"And, Oakley, you must get used to keeping Evie's confidence, it's extremely vital that—"

"I would never betray her. I haven't breathed a word of anything she's told me to anyone and I have promised her that I won't."

"Again," Noel said. "I must emphasize that it may be something less significant than events with Beth, these sessions, or her anxieties… Don't share what she tells you without her permission. Nothing."

"No one even knows we're having sex," Oak muttered. "I'm good at keeping secrets."

"It bothers you," she said, twisting to look at him. "You want people to know."

"I would find it easier if they did," he said. "It would be easier for me to include you if they did."

"Because you'd invite me into more meetings?" she asked. "I won't be at MatchMate forever, and people will resent me if they think I'm manipulating you. Look at what Kody said about my tits during that Regent meeting… And Taylor, she needs both of us right now, she should think we're there for her, not creeping off at night to talk about her."

"I have to say," Noel said. "Openness is going to be vital in your relationship with each other. But I have to support Evie's need for privacy at this time. I don't think you should have an extended period of secrecy, no more than a month or two. But for now, there may be questions that neither of you will be comfortable answering."

"Questions?" Oakley asked.

Evie answered. "What if Taylor wants to come to your apartment for dinner?" she asked. "You guys eat together all the time, right?"

"Yeah."

"So, what if she asks me to join her? Why wouldn't I stay the night with you? Why wouldn't I want to go out to dinner with you guys and then go home with you? Why would I be happy to have sex with you in the office in the middle of the day or take a room with you here, but I won't share a hotel room with you if we're away as a group?"

"Exactly those questions," Noel said. "Evie shouldn't have to tell everyone about her past. It's a big deal that she told you and you've already acknowledged that."

"I understand," Oak said.

Evie was impressed by how he was taking this in his stride, accepting and adapting to everything that was being said to him.

Leaning forward, she kissed his lips. "You're making it very difficult," she murmured, and he smiled before kissing the end of her nose.

"But, Miss Dewar, don't think all of the onus is on Oakley."

Oh shit, that made her spin away from her man fast enough. "What do you mean?"

"This is going to be hardest on you and I'm going to demand the most from you… At the moment, no one is asking you to put language to this, but that will have to change. You will have to start thinking of yourself as being in a committed relationship whether you say the words out loud or not."

"It's not like I was having tons of sex before this," she said. "I think Oakley can be assured that I'm not going to be sitting on any other cocks any time soon."

"Just like I said to Oakley, this is not about sex," Noel said. "Those needs will be fulfilled. You have already proven that you will take what you need from Oakley. Of course you shouldn't sleep around, that goes without saying. But beyond that, you must include him in your life."

"Like sending him my notes."

"Yes," Noel said. "And you must be open to

discussing them. You must listen to his hopes and fears too, not just for this relationship but in all areas of his life. Compromise, Evie. You have to think of yourself as an involved woman, decisions should be made as a couple, even if they only seem to involve one of you. Picture your future with Oakley, think about what you want, how you want it to look. You don't have to express the details to him now, but you should make yourself comfortable with the notion that he's going to be around for a while."

Thinking about this, Evie shivered when Oakley leaned in behind her to whisper, "A long while."

Perking up at the opportunity he'd lined up for her, she grinned. "A long, hard while?"

Noel wasn't impressed, but Oak pressed her hand to his thigh, so she took that as his approval.

"No one wants you to change who you are," Noel said. "Either of you. But more than most couples, you're going to have to make the effort to integrate each other into your lives, especially since your relationship is secret at the moment, that will increase the intensity of it, and ultimately nurture your intimacy, which is a positive, but it will be difficult."

Hmm, he probably didn't use the word 'hard' on purpose. "We will try our best, Doctor Brewer," she said, nodding like the dutiful student. "Tell him we'll try our best, Oak."

"We will try our best," Oakley said.

Noel smiled, and she hissed at herself. "Shit. I just did it again."

"It's okay, Thirteen," Oak said, rubbing her hand on his thigh. "I don't mind being your bitch. You let me take the lead where it matters."

"Sex?" she asked over her shoulder.

"You seem to be in charge of oral, but I'd say I take the lion's share of the work in… other areas."

It was so funny that he didn't seem to like being explicit in front of Noel. Oak would get used to it, she was sure, not just because her language was explicit with the doctor, but because the more time the men spent together, the easier it would get to be blunt.

"The largest hurdle you are going to face, and the one that will likely cause the most frustration for both of you, is Evie's issues with spending the night away from her apartment."

"It's not the apartment that's the problem," Evie said. "It's my… setup."

"Would you feel comfortable in my place if we set it up like yours?" Oakley asked.

Sweet of him to ask, but she shook her head. "I would never do that to you… You can't sleep with the light on."

"Why not?" Oakley asked. "I've never tried. I'll adapt and if I don't, I'll buy a sleep mask or something."

"And if someone comes in while you're wearing this mask?" she asked.

"Interesting," Noel said.

She growled aloud and threw her hands up, though one was still connected to Oakley so it came with hers. "What? What did I say?"

"You are as concerned for Oakley's wellbeing as for your own."

"Yes," she said. "I'm worried I might accidently stab him while I'm having a nightmare too." That admission was meant to be tongue-in-cheek, but as she considered it, she sagged. "Oh, God, what would I do if *I* was the one to hurt him?"

"Your nightmares are less of a problem now than they used to be," Noel said. "Far less… And if you let me prescribe—"

"No," she said, straightening a finger. "I won't take drugs. I can't be out of it. If I'm attacked—"

"Like I said, this is going to be the greatest hurdle," Noel said. "Spending the night together is not about the physical act of sex, it's about a sign of the relationship and that Evie is mending. How can you marry or have children if you can't live together? How can you have children if Evie fills their bedrooms with razor blades and makes them terrified of imaginary intruders?"

"We just got past, 'no one is asking you to put language to this relationship' and now you want us to have children?" Evie asked. "Can we please take a step away from that for a second and just focus on the fact that I'm even in a relationship at all? I mean, what the hell, Noel, did we ever think I would get here?"

"I always told you that you would, but I understand what you're saying, and you're right. This is significant enough for the moment." Everyone relaxed. "Now, Mr. Orion, since we are going to be spending more time together and you know so much of Evie's past, please, tell us something about your own. Let's focus on getting to know you."

So they did. For the rest of the session, Oakley was honest about his family and his upbringing. There wasn't time to go into everything, but he spoke about his father's death and how he'd adapted to taking care of his mother and sister.

Evie listened to every word. His story was intriguing and amazing; he'd stepped up for the family, and taken on every responsibility so that his mother and sister wouldn't have to.

At first, Evie was annoyed at herself for making their relationship so much about herself. She hadn't taken much time to get to know him.

But the more he spoke, the more worried she got. Was she just another responsibility? Did Oakley need someone to take care of and now that his mother and Taylor were moving on, was she the next crutch?

Evie was proud to be with him, and awed by his strength and fortitude, but she wondered what she'd ever be able to do for him that he couldn't do for himself. How would he ever need her or rely on her when he was so sane and she was so… not?

TWENTY

THAT HAD BEEN AN INTERESTING lecture. MatchMate events were always interesting, in one way or another.

Evie was standing at the edge of the conference center beneath the long row of screens that displayed events that were going to be on over the next few weeks. Noting down the ones that she thought looked interesting, she knew she had some time to kill before the next event.

It was a workshop, which usually meant she'd be forced to participate more than she wanted to, but there was another lecture after and she was looking forward to it, so she'd hang around.

The lecture this morning had been about confidence recovery after relationship loss. After the speaker gave the initial lecture, participants were invited to come to the stage to share their experiences. It was interesting to watch. While she hadn't lost her own intimate relationship, she'd lost familial ones.

The guy running the lecture was a therapist of

some kind and he offered advice to those who shared their stories. Comparing her own therapy experience to this one, Evie found her emotional distance from the participants on stage to be useful in figuring out how she felt.

She hadn't gone on stage to share, but she'd taken a bunch of notes and learned a lot about herself as well as gaining some perspective on her "relationship". Damn. She really had to stop thinking of that word with permanent inverted commas around it. She wasn't in a quote, end quote relationship with Oakley. It was just a relationship. There. She'd done it and she underlined her achievement with a deep breath. Good. Progress.

Except all the progress she'd made since their joint session with Noel yesterday had led her to one conclusion.

It was never going to work.

She couldn't be Oakley's girlfriend.

It wasn't that she considered herself inferior to him; it was simply that she didn't think she had the ability to give him what he needed.

Telling him it was over would be difficult, but her decision had been solidified during the lecture this morning. Evie hadn't been able to ignore what she was hearing. Those people lost their confidence as they gave so much of themselves to their partners that they didn't know who they were when the relationship was over.

Listening to Oakley yesterday had made her realize how selfish she'd been. Evie should have taken the time to question him about the difficulties he'd faced in his life. That she hadn't, didn't make her feel guilty as much as it changed her perspective, she just didn't have the emotional maturity or capacity to be a fully committed girlfriend.

She wasn't ready.

Evie couldn't ask him to deal with her

insecurities, to give all of himself to her when she had nothing to give him. Yes, her heart hurt when she thought about hurting him, but she'd do whatever it took to free him from the trap of his feelings for her and that's what they were; a sticky quagmire that would drag him down and smother him before he realized he'd been consumed.

"You're going to be a busy girl."

The sensation of Oak's breath on her neck came before the scent of him hit her. Evie shivered; this could be the last time he ever stood so close to her. Turning around, she was ready to lay it out for him. She hadn't expected him to be here, but talking in public was better than talking in private.

But her inhale didn't end with a cutting remark when she saw that not only was Oak standing there, but Lana was with him, and their arms were linked. The couple were smiling, and Evie was stunned by how they looked together.

"Wow," she said. "You make a really attractive couple." Lana beamed, but Oak's smile faltered. Yep, Evie, this was it. Ignoring her internal struggle, she had to take a deep breath. She cooled her eyes and curled her lips. "Did you enjoy the lecture?"

"Yes," Lana said. "It was interesting to learn what pitfalls to avoid."

Snapping her notebook shut, Evie turned it into her palm and pointed it at Lana. "Yes, exactly. That's so funny because that's exactly what I was just thinking about."

"It…" Lana glanced at Oak, probably worried about Evie's exuberance, but Evie cared less about her and more about the darkening scowl on Oak's face, though she kept herself loose. "It was?"

"Yes," Evie said, resting an arm beneath her breasts, tucking her notebook against her body. "I was thinking about how listening to all those wa-wa whiney stories is probably the best commercial ever for staying single."

Lana paled, and Oak looked pissed. "I think that…" Lana was nervous but obviously felt the need to say something. "Some people join agencies like MatchMate to find their confidence again after they've come out of long-term relationships."

"Yeah," Evie said. "So it's full of the dregs looking for a rebound lay, right? I mean we ladies want a real man, don't we? Not some sniveling loser who's crying about how his ex-girlfriend couldn't orgasm in bed, right? I mean if he can't get her off, why should we want her cast offs? I am going to that speed-dating thing across town tonight, and seriously, if I see one guy there who was here today, whoosh, I am out of there, like a fucking shot, right?" Evie laughed, but she was the only one. "You guys are lucky you have each other now, so lucky… Just spare a thought for those of us who are still wading through the swamp." Flashing her grin to each of them, she gave them a nod too. "You guys have a good day out."

Turning around, she strode off. Was that enough to give him the message? Did he think she was playing? Nope, she wasn't. Well, she was in one way; she didn't think any of the guys in the lecture were losers, quite the opposite; her heart went out to them. But when in doubt, and when trying to make a point, switch on the bitch.

Someone caught her arm and it didn't take a rocket scientist to figure out who was pulling her to a halt. "You want to tell me what that was?" Oak asked.

"Where's your girl?" Evie asked, playing innocent, scanning around for Lana.

"Standing right in front of me," he said, putting a finger on her cheek to make her look at him. "What's wrong? I came here to surprise you. Lana sat down beside me, I didn't even know she was going to be here."

"Less than a day after Noel tells you not to surprise me, you think it's a good idea to surprise me?"

"What?" he asked. It seemed that he didn't know whether to be apologetic or playful. "That's not what he said, he told me not to keep important things from you. I didn't know I wasn't allowed to surprise my girlfriend."

Folding her arms, she sighed. "That's just it, Oakley Orion. I'm not your girlfriend."

"Lana isn't—"

"This isn't about her," she said, doing her best bored shrug. "I'm just not that into this."

"Excuse me?" he asked and grabbed her arm. "I don't believe you. Whatever happened, you can talk to me, we'll call Noel and—"

"No," she said, picking his fingers from her arm like she was done humoring him. "I figured this out because of him. All that talk yesterday… it made me see it… I wanted to fuck you… and I have… All the rest of the bullshit—"

"Bullshit," he said, "like my feelings for you?"

"Aww," she said, playing it with amused pity. "Sweetie, you're a special guy, really special. You'll find yourself a wonderful woman who—"

"You are my wonderful woman."

Flattening her smile, she raised her brows. "No, Mr. Orion. I'm not."

Turning her back on him, she strode away. He wouldn't make a scene here. Oakley had seen how their scenes ended. In the dining room of the Washington hotel, they'd had the cover of people around them, this was an exposed space and Lana was somewhere, probably watching. He had to let her go.

The other time he'd made her mad, she'd lost it and broken down in front of him. Evie knew there was no chance of that happening today. If Oak pushed her she'd turn her bitch up to eleven. She'd embarrass him, make a drama queen of herself, and have the office talking about them for weeks. Neither of them wanted that.

Just as she thought, he didn't come after her, and didn't pull her back. But Evie knew he wouldn't give up that easy. So she had to fight hard if she wanted him to be free of her.

***

AND THERE SHE WAS. His woman.

Oak hadn't expected Evie to make the declarations in the conference hall that she had earlier that day. But he should have. Things were serious between them now and the session with Noel had gone so well that while he was encouraged, she was probably freaking out.

It didn't take much effort to get himself put on the roster for the speed-dating event that she'd referenced, and now here he was, on the guys' side of the bar, waiting for the night to begin.

Evie hadn't noticed him yet.

She was leaning on the bar, drumming her fingers on it, with one foot propped on her toes behind the other leg as she chewed on a fingernail. But she wasn't nervous; she was playing the innocent virgin or the clueless bimbo. The only way he'd find out which, was to go over there.

The metal strip on the floor was meant to separate one side of the bar from the other, giving men and women equal space to mingle in their own genders before and after the dates. As luck would have it, Evie was right next to this line on the female side.

Sauntering up to the bar, Oak slid his hands to the center. "Did you think it was going to be that easy?" he murmured.

Angling herself toward him, she grinned. "Oakley Orion," she said like she hadn't seen him for years. "You know, we really should stop running into each other at events like this."

"Do you want to talk to me?" he asked, keeping himself calm to show that he wasn't going to play her games tonight. "Do you want to tell me what scared you?"

"Scared me?" she said on a scoffing laugh and leaned over to nudge him. "What scares me is how long this bartender is taking to pour martini… you think there are guys on your side of the line who pay him to drug the women? That would be a pretty good move, don't you think?"

"This is a MatchMate event, you don't have to worry about anyone taking advantage of you or spiking your drink."

She waved a loose hand. "I'm not worried," she said. "I haven't been high while having sex since college, might be a nice trip down memory lane. Everyone likes a bit of nostalgia, right?"

If she didn't want Noel prescribing her drugs, then she wasn't going to be taking the recreational kind. "You don't have to hide from me, Thirteen. I thought you trusted me enough not to push me away… talk to me, Sweet."

Leaning to the side, she looked past him. "You think number six would be a good choice?"

It was difficult not to sigh at her, but he was fed up with her façade. They didn't have much time and he wanted honesty. "Good choice for what?"

"Sex," she said.

That made him smile. "You want me to think you're going to sleep with a random guy you meet tonight?"

She prodded his chest once. "That, my friend, is

exactly what I'm going to do," she said.

The bartender came over with not one drink, but two, and she started to gulp the first down.

But he didn't believe her, not as he watched her consume her Dutch courage. "Evie, I can see that you're anxious."

"Not anxious," she said, finishing the first drink and as she slid the glass away she did seem… positive. "I am actually feeling really good, Oak. And do you know something? I have you to thank."

"Me to—"

"You broke the seal," she said, shimmering with excitement. "I've done it! I had sex, I'm cured… I think I was feeling weird yesterday 'cause I realized, I'm not ready to tie myself down, you know? I used to have boyfriends, back in the day, I liked dating, liked men. Now I've got my confidence back and I know I can do it… I think it's about time I had some fun." The bell rang to signify the women should take their seats. Her shoulders rose, and she winked at him. "Ding, ding, my friend. Ding, ding."

As she began to move away, he took a step toward her. "Evie—"

"Ah," she said, nodding at the line on the floor. "There's a line you can't cross, Mr. Orion… not anymore."

***

EVERY DATE SEEMED to drag. Six minutes had never seemed so long. But it didn't matter to Oak that he was impolite to the point of being rude. He wasn't here for a date; there was only one woman he cared about getting to.

How the fuck could she say that to him? Noel had told her to start thinking about their relationship seriously, and she'd… dumped him and declared she was off to sleep around. What the fuck? How was he supposed to keep his cool when she said something like that?

His mood only got more sullen the longer he had to wait. When he found himself in the position next to hers, it took every ounce of his restraint not to grab the guy seated beside him to punch him right in the chops.

Evie was laughing, flirting, using that smooth purring voice that he wished was only reserved for him.

When the bell went, Oak surged up and marched to the next table. Evie's table. The previous guy was lingering, looking at her, even though she had her face buried in her phone. Instinct made him shove the guy who was so surprised that he almost stumbled. Oak didn't even care, he just glared at the guy until he moved on.

Seizing her phone from her, Oak wasn't feeling patient anymore. "Hello, Oakley," she said, folding her arms. "I forgot you were here."

Hoping to get some insight about what the hell was going on, he looked at her phone expecting to get a glimpse of her emotions. To his horror, all he read were notes exactly as she'd described before, each guy was rated, she'd made notes about seduction techniques, possible cock size, everything he didn't want to see.

Sinking into his seat, he was devastated. She meant it. She fucking meant it; his woman was actually going to have sex with another man.

"Evie," he exhaled, his shock taking all the strength from his voice.

"I don't suppose we really need to talk," she said. "You're not on the shortlist. Do you want to get me another drink with your six minutes?"

She couldn't really think that he was just going to stroll over to the bar and order her more alcohol.

Slamming the phone onto the table, he kept his fist tight around it. "You're not going to do this. I don't know what the hell happened. I don't know what changed between us having sex after our session with Noel and this morning, but something did, and I want to know what it is."

His tension level was rising, but she was cool and calm as a millpond. "You know, I think there's some rule about exes stalking through MatchMate events," she said, like it was no big deal. "If you give me my phone, I can make a call to the complaints line and—"

"I'm not your ex and this is not stalking. I'm trying to stop you from doing something you'll regret."

"Seems like you're the one who's going to regret it. I'm looking forward to tonight."

And damn her, but she really looked like she was excited. "I'm going to buy you a big present, a big box of candy or something. You know, it's amazing, I'm looking at guys again in a way I haven't looked for a long time and shit, Oak, there are some real prospects in MatchMate."

His anger was so potent that it was making him feel sick. "I thought they were all sniveling losers who couldn't satisfy a woman."

Her eyes slunk from left to right as her lips slanted. "Not tonight… One or two seem, you know, decent. Great prospects for some against-the-rules fun. I might actually fill out one of those card things tonight, cool, huh? You really fixed me, Oak. Maybe you should list your cock as a special event for reluctant women… Though, hmm, Lana might not like that… I'd definitely ask her for permission, signups would go through the roof."

"What is wrong with you, Evie? What the hell happened that made you switch off?"

Pushing her shoulders back, she shook her hair.

"I feel damn switched on, Mr. Orion… I feel more alive than I have in years. This is amazing progress for me; I'm proud of myself."

"And how will you feel when you have a stranger on top of you?" he asked. "Are you going back to his place or taking him back to yours?"

"Neither," she said. "We might just do it right here in the parking lot and if he's good, there are hotels just a few blocks in every direction."

If he'd hoped to hear she had no plan or to plant a seed of doubt in her mind, he'd fucked up. She not only had a plan but was determined that this was a good idea.

Softening, he wanted to reach her. "Evie," he said and tried to take her hand, but she pulled them from the table.

"You're not allowed to touch me."

No, the rules of the night meant they weren't supposed to touch and yet she was talking about having sex with a guy who was in this very room, sharing oxygen with him. There were some things too precious to him to share and Evie was one of them.

"I love you."

She laughed a quiet titter. "That's a helluva line, did it work with the other women tonight?" Pushing herself upright, she looked one way along the line over the top of the screen, then the other. "Do you want me to provide references for you? I won't tell Lana. I'll be like your wingman."

"I came here for you," he said. "And I won't leave without you."

The bell went. "Yes," she said. "You will."

He didn't move, even after she slid her phone out from under his hand. But instead of taking notes, she put it in her purse and tipped up her chin to flutter her lashes at the guy now behind him, waiting for Oak to vacate.

Balling his fist, he slammed it on the table and

leaned as he stood, pinning her under his glare. But she was soft as putty.

He didn't want to intimidate her, didn't want to scare her, he just wanted her back.

TWENTY-ONE

OAK WATCHED HER after the dates were over. She did wait to fill out her card and was laughing and chatting with the other women like she wasn't ripping out his heart and chowing down on it.

She didn't look at him. Not once.

He caught her looking at the male side of the bar several times, but he was never the focus of her flirtations. Evie made eyes at a few of the guys, whispering things to the ones she got in earshot of. But every time he tried to intercept her or speak to her, she turned on her heels and sashayed off like he was invisible.

Oak never thought he'd see the day he'd be happy for Evie to leave. But he was happy when she left the bar at the same time as the other women. Rules dictated that the women departed a half hour before the men, so he was stuck here with the guys, all of whom had mentioned his woman. Not that they knew that was what they were doing when they started their leering and commenting.

It pissed him off. He wanted to warn all of them

to stay away from her. For a brief minute, he considered telling them she was a viper that they'd be smart to avoid. But if he did that, he'd be tagged as an ex and would be precluded from attending future dating events with her, like this one.

Pure chance was all that made him leave at the back of the pack when it was time for the men to go. One of the employees had recognized him and waited until the end of the night to compliment him on his use of MatchMate services. The conversation was short, but it was enough to hold him back.

Leaving the bar, he saw the other guys were already in their cars, getting into cabs or walking away down the street. All except one.

Number six.

Six was standing in the dark parking lot holding both hands of the woman who stood in front of him. With her head tipped all the way back and her face lit in a smoldering smile, there was no mistaking the woman's identity.

That was his woman.

Oak only watched for five seconds. The couple exchanged a few words and a laugh before Six dropped one of Evie's hands to begin leading her toward a vehicle at the back of the lot.

A perverse and silent laugh made Oak shake his head and look at the ground. Yep. This was going to happen.

Striding in the direction of the couple, Oak saw the lights on a car flash, but he kept on going and only called out when he saw them move down the passenger side of the vehicle.

"Evie," Oak shouted.

She heard but didn't look at him. "Go home, Oak," she responded.

Six was the one to stop and look at the man who

was following them, giving him a once over with his gaze when Oak came to a halt between the headlights. "Who the hell are you?"

Evie moved to press herself against Six. "He's the MatchMate guy," she said, in her pouty, innocent voice. "He's here to get us into trouble for breaking the rules… Do you think I'm worth an official warning in your membership file?"

Six made the mistake of looking down at her. Once the guy was in the focus of those simpering eyes, he wouldn't be able to think straight. Oak knew their power; he'd been ensnared by it himself more than once.

"Oh, yeah, I do." Hooking an arm around Evie's neck, Six waved at him. "Sorry, dude, she's a ten."

Six opened the passenger door of the car. Evie peeked over it. "You hear that? I'm a ten."

"I didn't need him to tell me that," Oak said. "Don't get in that car, Evie, I'll slash every tire before I'll let it leave this parking lot."

She shrugged like she couldn't care less. "So we'll have our fun right here, who needs to go anywhere? You want to watch through the windows? That has a name doesn't it…?"

Tapping her finger on her lip, she seemed to be considering what that name might be.

Oak wasn't playing. "This guy doesn't want me smashing out his windows and scratching his paintwork," Oak said and was pleased when the guy tensed to turn on him.

"Hey, you don't fucking think about touching my baby," Six said and started toward him.

This guy might care about his car, but that would be nothing to how Oak felt about Evie. "You don't touch mine and we won't have a problem," Oak said.

Adrenaline made him stand his ground. He'd take a beating, or he'd beat the crap out of this guy;

whichever way it went, he didn't care. By the time the cops were called, and they were hauled away to the station, Evie would be tucked up inside, probably waiting for Taylor to show up. He'd be a prick. But his woman would be safe and untouched. That was all that mattered to him.

"That what this is?" Six asked. "You wanted this girl? Well fuck you, she chose me."

Oak heard the car door close and hoped to God that Evie was on the outside of it and not the inside. "You don't have a goddamn clue what you're doing," Oak said to the guy, matching his stare as Six came to bump his chest against him.

It had been years since he'd been in a fist fight, but he was pumped, ready to go, and when Six shoved him, he shoved right back. "No," Evie called out. The proximity of her voice was enough to throw Oak from his game. Six's punch blindsided him, but it didn't knock him off his feet. For a big guy, he had a weak right hook. "Oh my God!"

Evie's panic fired Oak's instincts and he swung back at the guy, getting him across the jaw in the same place he'd been hit.

"No!" Evie screamed out. "Stop it! Don't!"

Her body came between them. Six pulled back his arm for another hit, seemingly oblivious to the woman who'd just got in the way. Throwing both arms around her, Oak took her with him when he twisted away, curling himself over her to protect her body with his own. The maneuver meant he was guaranteed to take another punch from Six, and sure enough it landed between his shoulder blades, but he'd take it over any chance Evie might be hurt.

Pushing her away, he spun back to face the guy who was coming at him again. "Get out of here, Thirteen!" Oak called, catching the guy as he threw his weight forward.

"Hey!"

"Hey!"

The security guys from the bar were running across the parking lot. Six saw them at the same time Oak did.

Backing away, Six glared at him and past him, probably at Evie. But he didn't think for long and was quickly scrambling into his car to speed away, nearly taking the security guards with him as he went.

Grabbing his jaw, Oak worked it and turned to see if Evie was still there; she was. She was standing about ten feet away from him wearing a blank expression.

"Hey! Who the hell was that? What the hell's going on?" Security Guard One asked as he and his buddy approached.

"Nothing," Oak said. "Just a misunderstanding, forget it."

Security Guard Two went toward Evie, but she took a reflexive step back. Was she afraid? "Are you okay, miss? You were at the event tonight. If you're a MatchMate member, you're entitled to report—"

Sidestepping, she walked away from the security guard without acknowledging that he'd spoken. With her arms folded, she approached Oak. Despite the ache across his shoulders and the throbbing in his jaw, he was most pained by the distance in her eyes when they met his.

"Oakley?" she asked.

Didn't she recognize him or was it an explanation she wanted? "I know you don't like violence, Sweet. I'm sorry. But I couldn't…" He tried to touch her arm, but she twisted from his reach. Her brows lowered a fraction. "I'm sorry."

"You put yourself between us," she murmured.

"You took that hit... for me."

"Yes," he said.

What the hell else was he supposed to do? Was she mad? Sad? Disappointed? Shit, this was worse than upsetting Taylor. He'd thought he felt bad earlier in the night, now he thought maybe he should've just let Evie have the night she wanted.

"Oh," she said on a rush of quiet breath and moved forward to caress his face with both hands. "Oh... My Oakley."

Pulling him down, she slanted her mouth and slid her tongue into his. Damn, she tasted good. He'd kissed her yesterday, but he felt like he hadn't kissed her for months. Hunching probably should've hurt his shoulders, and maybe it did, but Oak didn't feel anything other than the slick heat of his woman's grateful mouth.

When she took her lips away, her fingers stayed stretched on his face, and he couldn't release the tension of his arms that pinned her to him. "Let me give you a ride home?"

Her nod was dazed. Her attention stayed on his mouth and he didn't argue when she kissed him again.

The security guards were gone by the time Oak made himself move her toward his car. With her pulled to his side tight, she probably wasn't really walking on her own, but he needed to hold her close. Easing her into his car, he didn't want to let her go, but had no choice once he put her into her seat.

Running around the hood, he jumped into his own side and put the key in its slot. But before he could push start, Evie's hand snaked to his inner thigh and began to rub his dick through his pants. He'd never been great at refusing her physical advances, but tonight he had to.

Taking her hand away, he laid it on his thigh and rested his other hand on the wheel. "Why?" he asked the badge in the center. "Sweet, I have to know why—"

"You were supposed to hate me," she whispered and when he looked at her all he saw was sorrow in her gaze. "You were supposed to walk away hating me."

Touching her face, he needed to understand. "But, why?"

"I thought if I made you mad that you'd hate me, like you did in Washington before I… before I told you about Beth… I wouldn't have slept with him, didn't even promise him that I would, all I said was that I wanted a ride home."

"You didn't kiss him?"

She shook her head. "I did flirt."

The corner of his mouth upturned. "You always flirt." Then he recalled their date. "Your phone? The notes you were keeping were—"

"I knew you would look at it," she said and twisted herself to face him. "Oh, I've been so selfish and I… I don't have the emotional maturity to be able to give you what you need. I can't be in an equal, adult relationship; I'm too caught up in my own crap."

Holding her face with both hands, he leaned toward her. "People who don't have emotional maturity don't say they don't have emotional maturity," he said. "And the last thing you are is selfish. Look at everything you've done with Taylor. You've looked after her, really got her through this Ethan mess. It played out exactly like you said it would. We had our fight on Wednesday."

"I know," she grumbled. "She told me that night when she came over, she was upset."

"And she apologized to me on the Thursday, I apologized too and… we talked, Evie, my sister and I talked… for hours, about stuff we haven't talked about for a long time. All of that was because of you… Yeah, maybe you and I haven't covered all my family stuff or my history yet, but there's no rulebook that says we have to do it all overnight. We've been together two weeks… There's still plenty I don't know about you, but we'll get there. We will. Evie? We will get there." Something like hope joined her sorrow. "But you can't do this again, understand? I don't mind the dating thing as long as it's helping your social therapy. But if you think you can break up with me again and then—"

"I won't," she said. He'd never heard such eager panic in her. Exploring her wide eyes again, he wanted to believe that she meant it. Oak couldn't claim he hadn't known what he was getting into. Everyone who knew the truth, including Evie, had told him that she'd do crazy, frustrating things. "You put yourself between me and him."

Why was that so incredible to her? Why did just saying the words make her eyes glisten? "I will always put myself between you and danger."

"But I was a bitch," she said. "I was trying to make you hate me. You were supposed to hate me. To walk away and live your life and be happy without me. Why would you take a hit for a woman who was so cruel to you?"

Was that what was tripping her up? It was sort of funny. "Didn't you hear what I said to Noel? Nothing can change how much I love you."

"Oakley," she gasped his name and then exhaled. "Push your seat back."

"Why?"

"Because I asked you to."

As he did what she said, he watched her lift her hips to wriggle out of her panties. Climbing over the center console, Evie sat on his knees, loosened his pants, and pulled his hips down the seat.

"We can go back to my place and—"

"It's too late. You have to take me home," she murmured, rising onto her knees and shuffling forward to sink down onto him. Both of them shared a silent inhale as their bodies joined. Everything seemed better when they were connected like this. "Oh… Oh, my Oakley."

The gratitude and devotion in her whispered words made his pelvis rise to help her in her effort.

Holding her hips, he gave her all the support he could as she rode him here in the parking lot. When he kissed her neck, she grabbed his head and pushed it back against the headrest, but she wasn't preventing contact, she opened her mouth on his and shared her devouring kiss as their pace increased.

Oak didn't want to think about how close he'd come to losing her. If he hadn't come here tonight, or if he hadn't noticed her with Six in the parking lot, this night might have had a different ending. Even if she had just got a ride home from Six, Evie would've made Oak believe the encounter had gotten intimate.

She'd said that she wouldn't have slept with Six and Oak believed that, she was incredible at faking her intentions, like how she'd made him believe that she slept around when they met. But that guy had a temper, one that might have put her in a vulnerable position.

Her panting became high-pitched; he recognized her pending release. He wanted her. Bad. Even when she was here on his cock, he was thinking about her in his bed, how he wanted to spend the night with her pussy wrapped around him.

Oak would give anything to take her back to his place now, or to be invited back to hers. He wanted to be able to sleep with her in his arms, to wake up and reach for her to sate the need he had for her even when he was dreaming.

Evie was his again, their separation might have been brief, but it was too long for him, and he'd do anything to make sure it never happened again.

TWENTY-TWO

IT WAS PROBABLY AUTOPILOT that made Oak answer his phone the next morning; he couldn't recall hearing it ring or picking it up. The sound of her voice was the first thing to slip through a crack of his awareness.

"Oakley," Evie whispered.

At first, he thought he imagined her voice. But he got more with it and realized there was a device at his ear. Lifting his head from his pillow, he looked at the screen. Yep, the call was connected to Evie… had she called him, or had he called her in his sleep?

Dropping her off at her place last night had been difficult. He'd been able to feel her internal conflict, either she didn't want to get out of his car or some part of her wanted to invite him up to her apartment. Figuring out the best course of action, given her issues, wasn't easy. But, he'd promised to be patient, so hadn't pushed for anything more when she kissed him goodnight and slipped out of the vehicle.

But he'd thought about her all night, dreamt

about her. Evie Dewar was never far from his psyche.

"Yeah, Sweet, what's up? What time is it?"

"About five a.m."

Clearing his throat, he glanced around at his bedroom to see vague light barely breaking around the edge of his curtains. "Are you okay? Is something wrong?" When she didn't respond, he sat up. Fuck, had something scared her? "Baby, if you need me to come over to—"

"I'm standing outside your front door."

What the hell? He stopped scrubbing his hand through his hair and tried to process that. "What?" he asked, leaping from his bed to rush across the room and out to the living room. "Why are you outside my door? Didn't you get the keys I couriered to you on Friday night?"

"I did, but I… I thought if I came in while you were asleep that I might scare you."

Scare him or fulfil his fantasy? "You don't have to call me. You don't have to knock," he said, frustrated with the door. He'd never remembered it taking so long to unlock the damn thing. "Shit, hold on." Pulling back the lock, he opened the door to see her standing there in his dim hallway. "Hi."

She hung up her phone and dropped it into her trench coat pocket… that was a trench coat he'd seen before. "You put yourself between us," she said, and he smiled.

How many times was she going to say that?

Taking her hips, he drew her forward and slid his arms around her. His limbs came up against a sports bag that was hanging across her back, but he didn't let that slow him down, he just squeezed his arms between her body and the bag and pulled her into the apartment.

"It wasn't that big a deal."

"It was to me," she said and unhooked the clip

of her sports bag to let it fall onto his floor. "Oakley Orion, you make it so very difficult for me to keep my clothes on…" Untying the belt of her trench coat, she shrugged it from her shoulders and yep, his woman was a walking fantasy. "Are you going to tell me to put my coat back on like last time?"

Bending to scoop it from the floor, he balled it as tight as he could and lobbed it into the dining room. "What coat?"

She laughed at his mischief. Scooping an arm around her waist, Oak picked her up and pulled her in for a kiss.

But as he took a step backwards, she pushed away. "Lock the door," she said. "Please."

He didn't put her down when he went back to the door and fastened every lock he had. "Done."

"Mmm," she purred at him. Running her hands through his hair, she nuzzled his mouth. "Thank you, baby."

Carrying her through to the bedroom, he reassured her some more, wanting her to know he took her misgivings seriously. "All the windows are locked, and there are phones in every room."

It wasn't completely dark out and she'd managed to overcome her fears enough to travel here; Oak had never been so proud and appreciative. She hadn't asked about the other things, but he guessed she was grateful when she kissed him.

"Thank you, baby," she whispered.

"And if you want to tie me down…"

Tossing her head back, Evie laughed, relaxing into his bed when he laid her down and moved on top of her. "I might take you up on that," she said, pushing his underwear from his hips.

Tasting her neck, he loved the way her body responded to his, rising and angling to better accept him as close as she could. "My woman," he said, kissing her throat. "My bed… five a.m… do you know what really completes this fantasy?"

"Mm?" she asked, clenching her fingers in his hair when he looked down at her. "What, baby?"

"It's Sunday."

Arousal and joy fueled each other and she grinned. "Yes, it is… no work."

"No plans," he said. "Just us."

"Yes," she said, smoothing her fingers over his jaw. "Just us."

***

THERE WAS SEX and sleeping… more sex… more sleeping…

It was almost noon and they were still in bed.

Oakley stretched and rolled away from her, but Evie grabbed his wrist and pulled him back. "No, don't get up," she said, climbing over to lay flat on top of him. He laughed and ran his hands down her bare back. "Please, stay in bed with me, I have to say sorry."

"Sweet, you've said sorry a lot this morning; so much that you've built up credit," he said, squeezing her ass.

"Does that give me permission to be bad?" she asked, caressing and kissing the redness on his jaw that wasn't quite a bruise, but was obvious to her because she knew to look for it.

"As long as you're being bad with me," he said, turning his mouth to hers.

"I'll never be bad with anyone else ever again, I promise. And I think I'll lay off the speed-dating thing for a while."

While pushing her hair from her face, he looked blissful and sleepy. This would be a perfect moment, if only he hadn't been injured for her. "I think that sounds like a good idea."

In her mind, she kept replaying everything that had happened last night. It wouldn't stop going around and around. "Do you think those security guys will tell anyone about what they saw?"

Oak wasn't concerned. "About us? Probably not, they left without giving us any crap. But I can go over there and talk to them later."

That would mean leaving her alone in his bed; her lips quirked. "Tomorrow," she said, resting her mouth on his.

He understood she was telling him she didn't want him going anywhere. "Yes, tomorrow," he said and pulled her legs apart over his hips. "Did I tell you how proud and honored I am that you came to visit me?"

It was sweet and flattering that he was so awed by her effort. "Oh, only a million times," she said. "I couldn't sleep and I… all I wanted to do was be in your arms, to tell you how sorry I was for…"

"It's okay, Sweet," he said, his voice so gentle that she believed he meant it. "I expected a freak out. And I'm kinda happy that it happened now, and that I was there to protect you."

"You're happy that it happened?" she asked, sitting up, still straddling him though she hooked her feet over his thighs behind her ass.

"I'm not happy that you dumped me or went off with another guy," he said, stroking her torso and her breasts. "But we got over it and I know you, Evie."

"What does that mean?"

"You've experienced it, you didn't like it, so you won't do it again."

That made sense, and she couldn't argue because he was right. "It taught me something," she said, pinching his chest. "It taught me that you're persistent."

Placing a hand over the spot she'd pinched, he gave it a rub. Evie pushed his hand away and bowed to kiss it, she didn't want to hurt him anymore. "You should've known that about me already," he said, stroking her hair. "And I wonder if there wasn't some part of your subconscious that wanted to push me, to make me mad enough that I might want to…"

Shit.

Sitting up again, she opened her hands on his chest. "Hurt me," she said, clarity made her gasp. "Damn, Oh, what if that's what I was doing? I wanted you to beat me…"

"I would never—"

"I know that," she said, sinking down over him to lick his lips. "Oh, my Oh. I thought if I was a pain in the ass enough that you'd say to hell with me."

Honesty like this, so raw and transparent was liberating. Evie liked it and didn't feel judged or that Oak expected her to be ashamed. He was letting her be her without punishing her for it; even though she'd been so unreasonable.

"Just like you did in Washington," he said. "You nearly walked away."

"But I couldn't. I couldn't walk out of that hotel room. I… I still don't know why I broke down like that."

Pulling her into his arms, Oak put her onto her back and kissed her. "I'm so happy that you did, Thirteen."

After another long kiss, she was so relaxed that she thought she might melt. She didn't even want to open her eyes. "This feels so weird and so wonderful," she exhaled.

His kiss moved to her jaw and down to her neck. "I hope one outweighs the other."

"It does… I might consider sneaking over here again."

"Use your keys next time," he said. "You have them for a reason. You won't scare me. I want you in my bed."

She laughed. "You're not worried about me walking in and seeing something you don't want me to?"

"Like what?" he asked and stopped kissing her to frown like he was thinking about what that might be. "The worst thing you'd ever see is me jerking off, and if you walk in on that… you know what to do…"

"Jump aboard?" she asked, coiling her limbs around him.

He laughed. "Exactly," he said. "Now will you let me cook you something?"

Pushing him aside, she sat up. "After you let me give you a massage. If you don't work out that shoulder you're going to be sore tomorrow."

He hugged a pillow and moved onto his front so she could straddle his back. "After all the exercise we've had today, I think we'll both be sore tomorrow."

"I want you to be happy sore," she said, bowing over him to kiss the back of his neck before she got to work massaging his shoulders. "You put yourself between us."

Evie got the sense he was sick of hearing her repeat the phrase. But that just betrayed to her that he didn't realize the gravity of what it meant to her.

"Say it again and I'll tickle you," he said, his mouth half in the pillow.

Squeezing her legs tighter around him, she objected. "I'm not ticklish."

Lifting his head from the pillow, his eyes opened. "Yes, you fucking are. Say it again and I'll prove it." Sealing her lips, she kept her laugh to herself, she would say it again and she would let him prove it, just as soon as she did her duty as his girlfriend. "Yeah, see, that's what I thought."

He relaxed again, and she admired how handsome he was there lying on his chest beneath her. Everyone had expected her to freak out, but she hadn't recognized that was what she was doing until it was too late.

The speculation had been right. All of her paranoias had come together to make her act in the way she had. But one thing she knew for certain was that she was never going to put Oak in that position again.

Never again.

TWENTY-THREE

SUNDAY'S BECAME THEIR THING.

Every week Evie would travel to Oak's as early as she could. Sometimes, if she slept, it was as late as eight a.m., but she'd managed just after four once. She'd been proud of forcing herself outside at an hour that early.

They'd be coming into the winter months soon and she didn't know how he would handle that time of year because with the longer nights, she spent more time in her apartment alone.

Seven weeks after spending her first Sunday here, Evie was back in Oak's apartment.

Alone at the kitchen island, she was sipping fresh coffee and reading back what she'd just typed when a yawning Oakley came into view from the bedroom through the living room.

"You're up early," he said, coming over to sink one hand onto the back of her stool and the other onto the island, so he could bow to kiss her. "Good morning."

Eleven-thirty was early for them on a Sunday. He

pushed away after their kiss and shuffled around the island to head for the coffee machine. "I have a kind of important report due this week."

"You're working? On our Sunday?" he asked like she was committing a sin.

Taking a drink from the mug he'd just filled with coffee, Oak came to the other side of the island and reached across it to try closing her laptop.

Evie caught the lid and edged her computer aside to open it and type some more. "I want to be thorough."

He yawned. "Put that away, Thirteen, come back to bed."

"You're not in bed," she said.

He drank more coffee before putting the mug down and heading to the fridge. "You want me to make breakfast? What do we have?"

"It's almost lunchtime," she said, her eyes moving over the words on her screen. "I had yogurt when I got up… and I finished the rest of my fruit."

"I thought I tasted peach," he said, licking his lips. "They're really sweet."

"Just the way I like them… they were past ripe," she said, typing some more then pausing to read something from her handwritten notes.

Oak rattled around in the kitchen for a minute, pouring cereal into a bowl then seeking out the milk. "How is it coming?"

"Hmm, it's okay," she said, trying to decipher her own scrawl.

"Do I get a sneak preview?" he asked and discarded his bowl to come around and bend over her. Trapping her inside his arms, he propped a hand on the counter on either side of her laptop to read over her shoulder. "MatchMate efficient… blah, blah… hard-working… fresh ideas… and my boyfriend is too nosy to let me work without snooping." He laughed and kissed her shoulder. "You're going to take that last part out of the final draft, right?"

Evie projected innocence. "It doesn't name you," she teased. He went back to his cereal. "I could leave it in."

"That might raise an ethical dilemma. Anyone outside MatchMate shouldn't be reading that, right?"

"So I'd have to admit to sleeping with a MatchMate employee," she muttered then shrugged and hit backspace. "Yeah, I guess I should take it out."

A moment of silence passed before he spoke again. "You know you only have a week left on your contract," he said, slurping up his cereal.

"I know." She gasped and clutched the edge of the island. "What will you do next Sunday?"

He didn't laugh, in fact he scowled and caught the milk that trickled from his spoon to his chin. "You have a week left on your contract with the company. Your contract with me lasts another seventy years."

Now it was her turn to try restraining a laugh. "You think you'll live 'til you're over a hundred?"

"Doesn't matter if I die when I'm forty," he said. "Your contract with me is forever."

"Yeah, right," she said, seizing an opportunity to tease. "You're not going to keep your dick in your pants up there in heaven. You think I don't know you'd be screwing around on me all over? Marilyn Monroe is up there… you think if she says, 'Come on, big boy!' You'll say, 'No thanks, and when my wife gets here she'll kick your ass for asking.'"

As soon as she said the words, Oak stopped chewing and his eyes lit up.

Oh, shit. Her mouth worked faster than her mind too often. Evie picked up a quick finger to warn him. "Don't."

He was only gentleman enough to let her type for

a minute before ignoring her request. "You do that a lot these days, Sweet."

It pissed her off. "I know," she mumbled.

Her subconscious made her do stupid stuff all the time, but her faux pas in the boardroom this week had been especially difficult to shrug off. She'd managed it… just. There had been talk of opening more MatchMate offices and even relocating HQ. The idea of LA had been floated on a kind of joke, but, like an idiot, Evie had declared to the room that she and Oakley would not be raising their children in California.

Oops.

Given that no one at work knew about their relationship, it had taken some fancy talking and sleight of words to get the hell out of that blunder.

His tone was cautious. "Do you think we should talk about it?"

Evie was less subtle, but she was annoyed at herself, so it was no surprise. "My stupid mouth? No," she said and kept typing. "I have to do this."

"Your presentation isn't until Friday and you can have as much of an extension as you want."

Oh, a chance to flirt, she did love those, and how they let her redirect the conversation. "I know how you love to extend for me, Oh," she said, and cast him a quick wink before returning to work.

Oak ate some more cereal before asking, "Is there anything major I should be worried about? You've played this close to your chest. I didn't expect to be so in the dark… I have no idea what you've been doing."

Once again, he was cutting her a break and not pursuing what he really wanted to talk about. Evie had struck gold with Oak; he was far more patient than any other man would be. Fair or not, she was happy to take the out. She just wasn't ready to face it.

In default mode, she kept playing. "That's 'cause

I haven't really done anything. I've spent the past eleven weeks getting my nails done and washing my hair," she muttered, reading her data.

"And sucking my dick so…"

Smiling, she wrote another few sentences. Oakley wouldn't even complain if what she said was true. He loved her so much, that he'd probably pay her the hundred grand anyway, just as a thank you for hanging out with him.

He loved her so much.

Glancing up, she saw him scraping his cereal together in the bowl and scooping it up into his mouth. How could watching a man eat cereal be a turn on? Was it the cereal or was it just being here with him doing something so… normal?

It had been nine weeks since they'd first slept together. Since she'd dumped him that once, she hadn't done it again. Yeah, she freaked out sometimes, and they had fights… oh, boy did they fight. But, she'd never considered trying to rile Oak or pushing him away in the same way she'd done that weekend.

The reason she'd broken up with him was because she wasn't sure she could give him what he wanted. They spent a lot of time talking, learning about each other. But it was about time she cut him a break instead of him always being the one to relent for her.

Evie was terrified but determined. "Okay," she said, slapping her pen on the island and turning her stool toward the empty one beside her. "Let's do it."

His confused eyes went side to side. "Can I finish my cereal first? I hate soggy cereal. And you'll have to go on top; I'll get indigestion if you make me do the work this soon after eating." But she didn't laugh despite his attempt to make her. "I'm sorry, Thirteen. Do what?"

"Talk about our future."

Just saying the words made her stomach flip and

she considered backing out until he threw his bowl into the sink, cereal and all, and darted around the island like she'd just said anal was on the agenda if he stuck it in within the next five seconds.

"Okay," he said, jumping onto the stool she was facing to grab up her hands and pull her closer. "Talk."

Right. She could do this. Except… "You go first," she said. "Tell me what you want from me."

"All I want is the obvious," he said. "I want you at MatchMate full-time, permanently. I want us under the same roof, marriage, kids… simple pleasures."

Simple. Yeah, maybe for anyone else, but the bitter taste of adrenaline flavored her tongue. "Simple."

He must have heard her anxiety because he slipped a hand onto her cheek. "I don't need it all tomorrow… We're talking long-term."

"We can't do kids until we can live together, and marriage is… complicated."

"Marriage is actually the easiest part of what I said," he said, smoothing his thumb across her cheek. "We have people on staff who can perform marriages. We get a license and could be married twenty-four hours later."

"Okay," she said. Even though he should know that because it was part of the MatchMate service, it was still a bit freaky that he could recite the details. "Let's put a pin in that for a second. You know we can't have kids if I can't…"

"Live with me," he said. Dropping his hands to her bare thighs, he stroked up to the hem of the tee-shirt she was wearing and down to her knees again. "I know."

"I would drive them insane and I'd drive you insane… If I'm this paranoid about my own safety, imagine how I'd be with theirs?"

"Sweet, I would love to have children with you," he said, but carried on fast when she tensed. "But if it doesn't happen, I'll get over it." Shaking her head, Evie couldn't imagine him foregoing having offspring because of her hang-ups. "We don't even know if we can have kids. We could find out my swimmers aren't up to speed. Would you leave me if that happened?"

"No!" she exclaimed and grabbed for him. "Geez, Oak, nothing could make me leave you now. I'm so in lo—" The expectation of his raised brows made her exhale and after a second, she conceded, "Yes, Oakley Orion, I fucking love you, okay?" Raising his arms, he balled his fists and held them high like he'd just scored the winning goal. "Don't be a dork."

When he brought one elbow to his chest and hissed in a "Yes" she grabbed the back of his neck and yanked him forward to match their foreheads.

"I can love you and not have sex with you for a month, you know," she said, like she'd consider punishing him for forcing her to make the admission.

But he hadn't forced her, it was well overdue, and he hadn't pushed for it, hadn't demanded she say anything, even in their weekly sessions with Noel.

"No, you can't," he said, cocky as he lifted her thighs over his before sinking his hands around to her ass and pulling her from her stool over onto his lap. "You can't resist riding me."

"So we're done talking about the future?" she asked, kissing him.

She wrapped her arms around his neck and drew her pelvis higher to line up with his.

"No, this is just a hug, we're still talking."

But he'd given her a chance of an out, and she wouldn't really be her if she didn't at least attempt to take advantage of it. "Ding. Ding. Ding. I'm not wearing panties," she murmured, pushing her mouth to his and rolling her hips. "You can just slide Pavlov right in, baby."

"No… Shit. Okay, rookie mistake," he said, lifting her up to put her back on her own stool. Evie whimpered and drew a fingertip around his knee, but he picked up her hand and put it on her own lap. "No touching Thirteen during serious conversations, Oakley, stupid. Stupid man."

Sometimes he was hilarious, other times he was so cute that she just had to laugh. "I love you."

He stopped talking to himself to grin at her. "Damn… I thought your 'very difficult' comments were tough to deal with in the office. Now you just found a quicker way to get me hard."

Excitement made her reach forward. "Really?" she asked, but he caught her hand before she could grab his dick. "You know it upsets me when you won't let me play with Pavlov."

"You got up early to work, you abandoned him," he said. "And you can play with him for the rest of the day after we finish talking."

"So talk," she said. "Marriage is on the table. Kids are a slim possibility if I ever manage to…"

"Spend the night," he said. "How could we make it more comfortable for you? Do you want me to spend the night at your place first? I know that inviting me over for dinner was a big deal, but we've done that a couple of times now."

"I'm worried about integrating that part of my life with you," she said. "Not because of why you're thinking… This is my chance to get out from under it. You are the new component. The push I need to get better. If I can spend the night with you without bringing that crap with me then I might be able to get free of it. If I bring my traps and my neurosis, then you can kiss goodbye to kids and anything else because I'll never have an incentive as strong as you to do it. If you're not enough, nothing else will ever be."

"Makes sense," he said and moved like he was going to pick up her hands, but he pulled his reach back at the last second before contact.

Witnessing him reminding himself not to touch her, provided too great an invitation to ignore. Teasing him was just too much fun. Leaning back, Evie stretched her hands above her head, feigning she'd been overcome with the urge to yawn. Opening her legs on either side of his, she pointed her toes and lifted them until they touched the curved back of his stool on either side of his ribs.

His half-dozen deep, sharp bursts of laughter made her blink her eyes wide with innocence. "What?" she asked and then looked down as if she'd completely forgotten that she'd just exposed her pussy to him. "Oopsy." But she didn't rush to conceal it. "Is Bell distracting you?"

"Nope," he said, because he wanted to win the game, except he couldn't lift his eyes.

"How about Friday," she asked, parting her knees further.

"What about Friday?"

"It's your birthday on Saturday."

"My birthday on—what? Shit." Grabbing her knees, he squashed them together although her feet were still on his stool back. "Please, Thirteen, cut a guy a break."

TWENTY-FOUR

EXHALING, she straightened and crossed her legs as she sat demurely. "Better?"

"Not really," he grumbled, still looking at her thighs. "Now I know she's there."

"She's always there," she said. "And that's what you get for denying me access to my Pavlov... When I ring the bell, he's supposed to drool for me."

"Oh, he's drooling, Thirteen. Can you tell me what you meant about Friday? Please?"

They'd started this conversation, so she figured they might as well finish it. "I'll come over on Friday night and I will try to stay."

"Friday?" he asked, leaping to his feet, though she didn't know why he was so excited.

Tempering his expectations, she raised a finger. "I said 'try', Oakley. I can't promise you anything."

"It's enough," he said, bowing forward to kiss her. "It's good. Thank you, Sweet." He leaned back to scrutinize her. "Are you sure Friday though? Your presentation will be on Friday, won't you be nervous? I don't want that to short you out."

That made her shake her hair down her back and relax. "I don't get nervous presenting," she said and traced her fingernail around his knee. "You're not going to grill me, are you? If I wear a short enough skirt, and go sans panties, you won't even be listening… It's your birthday party on Saturday night, you'll probably have people back here for drinks."

Her poor baby was at a loss. "I will?"

He might be left out of some decision-making, but she was on top of it. "Let me rephrase: Taylor is planning on having people back here."

"I thought we were going out for dinner," he said, seating himself again.

She explained. "Your MatchMate people are going out for dinner—I won't be MatchMate on Saturday."

Panic made him tense. "But you are going to be there, right? If you're not going to be there, I'm not going to be there. I'll be wherever you are."

As sweet as it was that he wanted to be with her, Evie wouldn't see Taylor's toil wasted. "No, you won't," she said. "Taylor put a lot of effort into this, you're going to go and have a ball."

"But if you're not—"

Evie put a finger to his lips. "It just so happens that Taylor asked me to be her date. So, yes, I will be there."

"You could be my date," he said, sweeping her hair back from her shoulder.

"Lana is coming… well, she's going to be there. Whatever she does to celebrate your birthday is—"

"This Lana thing is getting crazy," he said. "We barely talk to each other, then we have to do these stupid interviews like we're in love. You know I think about you when I answer their questions."

"I know, you told me," she said, turning back to her computer and picking up her coffee. "It's working, membership has increased."

"Yeah, and how will those members feel when they find out it's a con?"

"Don't be silly, it—"

A thought made her stop, then she exhaled a laugh and looked at him.

"What?"

"We're a MatchMate couple."

"Yeah," he said, smoothing her hair. "We knew that. But you said you weren't up to doing the whole media thing and—"

Grabbing his thighs, she got excited. "We get to go to the Valentine's Black-Tie event!" He nodded. "I've always wanted to go to that. Do you always go?"

He nodded again. "Took Taylor last year."

Sucking in a breath she bit her bottom lip and started to think about what she could wear. "We better be out by then because I want to go next year, we can go as a threesome."

"It's in five months, so, yeah, we better be fucking out," he said. "And Lana won't be around to—"

"I meant Taylor," she said, prodding his knee with a fingernail. "You can take me and Taylor… you can do that right?"

"I can do anything I want. Taylor is organizing it. She can get you as many extra tickets as you want."

She waved a scolding finger at him. "No, this is an exclusive event."

He shook his head and smiled at her. "You care about the weirdest things."

Pushing her hands to his thighs, she levered over for a kiss. "I care about you. Are you weird?"

"The weirdest," he said and kissed her again.

"You know I appreciate this, and the effort you make for me. You don't have to."

"You've been spending too much time with Noel," she said, smiling into their kiss before pushing away to return to her computer.

"I mean, I want you here every night, all night, but that you're willing to even try, it means a lot and I want you to know that."

"I might not make it," she said, typing again. "Don't be disappointed if I don't."

"We're starting, that's something. You stay as late as you can then next time you stay two minutes later and so on. I told you, one step at a time."

One side of her mouth rose, and she peeked at him. "You should've said one inch at a time… Are you worried about saying anything that I might construe as sexual?"

"Thirteen, you construe everything as sexual, it's one of the things I love about you," he said, "but while you're working like that, I'm not sure you know I'm here."

When he tried to lean in to sneak a peek at her work, she grabbed the top of her screen and pulled it down. "You get your report on Friday, Mr. Orion."

"Oh, come on," he said. "I'm dying to know something… Don't tell Orion, tell me. Tell your boyfriend, not your boss."

"I wouldn't reveal proprietary information to outsiders," she said, enjoying that she could flash him a mischievous grin before opening her computer again.

"If I finger-fuck you, will you tell me?" he asked, walking his fingers across her thigh. "What if I eat you out while you work?"

Evie played it straight. "Do you offer that to all your contractors?"

He shrugged and picked up her coffee to drink

some. "Standard practice… Come on, Thirteen, you love me."

Typing faster, she wanted to finish her thought before she knew they'd go back to bed. When he got his fingers to her clit, she slapped the top of her laptop down and spun to face him. "Six need to leave immediately. Twelve can be given notice and there are forty-two others who either need to be filtered out or retrained."

Stunned, it took him a second to catch up. "Wait, that's… that's sixty people, that's almost an eighth of my staff."

Folding her arms, she shrugged. "Twelve percent, pretty average."

"Average?" he asked, slumping against the back of his stool as the mug in his hand dropped to the counter. "Forty-two? I mean, fuck, Evie, forty-two?"

"Those people aren't lost causes," she said. "If you're willing to take time, you can help them to improve. I'd recommend introducing a mentoring scheme. It depends how much time and money you want to spend… I have outlined a full training plan for each of them. Though there are training needs in every department. Again, average." She meant to reassure him because he was starting to pale. "I have step-by-step plans for everything that will need to be done and your HR manager will—"

"Heather is going on maternity in three months," he said. "She doesn't even know if she's coming back. I said we'd keep the post open but…"

"Don't panic," she said, squeezing his knee. "Everything is in plain English and I have a short list of prospective candidates for every vital vacant position. And remember what I said at the start of this, you don't have to take any of my recommendations."

He scowled at her. "You also said if I didn't that it would affect the chances of us working together in the future. You said something about respect and wasting your time."

"A lot has changed since then," she said, sliding off her stool to stand between his thighs and drape her arms around his neck.

"Yeah, we fell in love. That guarantees I'm going to do everything you write in that report because I value your advice over everyone else's."

"All I want to do is make MatchMate stronger," she said and when she touched her lips to his, he did respond, but his mind was somewhere else.

"And what about these six?" he asked. Of its own accord, his hand moved from the counter and slid under her tee-shirt to cup her ass cheek. "Should I be worried? If they need to be out, you need to tell me now, today, and I'll make the calls."

"Baby," she said, laughing as she brushed her nose over his. "You're freaking out. Don't freak out. I promise, it will be okay."

He searched her for a second. "You have to come work with me," he said and when she tried to pull away, he grabbed her ass with his other hand too and pulled her closer. "It's insane for you not to, Sweet. We're going to get there. I know we are. You didn't think you'd ever be able to love me and here you just said you loved me."

Evie sighed. "Loving you is easy," she said. "Giving you the life you should have is harder."

"You do," he said like he was aggravated by her. "But this is business, and MatchMate is as much yours as it is mine and Taylor's. Think about it. If we do have kids, even if it's in ten years, this company is going to be handed down to them. Don't you want to be a part of building our children's inheritance?"

"Yes, but—"

"I need an HR manager," he said. "That's what

you are! You could do the job standing on your head. And I'm not going to limit you, you can still work for your other clients, your regulars, I trust you to balance your workload I just… I want MatchMate to be your priority."

"You are my priority."

"Good," he said, pulling her to him. "Great! Then come work with me."

Drawing in a breath, the expansion of her lungs forced her breasts into him. "Oak, you haven't even read my report."

"Did you write bad things in there?" he asked. "Did you find something negative that you think will piss me off? Is it about the top-tier staff?"

"No," she said and gave him the kiss she'd wanted to give him for a while. "You, my love, are in the top ten percent. I'm so proud of you."

"Top ten percent of—"

"I won't recommend any salary deductions from top-tier staff and you don't even take a year-end bonus." Squeezing her closer, she whispered on his lips. "You might have been a little generous with Taylor's bonuses, but that might have accidently not made it into the report."

He groaned and opened his mouth to kiss her. "How can you not believe you're part of MatchMate?" he asked. "You are meant to be with us."

"I've written reports on some people that will not be appreciated," she said. "You can't ask me to judge these people and then manage them after they've read my negative comments about them. They'll never believe I've given them a fair shake."

Thinking about this, he came up with a solution. "Then omit them from the final report. You can send me the full final so I know the script, but we'll censor the public version… At least, we'll just omit those details. It would be unfair to publicize comments that may be read by peers anyway, it may unduly influence their colleagues' opinions."

"You're that desperate to have me on staff? Oakley, I can't—"

"You can write your own ticket," he said, not ready to give up. "No messing from me, I promise."

"I get to write my own contract?"

He shrugged. "Sure, if it secures you with MatchMate. I know you're fair."

"And if I demand that the boss has sex with me every day after the morning briefing?"

"I'd ask you to stipulate that it happens after the others have cleared out the boardroom." She didn't know if he was serious, but she'd bet if she actually wrote it, he'd sign it. "You fit in. Ian has operations, Kody, marketing. Taylor does the events. I deal with finance… Someone needs to round out the team. Someone who cares about MatchMate… You'd have an equal vote with me and Taylor… And you know, Tay wants another woman in the boardroom with her. Heather was always too interested in punching a clock, she never cared. We've never been able to find anyone who cared."

"And if Heather wants to come back?"

"As long as we don't reduce her salary, I'd bet Heather will be happy to take on less responsibility." He peered at her. "And I'm guessing from the look on your face that you know something I don't anyway."

She sighed and sagged into his arms. "Heather isn't coming back, she just wants to make sure she gets her maternity pay, that's why she won't tell you yet… And you better give it to her, Oakley. Raising babies is expensive work… it would be decent of you."

"Whatever you want, Sweet," he said, trying to tempt her mouth. "Does that mean you'll take her place?"

"I'll think about it," she said and when he inhaled to keep trying, she pushed her hand over his mouth. "I said I'll think about it, Oakley Orion, that's more than you've had from me in seven weeks. I just told you I loved you and said that I'd try to spend the night with you, that's a lot."

His frame expanded, but only for a second before he slouched again, giving in... well, sort of. "You're right, future Mrs. Orion."

"Yeah, well there's that too," she said, happy to wrap her legs around him as he stood and picked her up. "You said something about eating me out... you ready for lunch?"

TWENTY-FIVE

IT WAS AFTER LUNCH on Tuesday when his office door opened and closed. Glancing up, he saw Taylor and so went back to his writing.

"You know those kids who ask their parents for a sibling, but they have no idea how babies are made?" Taylor asked.

Okay, this was going to be one of these. "Yeah," he muttered.

"They have no idea how expensive a kid is, or even that daddy has to bounce around on mommy and get all sweaty. They don't know that it's difficult and stressful," she said, sinking down into the chair on the opposite side of his desk. "Those innocent little kids don't know that pregnancy is emotional and taxing, or that labor is exhausting and painful. They just want the prize at the end, the cute little baby."

If Taylor was in a relationship, he was sure that Evie would've told him. Even if she'd just hooked up with some guy, Evie would have told him… maybe. But, somehow, he doubted his sister was about to confess that she'd been knocked up. That was definitely something Taylor would confide in Evie before she told him. And Evie would give him a heads up if Taylor was pregnant, if for no other reason than to make sure he tempered his reaction to the news.

Putting down his pen, he linked his fingers and peered at his sister. "Tay?"

Slumping into a petulant hunch, she whined. "I want a new sister!"

"Goddamnit, Tay," he murmured. She threw herself on his desk, stretching her arms toward him, whimpering and whining like a toddler. "Lana is not—"

"Not Lana!" she said, staying in her slump though her hands flattened. "Evie! I want you to ditch the square and get with the rock chick who drinks in the corridors and makes out behind the bike sheds! I love Evie!" Taylor pretended to cry, turning her face to the desk. It was so hilarious that he didn't even know how to react. Taylor sucked in a breath and sat up straight. "If you don't grab her now, we'll lose her! She's leaving at the end of the week, do you get that? Don't you think she's pretty? Evie's so pretty! And she's smart! And I know you're not that into boobs, but she has nice ones, I've seen them!" So had he. "And she has legs. You like legs, right? And I'm sure if you just—"

When he raised his hand, she stopped talking and sealed her lips. Trying his best to remain stern, he locked his finest parental stare on his sister. "You want me to get with… Evie?"

Taylor nodded fast, giving him a broad, innocent grin that Evie would be proud of. Reaching to his phone, he hit speaker and dialed Evie's line.

"For the last time, Mr. Orion, I will not send you an up the skirt shot and it's inappropriate that you keep asking," Evie chirped down the line and he heard her keyboard working.

"Can you come here?"

"Hmm," she said like she was pondering it. "Come? I'm sure I could if I closed my eyes and thought of something sexy like licking peach juice from the testicles of a ripped dating agency CEO… Hmm… interesting… that's already working."

He tried to restrain his smirk. "Evie, just come to the office."

"Okay," she said, like it was inconvenient. "But you'll have to wait five minutes for me to finish blowing this UPS guy. He asked me to wear a FedEx cap… do you think that's weird?"

"Soon as you can."

He hung up the line and Taylor presented both hands to the phone. "How much fun is she? How can you not be attracted to that? I know for a fact there are a bunch of guys in the office who have asked her out."

He knew it too. "And she turns them down."

"Yeah, but they're not you," Taylor said. "You two are… I don't know, sometimes it's like there's fire between you, like you're super attracted, then it's like you hate each other and the air around you gets frostier than the icicles in an Eskimo's pussy."

With a slight disapproving smile, he tilted his head. "You've been spending too much time with Thirteen."

His sister wasn't apologetic, not that he really wanted her to be. "She's great! And if every other guy sees it, why can't you?" Taylor whined. "Oakley, please! I never ask you for anything! I'm asking you to try, okay? When she gets here, you just… you look at her and see if you feel anything."

He felt a bunch of things when Evie was around. Horny was usually number one, especially in the office when she was playing everyone like a cheap club showgirl did her clients on heart attack night. Hmm, maybe he'd been spending too much time with Thirteen too… Never.

"Taylor—"

"If you don't at least try asking her out, we'll never know, will we? I know Lana complicates things, but there's no spark between you two and… Evie is all spark, with everyone… even I'd sleep with her!"

"She said the same thing about you."

"There you go," Taylor said, and banged on the desk. "If you don't snap her up, I'm taking her." He must have smiled because she sneered. "You laugh all you like, Oakley Orion, but this is no joke. If you don't ask her out, she's going to say yes to another guy and you'll have lost your chance."

But, Oak wasn't worried. "She's not going to say yes to another guy," he said. "She hasn't done it yet, has she?"

"No, because she… because she's…"

Watching his sister trying to come up with an answer was the cherry on his cake today. "Because she's in a relationship."

Taylor's mouth opened twenty seconds before she gasped. "She is not! She would've told me!"

Folding his arms, he swayed in his chair, trying not to be smug, though it was tough. "No, she wouldn't."

"Why wouldn't she—"

"Because we agreed not to tell anyone," he said. Suddenly, Taylor had nothing to say. "Evie and I have been together for weeks… Nine, actually."

Again, Taylor's mouth fell open and while he was initially relieved to be telling the truth, his worry began to pique with each silent second that stretched between him and his sister.

The office door opened. Taylor turned her chair as Evie came dashing in. She closed the door and got three paces toward the desk when she stopped and eyed

Taylor, then him, then Taylor again.

"Do I have something on my face?" she asked in a monotone then stamped her foot and wiped the corners of her mouth. "Shit, I told him to aim for the tongue, he said I was clear!"

Leaving the desk, Oak went over and slid an arm around her waist. While she drew back a fraction and frowned at him, she didn't whoop and run away until he tried to kiss her.

"Evie," he said.

In her usual theatrical way, she brushed her clothes and smoothed her hair like she was offended. "I don't know what kind of business you're running, Mr. Orion—"

"I told her."

But Evie didn't get it, or at least she pretended not to get it. "Told who what?"

"I told Taylor about us."

"Us," Evie said, drawing out the word, she narrowed her eyes, acting like she had no clue what he was talking about. "I don't know what—"

"Evie, it's time to tell her," he said. "You know that… others agree." Noel had said it was time to start including others in their relationship. "She came in here and told me to ask you out, what was I supposed to say?"

If Evie flat out denied it, he was in trouble, Taylor might think he was making fun of her and that he'd expected Evie to go along with the ruse just to mock his sister. He'd never be that cruel. But what else could Taylor think if Evie denied it?

But when Evie's eyes slunk to Taylor, he turned to see his sister still sitting there gaping, stunned. "She doesn't look like she's taking it well," Evie said, sealing her own mouth under a frown.

Taylor gasped so loud the inhale was almost a scream. It was like she'd just broken water after three minutes holding her breath.

Shooting to her feet, Taylor held out her arms to shake her hands at them. "Kiss him!" Taylor screeched at Evie.

"No!" Evie said, pushing his chest when he turned to her. "You kiss him!"

"Please, Evie!" Taylor said, clasping her hands together. "Please! Please, please…"

Okay, so the toddler-like begging hadn't finished.

Evie lifted her triumphant chin and folded her arms. "The blinds are open. He doesn't let me kiss him when the blinds are open."

"Oh my God, it's true," Taylor said.

Oak stopped breathing when he saw the tears in her eyes. "Tay, why are you crying? I thought you wanted—"

"They're happy tears," Evie explained. "Because she thinks we'll live happily ever after." Bending toward Taylor, Evie kept her arms folded. "We won't. He snores and hogs the blankets and he never lets me win naked bingo."

Smacking her ass, he was pleased that she tossed a smile over her shoulder at him. "You watch what you're sharing, Thirteen."

"Oh!" she called as she swaggered the half-turn to face him. "Oh, isn't that rich, Mr. Orion? Who just told a whopper of a secret without consulting fifty percent of this partnership? And am I freaking out? No!"

"You're going to make me pay for it later," he muttered, wearing a smile.

She half-shrugged and didn't hide the truth. "Of course I'm going to make you pay for it later, I think Pavlov might be very hungry this weekend."

"It's my birthday this weekend, you can't withhold sex on my birthday."

Swinging her hips, she took slow steps toward

him. Evie kept on coming until her body made contact with his. Still her arms stayed folded and she hitched up that stubborn chin again. "You want to watch me withhold sex on your birthday?" she asked. "I will be withholding all over the damn place. Withholding at your apartment, at mine, here in the office, at the restaurant, in your car, in the hotel and any other damn place you can think of."

Lowering to murmur in her ear so Taylor wouldn't hear, he curled a hand around her hip. "And how powerful will you feel if the first thing I have to do on my birthday is eat your delicious pussy?"

When she leaned back, her hips pushed into his. "Want me to put a candle in it?"

He laughed. "No, the blowing is your job," he said and lowered to kiss her.

But Evie slapped a hand on his chest to stop him. For a second, she examined his expression and he couldn't figure out what she was thinking even after her saucy smile got naughty. Turning him to the side so that they were both in profile to Taylor and to the window, she grabbed his neck, and leaped up to wrap her legs around his waist as she sank her tongue into his mouth.

Well, they weren't just out to Taylor now, they were out to the entire company. That's what he got and exactly what he should've expected from his woman. He took the liberty of an inch, so she grabbed a fucking mile.

He fucking loved her.

Yeah, they were together, they were in love, and now they were official.

Driving his hands under her skirt, he cupped her ass knowing that he'd probably just revealed her underwear to Taylor, but the others would be too far away to see it… he hoped. When Evie pulled away from the kiss, she tossed her head back and he had to grab for her weight to stabilize her. But she sighed out a long breath and he wondered if she didn't feel kind of relieved too.

He hadn't heard the blinds opening, but there was Taylor in the corner by the blinds cord. She'd pulled them all the way back so there was no obstruction to the view of their kiss to the rest of the office, who were currently suspended in surprise, watching the show in the CEO's office that was playing out like it would on a cinema screen.

"Should I get my tits out?" Evie asked when he waved at the office when everyone began to applaud and cheer.

"No, they stay in the bra until we're alone," he said.

Taylor laughed, and Oak gave Evie back her feet and positioned her in front of him as she curtsied to the office and gave everyone a droll wave like she was the fucking Queen of England. All he could do was worship his woman and her confidence. Kissing her neck, he put his arms around her waist to hold her from behind.

"Can I go back to work now?" Evie asked out the corner of her mouth.

He was about to say yes, when Taylor pulled the blinds over and closed them.

"No, no," Taylor said. "We have to talk about this… We have to talk about the future."

"Oof," Evie said, losing her rigidity in a slump. "What the hell is it with you Orions and the future?"

"Evie doesn't like talking about the future," he said, adjusting his slacks as he went back to his side of the desk.

"I want to know everything," Taylor said, grabbing Evie and pulling her to the desk to seat them both on the guest side. "When did you first kiss?"

"Uh…" Evie raised her attention. "Washington."

Taylor gasped, and slapped the desk. "I knew something happened when you two slept together on the couch! I knew it!" His sister glared at him. "You are such a liar!"

But he held up his hands in surrender. "I am not! We didn't do anything on that couch… that night."

Evie picked up Taylor's hand. "He's telling the truth… I think. We'd already had sex by then."

Again, Taylor inhaled; if she kept this up she'd have a sore throat later. "No way! When the hell did you first have sex?"

"We had sex before Washington," Evie said, dragging her fingers across the back of Taylor's hand in a pronounced stroke.

He heard how bad that sounded and from Taylor's humph, she was putting pieces together. "You had sex before you kissed?"

Evie took a second then grinned at him. "Oh, wow, we did."

"You're just figuring that out?" he asked. "I thought women cared about that kind of shit."

"Other women," Evie said, waving a dismissive hand. "Other women wouldn't have been fine with you dating outside the relationship."

Oak pointed at her. "Hey, you date too," he said because he didn't want Taylor to think he'd pressured Evie. "And you were the one who said Lana—"

"Lana!" Taylor exclaimed, grabbing on to Evie's hand to tug them closer to each other. "Oh, God, how have you handled seeing him with Lana?"

Evie tucked Taylor's hair back behind her ear almost like a mother would. Oakley was amazed that she'd ever think she might not have it in her to parent when she was so amazing with Taylor. It would be better if the women took their conversation out of his office, but he wasn't going to shoo them.

Letting them have their gossip, he returned to proofing the contract he'd have to send out later, doing his best to ignore them.

Picking up his pen and the document, he went back to making notes for his assistant who'd make the updates.

"Lana was never a problem, she was business," Evie said. "It's not like Oak wanted her and I've been more relaxed about it since, well… you know…"

"Yeah." Taylor was nodding like she totally got what Evie was talking about. "Now I understand why you were so casual about that."

"So casual about what?" he asked, circling a section and making a notation in the margin.

"You didn't tell him?"

When he shifted his eyes upward, he saw Evie shrug, but Taylor was too shocked for him to just let it go. "Tell me what?"

"Kody had sex with Lana," Evie said.

The pen fell from his hand. "When?"

"A couple of weeks ago," she said, drawing a fingertip along the edge of his desk.

Hitting the speaker button, he dialed Kody. "Hey, boss."

"Where you at?" Oak asked.

"In the elevator, just getting back from the Regent meeting. They're going to follow the plan you created for them, Charley and Ed are grateful. They're going to make it. Are you looking for me?"

"Yeah, come to the office," he said and smacked the disconnect button as he glared at his girl.

If she'd had information like that, she should've shared it with him. Something flew across his vision and he turned to see Taylor throwing paperclips at him.

"Are you jealous? You can't be with Evie and be jealous that Lana is looking elsewhere. Geez, Oakley, you're supposed to be my role model for guys! You're just as bad as the rest of them. Is there any hope of finding a decent guy?"

"Oh, sweetie," Evie said, putting an arm around Taylor to hold her tight. "Oakley's driven by his dick just like every other male on the planet. It's pride. It's machismo. It's—"

"Bullshit," he said to Evie who immediately lost her condescension to a smile. "You know I don't care who Lana fucks and I know why you didn't tell me she was sleeping with Kody."

Taylor rolled her head on Evie's shoulder. "Why? You guys don't talk to each other?" She sighed. "Please don't break my heart and tell me this is a casual fuck fling."

"Oooh," Evie said, parting from Taylor to smile at her. "Fuck fling. I like that. I'm using that… I just need to find a guy who I can have one with."

When Evie batted her eyes at him, he knew to stay stern, but she made it difficult. "No," he said. "Weren't we talking about marriage forty-eight hours ago?"

"Ah, no," she said, pointing at him and then a squealing Taylor. "He was talking about marriage. I was talking about him fucking around."

When the hell had that happened? "You were not!"

"Uh, hello? Marilyn Monroe." Yeah, okay, they had talked about that. Kody came into the office and right over to the desk, smiling at everyone. "Hello, Kody," Evie purred in a deep, seductive lilt; she leaned back and traced a fingertip around the neckline of her top.

"Hi, Evie," he said, his smile growing nervous. "What's up?"

The marketing manager would have taken an

answer from anyone, but Evie leaned toward him and threaded her fingers through his. "I heard you have a thing for Oakley's women…"

"Okay, Thirteen, enough," Oak said. Taylor wasn't helping with her giggling. "Are you fucking Lana?"

Kody blanched, his jaw swung loose and he searched for something to say. Oak kind of wanted to make the guy sweat for a while. Not because he cared who Lana was hooking up with but because he was pissed at having been kept out of the loop as seemed to be a habit these days. The women in his life were taking over his company.

"I… I'm sorry, man, it… just happened and—"

"Thank fuck for that," Oak said.

Evie snapped her fingers at him. "And that's exactly why I didn't tell you," she declared. "I knew you'd use it as an out. You're going to dump her now, aren't you? I fucking knew it, Oakley Orion. You're as transparent as that fucking window back there. You've been looking for an excuse to—"

"I can't keep seeing her if she's screwing another guy," he said, but could tell she was never going to buy it.

"Don't give me that crap," Evie said. "She's been seeing you and the whole time you've been screwing me!"

"That's not even—"

"Wait, what?" Kody asked, cutting him off. "You've been… you two… you're… Fuck me!"

"Well, apparently, I'm on your list," Evie said, holding up two sets of crossed fingers.

Kody didn't really seem to react to Evie's tease, though he was probably still surprised. He wouldn't have seen the kiss if he'd been out of the building.

Just to be clear, Oak slapped a hand on the desk.

"Yo, buddy, the fake girl's all yours. Congratulations. Be happy. My real girl, is out of bounds. So you watch what you're looking at."

"You never let me have any fun," Evie huffed and folded her arms; she slumped in her chair.

"Wait, your real girl?" Kody said, moving closer to the end of the desk. "You're actually… you guys are together?"

"They are totally together. As together as you can get, together," Taylor said, brimming with excitement. "Getting married, together."

Shock jolted Kody's whole body. "You're engaged?"

When Evie lifted a finger and straightened, Oak lost control of his smile, letting it fly. "Sometimes a game just gets away from you, Thirteen, gotta go with the flow."

For a second, she struggled, then she held up her hand in triumph. "No ring, ha, I can't be engaged without a ring."

Taylor squealed and lunged over to scramble for his hand. "Can we go ring shopping? Can we, Oak? Give me your credit card! Evie and I will pick out something perfect."

Lifting from his chair to reach for his back pocket, Evie growled. "You take out your wallet and you'll be a brave man to ever put your dick between my teeth again."

Sniggering, he lowered again and linked his fingers as he shrugged at Taylor. "You heard her, Tay… You want nieces and nephews, right?"

Pushing her hands onto the table, Evie rose to her feet. "I am going back to my office," she said. "Mr. Orion, you're not getting laid tonight."

She went to kiss a grinning Taylor's cheek, smiled at Kody, and gave him a shoulder punch before turning for the door.

Pushing back in his chair, Oak opened his arms. "Where's my loving, baby?"

Pulling open the door, she kept hold of it as she hung back into the room. "Left it in my other panties," she said. "You know the ones that say, 'My boyfriend is a masochist and sadism suits me.'"

"I love you," he called out, but she just waved at him over her shoulder and carried on down the stairs.

Taylor squealed again. "She called you her boyfriend," she said. "This meeting couldn't have gone any better for me!"

True, but Evie would enjoy teasing him about it for a while. Taylor leaped up and began to scurry for the door.

"Where are you going in such a hurry?" Oak asked.

"Sister time!"

Taylor was as dismissive as Evie had been. He guessed he should be happy that they were taking their chattering out of his office since that's what he'd wanted.

Finding himself alone with Kody wasn't part of the plan. Returning to his work, Oak figured the guy would get the message and leave too, but he hung around.

"So... are we... okay?"

"Fine," Oak said.

"I need you to know, I didn't mean for it to happen. I don't think she did either and—"

"Kody," he sighed, shifting his concentration. "I really don't give a fuck. I was ready to finish the stupid charade before it even began. Congratulations to you both."

"So I should tell her that... it's over?"

"Between me and her, yeah," Oak said. "I don't care that you two hooked up, but it seems dumb for her and I to keep seeing each other if we're both with other people." It wasn't until he saw the light of hope in Kody's eyes that he realized what the guy was actually asking. "You can keep seeing her if you care about her. It's nothing to me. Lana and I were business, nothing ever happened between us."

"She said that," Kody said.

"And I can back that up," Oak said. "I was with Evie before you introduced me to Lana in Washington."

"That's why you wanted her out," Kody said, putting the pieces together. "Why you tried to get out of the deal."

Oak nodded. "It was only 'cause Evie said it was a good idea that I stuck with it. And Lana did good. We've increased membership, the press spread the story, we're good."

Kody grinned and held out a hand to shake his, then started for the door. Before he got there, he stopped to turn back. "But I don't get it, you met Evie through MatchMate… why wouldn't you just use her for the press?"

The honest answer was because Evie wasn't up for it, but there was another reason too. "Exploiting a setup is one thing, but asking the woman I love to do interviews about our relationship…" Oak shook his head. "It's not right. It wouldn't have been right… No, what Evie and I have is real and I don't want anyone to take advantage of it."

Nodding, Kody slipped his hands in his pockets and smiled like he got it. "Thanks for being cool about Lana and me."

With a conceding chin drop, Oak said nothing else and watched Kody leave.

It was a shame the guy had been stressed and probably worried about his job. Kody would've been concerned with the prospect of losing his position or souring his relationship with colleagues he was close to.

If Evie or Taylor had told him the truth, then the whole mess could've been cleared up weeks ago. But Evie was right, he'd have taken any opportunity to get out of seeing Lana because every minute he spent with her was one he could've been spending with the woman he actually loved.

Putting down his pen, he leaned back in his chair. Taylor knew. The world knew. His relationship with Evie was public. He'd invite both women to dinner tonight, answer all of Taylor's questions with Evie's support, and they could start getting used to being a family.

Evie was going to try her best to stay at his place on Friday night. Saturday would be his birthday party, which would bring together all the people he cared about most in the world.

Life was good. He was a lucky guy.

Nothing could go wrong.

TWENTY-SIX

EVIE ADJUSTED HER CUFFS and the hem of her skirt as she settled on the couch in hotel room number thirteen later that afternoon.

Noel's eyes were boring into the top of her head. She didn't appreciate her therapist making her feel nervous, especially on today of all days.

"You didn't tell him," Noel said. "Did you?"

Taking a deep breath, she wasn't going to shrink or apologize. "No, I didn't."

"You assured me that you would tell Oakley about the importance of this date."

"And I intended to," she said. "I was going to tell him, but Taylor just found out about us… It's not the right time to talk to Oak about this… I'm sure it will be fine… It will be fine."

It wasn't Noel's fault that she felt edgy. She shouldn't get defensive, especially knowing how wrong it was to let emotions rule on this day that always brought her sensitivities to the surface. She should've stayed in bed; it was the only way she wouldn't flip out and do something insane.

"Every year on Beth's birthday, you have some kind of episode. It's as if the date itself is a trigger for you. How have you handled it today?"

"It's been rough," she said, pleased with herself for being honest. "Before I opened my eyes this morning I wanted the day to be over. I didn't sleep well last night, I rarely do, but, it was like I was watching the seconds ticking by, I was just waiting for myself to lose it. It's always worse when I'm tired, but anyway... I got up and went to work, went about my day and here I am."

"That's it?"

She opened her hands. "That's it, doc. No episode."

"And what about tonight? You'll be finished work after this session? Are you spending the evening alone at home?"

"Oakley is taking Taylor and me out for dinner."

Noel wrote something in his notebook. "Do you think that's wise?"

It frustrated her that he could be so calm and detached when she felt like there were ants crawling under her clothes. But she was really trying hard not to let her anxiety show.

Life had a way of carrying on despite her issues. So, even though this wasn't the most convenient of days, there was nothing she could do about the fact that it was the one Oak had chosen to out them. He hadn't known what day this was or how significant it was for her.

"Taylor has questions; both of us have lied to her for weeks. It's only right we answer them. She's like a sister to me."

Her therapist's discerning look deepened. "Like a sister," Noel said. "And you think it's wise to spend time with this woman you've adopted as a sister on Beth's birthday?"

It was difficult not to be sassy. But, Evie knew Noel would make sarcasm out to be a cover, and she didn't need to be analyzed today, she just wanted to get out of there.

"On the day I usually always have a breakdown?" she asked and thought about how to put her feelings into words that weren't defensive or teasing. "Things have been going well with Oak and, yeah, I was nervous this morning, but when I got to work, I felt better… what can I say, MatchMate makes me calm. Oakley and I even talked about the future at the weekend. I'm getting better, Noel. He's helping me to get better."

With his astute eyes set on her, Noel said nothing for a minute. "You can't rely too heavily on him or your relationship for your recovery. You do still have a way to go. You can't be complacent."

"I said I would try to stay with him on Friday," she said, and his expression became something verging on worried. "Really, Noel, you have nothing to stress about. I told Oakley, I'm not promising anything. I'm being careful, Noel, don't worry about me so much."

She flashed him what was meant to be a dazzling, optimistic smile, but the look on his face told her he wasn't convinced. "If your flashbacks take you by surprise, they could devastate you. Until now, you've been braced, expecting the worst, but you've dropped your guard and that's good. You have a man you can trust at your side, but… today, on this difficult day, just be careful for me, okay?"

Huffing, she rolled her eyes and crossed her legs like she was bored of the conversation, which, in truth, she was. Evie had made it this far through the day without screaming her head off or descending into the darkness. She was confident she'd make it to the end.

"Yes, sir," she said and bent forward to retrieve her notebook from the front of her bag. Waving it at him, she grinned again. "Want to read my innermost thoughts? There's a lot of sex in there this week."

He leaned forward to take it from her. "There's been a lot of sex in there for weeks. If there's one thing you and Oakley don't need to be coached in, it's that."

Raising her brows, she bit her lip. "Oh, you got that right."

The doctor was telling her to be wary because it was his job. Evie was feeling good and it had been a long time since she'd been able to say that. She didn't want this feeling to go away anytime soon and would embrace every second of it as long as it lasted.

TWENTY-SEVEN

OAK WOULD END UP cursing himself for having his thought about nothing going wrong.

Just thinking that life was perfect and indestructible was enough to ensure it would shatter. He'd jinxed himself and damned the woman he loved more than any other.

Inviting the women to dinner was a great plan, they chatted, Taylor got all her details, and Evie had fun riling him with her jokes and flirtations.

Driving up to Taylor's apartment block, Oak wasn't surprised when Evie put her hand over his on the wheel. "We have to walk her upstairs," she murmured.

He understood that Evie's insecurities extended into protecting Taylor, so he didn't object, just picked up her hand to press his mouth to her knuckles.

Evie cared about Taylor, she loved her, as a sister would love a sister. Yes, maybe Evie was a bit overprotective, but he couldn't argue with that, he was overprotective too. He would rather that than the alternative.

So, they went up to Taylor's place together and waited at the door for Taylor to unlock it. Evie shivered as Taylor opened the door.

"Let Oakley go in and look around," Evie said, staring into the dark apartment.

There was something odd about the expression on her face, but when she looked at him, he nodded. If she was worried about Taylor being safe, he was going to do everything in his power to make sure both women were at peace.

"Why does he need to go in?" Taylor asked and began to move forth, but Evie pulled her back.

"Just a minute, honey," Evie said, and looked at him again. "Be careful."

Why did she look so pained? It wasn't worry in her eyes or even fear; it was like a dread of resigned anxiety hung around her. After kissing her forehead quickly, Oak went inside and looked through the apartment. He found nothing out of place and was checking the last closet in the bedroom when he called out.

"We're good!"

Oak didn't want the women hanging around in the hallway alone longer than they had to, so was pleased when he came out to see Taylor sitting on her couch freeing her feet from her shoes. But, when he glanced around for Evie, he saw her just inside the doorway, frowning at the scene.

"Sweet?"

Raising a finger, she didn't say anything, just silently asked him to pause and he did. Oak stopped just outside the bedroom and waited. Taylor didn't seem to notice Evie's growing discomfort, maybe because they'd had such a good night or maybe because she'd had one too many drinks.

His sister flopped onto the couch on her back

and groaned. "I think I'll go to sleep and never wake up," Taylor said, straightening out and letting an arm hang off the side of the couch.

"Tay, sit up," he said and went over to pull Taylor into a seated position.

Something was on Evie's mind, he'd never seen her so tense or so pale, and he'd been with her when she woke from a nightmare once. It seemed that she was forcing herself to move forward when she took a step and then another.

Whatever was going on inside her, she was trying to fight it. The last thing Evie needed to see was Taylor strewn out on her back like she was passed out or worse… like Beth.

Evie hadn't made it ten feet across the room when Oak noticed a shadow in the open doorway behind her. It hadn't been his intention to tense or to draw attention to it, but Evie must have noticed his change in expression because she flipped around just in time to see someone walk into the apartment.

"Ethan," Taylor said and shot to her feet. "What are you doing here?"

Ethan didn't look at Evie, he strode straight past her to head for Taylor. "Sweetheart, I had to see you," he said and lifted an arm.

Before Ethan could make contact with Taylor, Evie jumped into action and sped across the room. "Don't touch her."

"What?"

Ethan was as startled as Taylor, but Evie didn't back down. She pushed Ethan aside and put herself between him and both Orion siblings.

"Thirteen," Oak said, reaching around Taylor to touch Evie's arm.

Her head snapped to the side, and she landed a glare on him that told him she wasn't going to budge.

The unexpected mass of tears weighing on her lashes made him draw an anxious breath.

Oh, shit. This wasn't good.

Something about this scene was reminding her of… no, this was more powerful than that, like a flashback. Was she hallucinating? Did she think that she was back there? That Ethan was…

Her glare vanished from his view when she turned back to Ethan. "Just stay back," she said, holding out both arms toward Ethan and moving backward, forcing him and Taylor to reverse. "Stay the hell away from her!"

"What the hell is going on?" Ethan snapped. "Who the hell are you?"

Getting angry wasn't going to defuse this situation. Oak moved quickly. Leaving Taylor behind Evie's back, he went around the coffee table to get behind Ethan so he could look into Evie's eyes, hoping to bring her back to the reality of the present moment.

Tears fell from her eyes, breaking his heart, but Oak stayed calm. "It's okay, Sweet. I'm here."

"Get away from him," she barked. "He's dangerous."

"He's an asshole," Oak said, pushing Ethan aside to try getting closer to Evie. But she opened her arms, herding Taylor further away from them. "But he's not dangerous. He's not Gemmell… Baby, I promise you're safe."

"Stop moving," she said, her eyes glazed with confusion.

He stopped trying to get nearer and let her get some distance. "I'm not moving, Sweet," he said, soothing her as best he could from the fifteen feet of space that grew between them. "But I want you to look at me, okay? It's me. It's Oak. Your Oak."

With her focus on the floor a couple of feet in

front of him, she was shaking her head. "No, no, I don't… don't come near her."

"I'm not going to touch Taylor," he said. "No one's going to touch her."

Ethan moved into his peripheral vision, Oak put an arm out to block him. "What the hell is going on?" he demanded.

Oak used his outstretched arm to push Ethan back. "Just stay quiet and back up," he hissed through gritted teeth, trying not to get angry or do anything that might aggravate Evie's confusion.

"Safe," Evie muttered, her words distant and confused. "Got to be safe."

Licking his lips, he tried taking one careful step toward her. "Sweet," he murmured. "Turn around, look at who's behind you. It's Taylor… My sister. Not yours."

"Her sister?" Taylor asked. "Evie is my sister!"

If Taylor thought that she was helping or defending her new friend, she was wrong. "Shut up, Tay," he snapped.

All he wanted was his together, happy Evie. Seeing her like this was scaring the crap out of him and he couldn't combat contradictions coming from other directions.

He had to keep his focus on Evie, but his sister had no idea what she was dealing with.

"Don't you shout at her!" Evie snapped, pressing her hands to her ears. "Don't! Don't shout!"

"No shouting," he said, lowering his volume again. "I'm sorry, Sweet… I love you. You're okay, okay? No one here is going to hurt you… You're safe."

"Not safe," she said. "Never safe… Never careful…"

"Oak," Taylor said, finally realizing that something big was happening, something worse than she'd probably thought. "Oakley, I'm scared. What's going on?"

Anxiety welled to new heights. Evie off her game was bad enough, dealing with an afraid Taylor too might be more than he could handle. "You're okay, Tay," he said, worrying about how he'd appease both women at once. "Just be quiet and stay there, okay?"

"But what's wrong with Evie, she's like... she's not even here."

He understood what Taylor meant, Evie was here, but it was like she was phased out of the moment. Her concentration on the floor was absolute, yet, something flickered around her; a mixture of pain and concern and terror all at once.

"Evie, baby," he said, taking some more careful steps. "You remember our Sundays? How you come to my place first thing and we spend the morning in bed? How I cook you lunch and you reorganize my closets? You remember that first morning you came over? When you called me and said you were outside my door? That was a dream for me, Sweet, having you there, with me, waking up with you." Her head began to shake slowly like she couldn't remember, like he was talking about someone else or a forgotten dream. Drips fell from her chin onto the floor; she was still crying. "You know I love you. I told you that weeks ago. I told you when we were in your hotel room, remember? When you showed me how you prepare for... everything. When I told you Pavlov needed Bell, do you remember?"

"Being afraid," she whispered. "I remember being afraid."

That wasn't what he wanted to hear; it pained him. But at least she was responding, that was progress. "Not there," he said, trying to keep his voice level. "Not in that room. You asked me to hurt you and I couldn't, do you remember, Sweet? I promised you that I would never hurt you and I promise you, I won't—"

"Never… never be hurt."

It didn't even occur to Oak to think about stopping her hand from sliding into the purse that was hanging across her body on a long strap. He was too busy concentrating on getting closer. He was almost there, just six feet away and he could almost—

Her hand emerged from her bag and what he saw in it halted him in his tracks. Evie extended her arm, holding a small black pistol tight in her hand, aiming it toward him and Ethan who was probably somewhere behind him.

Taylor screamed, and Ethan cursed, but the exclamation only made Evie twist to grab Taylor, holding her against her side while she aimed the weapon.

"He won't hurt us. I won't let him hurt us," Evie said and the venom in her eyes was enough to make him worry that she might just pull that trigger.

"No!" Taylor screamed out. "No, Evie! Please! Oakley!"

"It's okay," he said and let his hands rise in surrender. "We're not going to get hurt. No one's going to get hurt… Evie, honey, look at me, baby. Do you want to hurt me?"

There was a shake in her hand, but not enough that she wouldn't hit something, or someone, if she pulled the trigger. But her head shook too, slowly, freeing more tears from her face.

"Oh," she whispered.

Good, he felt like he was getting her back. But that weapon was still there between them. "What do you want? Do you want me to get Ethan out of here?"

He wasn't wild about the idea of leaving Taylor alone with Evie. His sister had no clue what was going on, or why Evie was acting this way. Taylor might get angry and lash out, but he was confident that Evie wouldn't hurt Taylor. This was all about protecting her.

"I want…" Evie said and shook the gun at him. But in the moment her eyes actually met his, something else shimmered across them. "I want… Oakley…"

When her voice cracked, her hand loosened, and he was sure that she was going to drop the gun.

Except Ethan chose that moment to bluster. "I'm calling the cops," he declared, and Taylor yelped.

Evie's arm strengthened again.

"You move a goddamn muscle and I'll shoot you myself," Oak growled over his shoulder at Ethan.

"Don't," Taylor said. "Ethan, don't move."

His sister was scared, there was no way he could deny that. But, she trusted him, Oak had never felt the weight of that trust more than he did now. "Thirteen, let Taylor go," he murmured. "Let the asshole go… Let's you and me talk about this."

"I want to protect her," Evie said. "We have to protect her."

Smiling at her wasn't as easy now as it was on other days, but he did his best. "We will, Sweet. We're an amazing team. You and me have done so much to protect her already… we love her and she loves us. We're family."

"I love her," Ethan declared.

Evie's frown deepened. "You hurt her. You're an asshole who doesn't deserve to breathe the same air as her."

"But you know I would never hurt her," Oak said. The last thing they needed was Evie to focus on the guy whose appearance had caused all this. "You know I'd protect both of you with my life… don't you?"

"Oh," she murmured.

"That's right," he said, edging nearer. "Your Oh… Now let her go, Sweet… Please, put the gun down and let her go."

The gun bobbed down once, then rose, but it

lowered again. Her arm must have loosened from Taylor too because his sister pushed away from Evie, inadvertently thrusting her onto the couch.

Taylor ran to him, into his arms, but he only soothed her for a second before urging her away. "Go into the bedroom," he said. "Go in there and wait. I love you."

"Oak, I—"

"Go, Tay!"

Taylor didn't say anything else, just turned and fled. When the door closed he could be assured that she was safe, but Evie wasn't as secure. Sitting on the edge of the couch with the gun in her hands, she was just… staring at it.

Before he could think about soothing his girl, he had to get rid of the other problem.

Spinning around, he grabbed Ethan's shirt in both hands to pull him close. "You are going to fuck off out of here and never come back. If you think about contacting my sister again or coming near her, we'll do a helluva lot more than ruin your finances and your relationship."

Ethan mouthed for a moment, lost in shock of his own. "You… you did—"

"That's right, I fucking did," Oak said, thrusting him away. "This is your last chance to get the hell out of here. I wouldn't mind taking you apart, so don't give me the excuse…" Ethan began to back toward the door. "And this never happened, asshole. Think about telling a soul and we'll have exactly the reason we need to bring you down!"

Ethan fled, slamming the apartment door, leaving Oak alone with Evie. When he turned back around, she was still staring at the weapon in her hands.

"Sometimes there's pain that lives in us," she whispered, somehow aware of him watching her. "I always thought I could make it go away, that I could make it move on… But sometimes it becomes such a part of us that without it… we're nothing."

"Sweet, look at me."

"No," she snapped and raised her attention to him as her hands trembled. But she curled her fingers around the butt of the gun; one slid over the trigger. "I love you, Oakley Orion." She swallowed. "And I love Taylor so much…"

Her voice drifted off in a squeal of pain that joined a sob when she looked at the bedroom door Taylor had used.

"I know, baby, and she knows it. Don't worry, we'll—"

"I always thought I would hurt you, but never like this," she said, gritting her teeth.

She shook the gun and squeezed her hand around the barrel.

"It's okay, flashbacks are normal after what you've been through."

He figured that was all that could account for her sudden change in behavior. He'd read up about PTSD and spoken to Noel about it too. Sometimes the symptoms were disparate and infrequent, but they could be powerful.

"Four years after?" she asked and shook her head.

He hated to see her punish herself like this; he wanted to comfort her. Figuring she was herself again, he took a step toward her, but froze when she chambered a round.

"What are you doing?"

"I always thought my mother was selfish," she murmured, her voice so quiet that he strained to hear it and with her focus on the gun, he couldn't even see her lips. "I thought that she took her own life and abandoned me… But I see now, it wasn't that… she did it because she didn't want to be this. She knew that there are some pains we're not meant to conquer, and losing Beth… We were never supposed to get over that."

Fear made his throat dry. He had no awareness of his heart, of what his body was doing because ice-cold terror numbed all of him. "Sweet, I want you to put the gun down, okay? Please, Thirteen, do it for me… We'll get through this. We'll—"

"I promised you I would never hurt myself," she said, keeping one hand on the butt as the other stroked the barrel. "But I never thought of what I'd do if I hurt you… Losing Beth was agony. Losing my mother was devastating. But if I lost you… or Taylor—"

"You're not going to lose either of us. It was a momentary blip. No one's hurt. No one's—"

"She'll never forgive me," she said, her gaze flicking to the bedroom.

"She will," he said. "She'll understand. Please, Sweet, just—"

"No," she said and shot to her feet. "I knew I wasn't ready. I should never have started this. I should never have started anything with you."

"You told me you wouldn't break up with me again," he said.

But she was shaking her head. "This is for your own good, Oakley. This isn't a game. I'm not pushing you away or trying to hurt you to make you hate me. This is me calm and rational telling you, we're through… over… forever this time."

She tried to walk past him, but he got in her way. "You think it's going to be that easy? That I'll let you go out there on your own while you're upset like this? That's not what family does."

"Family doesn't hurt each other," she said. "They don't threaten and scare each other… I'm not your family… I never was… I never should have let myself believe I could be. Normal isn't for screwed up people like me."

"No," he growled because he couldn't let her disappear, not like this. "You're upset. You don't know what you're saying."

The loaded gun was still in her hand, and as much as he wanted to touch her, he feared that any sudden movement might make her tense and fire the gun. "Shit, Evie… I love you. I can't lose you." But that didn't influence her. Her gaze was so cool, it was icy. Much like he'd seen in Washington before she told him about Beth, she switched off all emotion in lieu of nothing but stark anger. "Damnit! Think of Tay! She's right through that door! What do you want me to tell her?" Evie sidestepped past him and began to stride to the front door. "Evie! Where are you going?"

Turning as she got to the door, fresh tears were streaming down her face, but her detached expression didn't match that involuntary show of emotion.

"To save your life, Oakley Orion… To save you from me."

She went out and closed the door, locking it behind her. Oak couldn't focus, his breath was all he could hear and even to his ears it seemed shallow and disconnected. Evie was… where was she going?

Fired by determination, he headed for the door, starting slow and picking up speed until he got there and tried the handle. But, the thing didn't give.

"Taylor!" he called. "Taylor!"

Though it wasn't smart to use such an urgent tone when his sister was probably still afraid, he couldn't think about anything except the panic coursing through him.

"Oak?"

Whipping around, he saw her meek figure by the

bedroom. Straightening an arm in a snap, he pointed to the door. "The key... I need to get the fuck out of here and it's locked."

Rushing to the couch, Taylor searched her clutch that was strewn there. But, the moment he noticed it was open, his heart sank. Evie must have slipped her hand inside and taken the key, which would explain how she'd managed to lock it again.

With wet eyes, Taylor blinked up at him, her hand still in the purse. "It's not here. Oak, what's going on?"

"Spares," he said, dropping to his haunches to grab her shoulders. "I need a spare. We need to get to Evie."

When Taylor shook her head, some tears skittered down her face. "I... I don't have any spares. Oak, please tell me, what's wrong with Evie?"

His sister fell forward into his arms and began to sob.

He'd have busted down the door if he could, but the confused Taylor was already scared enough, so he tried to maintain calm while soothing her and making plans to call a locksmith. Except he already knew that by the time the tradesman got there to do his thing, Evie would be long gone.

***

FROM THE MOMENT they'd gotten Taylor's apartment door open, Oak had been trying to track Evie down. But, he couldn't find her. Oak didn't see Evie the next day, or the next. A form of hope came when her final personnel report was emailed to him. He tried to respond to it, but got a returned message stating that the email address no longer existed.

He called Noel, but the therapist shut him down

by saying he couldn't discuss patients. All he offered was an assurance that he'd spoken to Evie and that he was sure she was not a danger to herself, which wasn't exactly a comfort. That's all Noel would say. Apparently, Oak had been shut out.

Evie's apartment was vacated. Her website shut down. She was just… gone.

TWENTY-EIGHT

FOUR MONTHS LATER

WALKING IN TO THE Washington hotel suite made Oak feel sick.

Taylor, Ian, and Kody weren't far behind him and they were all talking about the weekend ahead. This convention was different from the other they'd been to, smaller and only for commercial dating providers. He'd almost made his excuses and decided not to stay in this particular hotel, in this particular suite.

But Taylor, as always, stepped up and slapped him, telling him that they'd always been loyal to this hotel and they were treated well, so they had to stay. She'd also reminded him that they had an account with the chain. They wouldn't want to upset the relationship, or it would have a domino effect on other areas of the business.

So, there he was, in the room he'd first kissed Evie. The room where she'd told him the truth about Beth. The room where he'd first spent the night with her. The couch that was there in the middle of the room had probably been cleaned, but somehow, he was sure he could still smell her in the air.

"Let's make coffee and get started," Taylor said.

The guys settled themselves in the armchairs, leaving him with nowhere to go except onto the couch he usually sat on… the one he'd shared with Evie.

Taylor had been a rock and shown real resilience since the night they'd lost Evie. It didn't matter that he knew she was alive, he still felt like he'd lost a part of himself. A part of himself had died that night.

He should have been able to help her. If he loved her, he should have been able to pull her out. To hold her up. To be the man she needed him to be.

At first, he'd felt guilty about telling Taylor the truth. He didn't go into details about things Evie had shared in therapy sessions, but he did tell his sister the facts. She'd cried. Broken her heart right there in front of him and begged him to find a way to help Evie.

Evie had thought that Taylor would never forgive her, when in fact Taylor understood the trauma completely. Perhaps because of their relationship, Taylor understood what it would be to not only lose him, but to see him brutalized and subjected to torture.

But, despite all their best efforts, he hadn't been able to find Evie. She'd moved out of state, that much was clear, and he'd even tried putting private investigators on Noel, but from what he could tell, Evie had cut all ties with the therapist too. She didn't want to be found and with no close relatives, he had no one he could appeal to for information.

"Okay, that leads us on to…" Taylor said.

The men groaned, which pulled Oak out of his funk. "What?" he asked, wondering why everyone was so grumpy all of a sudden.

Taylor leaned over to show him the next item on the agenda. The last item. The item that had been on every agenda for a month and he'd ducked it every time.

"A new HR manager," Taylor said.

"Why do you even bring this up?" he asked. "You know I'm not ready to—"

"I bring it up because the guys and I have put it to a vote and we've decided to hire someone."

"What the hell?" he asked. Was it something about this damn hotel that made everyone think he was suddenly senile? "I said no new manager, didn't I? Heather left a month ago. We have time to—"

"We need someone," she said. "We're still floundering since the report…"

The report was what everyone had taken to calling Evie's report because they didn't want to say her name in front of him.

"We're working through it," he mumbled and felt himself begin to withdraw.

"Yes, the report is great," Taylor said. "You know that we were all impressed, but we need a strong hand to keep an eye on things in that department or we'll end up in the same position all over again. You read the conclusions and the way that Evie summed up complacency."

Just the sound of her name made him look up to see both Ian and Kody were braced as if he might flip out, and hey, he just might. It seemed to be what they were all expecting, and, in this case, he didn't mind giving the people what they wanted.

"Fine," he sighed, resigning himself to sanity. "I'll look at a shortlist and—"

"No shortlist," Taylor said, checking something on her phone when it buzzed. "We already picked the perfect candidate."

But he wasn't quite ready to be pushed around. Fun as they might think it was to tease him, he had to assert himself sometime and now was it.

"No," he said, "I'm drawing a line, Taylor. You cannot make a unilateral decision about something this important."

"Something this important that you've ignored for a month," Taylor said, getting up to head for the door. "It can't be that important if you can blank it off the agenda, meeting after meeting. Well, I'm sorry, brother, but this is the day you've been dreading, you've run out of White-Out, no more blanking. Meet your new HR manager."

Opening the suite door, Taylor reached into the hallway and grinned as she pulled someone into the room.

Someone.

Not just someone.

Oak surged to his feet. "Evie," he inhaled her name.

The moniker stuck in his throat, blocking his windpipe.

Evie and Taylor hugged, one whispered something to the other and then Ian was moving away from the living room with Kody. Both men left with Taylor in their wake.

Alone with Evie, Oak still hadn't figured out what the hell he was supposed to say.

"Taylor told me that as soon as I saw you, I'd know what to say," Evie said, her hands loose at her sides. "Usually I always have something to say, but… All I can come up with is… I've missed you."

Was this real? Was she really here? "Evie," he said again, torn between his need to grab her and his need to ask a million questions.

Except he couldn't order his thoughts, or any words, and he didn't know where to begin.

"I called Taylor about a month ago," she said. "It was part of my therapy. I apologized, obviously, I explained some things, and I thought that would be it. But when she asked to meet me, I… Hell, Oakley, I pointed a gun at her brother in front of her, I figured I owed her one… I could never have imagined that it would lead to this."

"The job," he muttered. "You're here for the job."

Sheepish and contrite, she licked her lips. "Not really," she said. "Taylor seemed sure that it was a great idea. I told her that it wasn't fair on you… It doesn't matter."

"Then why are you here?" he asked. "If not for the job? I… I mean, what the hell happened, Evie?"

"I don't know, I guess… Something that night snapped, I was in the hallway outside the apartment and I just got this vision… I thought I could shrug it off, I've had memories like that before. Memories that are more than mental pictures, they're like nightmares, more than visceral, tangible flashbacks… I could see it, Oakley, I could… I could taste the blood in the air, feel the humidity on my skin, it was… real… Don't ask me to explain how because I can't."

"And then that asshole showed up… Taylor ripped him a new one by the way, promised never to go near him again."

"She told me… he's an asshole, but I… I probably shouldn't have pointed a gun at him either." Oak shrugged. "I've always hated guns," she said, folding her arms around herself. "I carried, but I never touched it, never acknowledged it until… God, Oak, I don't know what I would've done if you hadn't been there."

"But, I was," he said. "Taylor and I were there, and we wouldn't have let you hurt anyone."

A wistful smile graced her lips. "I think it was the smell of Taylor's hair… I looked into your eyes and I smelled her hair and I… I was myself again. But I hated myself. The thing I'd feared most was hurting you. I know it was Ethan I was aiming for, but… you were in the line of fire. I really can't… I can't forget that. In the early days, after Beth, I trashed my apartment when I was having nightmares and I had no memory of doing it… Another nightmare like that might have made me hurt you, I couldn't have stayed, Oak… I couldn't. When we started, I think I tried to convince myself it wouldn't happen… but it did. I hadn't wanted you with me, staying at my place for that reason."

"You could've told me that. I would've told you—"

"What? That it was worth the risk?" she asked and shook her head. "No. No chance. After that flashback, I knew it was a possibility; that it might happen. I had to get away."

"From me."

"From me," she said, and determination lit her eyes. "Oakley, I knew I wasn't ready to be with you when we started together, but I… I loved you so much that I silenced that voice. I wanted to be with you so badly that I made myself believe that I could do it."

"But you can't."

"I couldn't, no," she said. "I had to fix me. Losing Beth was tough, but I think I switched some part of myself off after that night. At first, it was to get through the manhunt, then to ignore my mother's death so I could get through the trial, then there were appeal hearings, and I had no one to talk to, so I bogged myself down in business. I put on the front that everything was okay, and I believed it… Until you… You made me feel. Opening myself to you opened me to every other emotion I'd ignored for four years. I never faced what happened to me. I never processed it. I only coped. Survived."

Moving toward her, he reached for her, but

dropped his hands without making contact. "But that's the point, Evie. You survived. You came through. You're so strong and so capable. I know you can beat this."

A smile that went beyond her lips warmed her eyes. "I have." He didn't understand. "I mean, as much as a person can… it will always be with me, but… I left you that night and I… I guess I had a breakdown. I called Noel, and he tried to coach me, but I got frustrated. I knew I needed more… I went away, to Florida if you'll believe, checked myself into a rehab place and I stayed there for three months."

"Rehab?"

"I know it sounds nuts," she said. "I felt nuts sometimes. But dealing with the trauma and with the grief of losing my sister and my mother has helped me see where I do need help. I'm still in therapy, and I'm taking medications now that help keep me calm, so I won't freak out like I did… I feel… better."

"Sleeping through the night?" he asked. She nodded. "Your traps?"

She shook her head. "I still like to be near a phone and I check all my doors and windows like a maniac, but… no razor blades in the vents or pressure sensors on the floor."

Oak knew what a massive step that was for her. He was impressed that she'd worked so hard to overcome her complexes. "I'm proud of you."

Of its own accord, his hand rose to her cheek. She was softer than he remembered, both in the way her skin felt and the way she turned into his caress and closed her eyes. She was so beautiful. It was tough to believe that she'd once been his… almost his.

"Thank you for listening to me," she said, sliding her hand over his to flatten his palm on her cheek, holding him to her.

It had been months, but not an ounce of his

feeling had diminished. He hadn't expected it to, partly because he didn't want it to. Evie had been a whirlwind in his life, but he wanted her to be a constant breeze, always there to comfort and soothe him. But she hadn't been. Before he'd been ready, she'd vanished, and he'd been left with a memory that he couldn't let go of.

Oak didn't want to stop touching her, wasn't sure he could let her go again. "I wish you'd called me."

"I needed to know you were free to live your life. I had no idea how long it would take for me to get my shit together, it could've been three months or three years. Spending some time in the sun, listening to other stories and talking mine out every day, it's made me feel so much lighter… freer… I wanted that for you too. No more darkness. No more woman telling you her sad story. I wanted you to be happy."

"Sweet," he breathed out her pet name and put his other hand to her face to pull her up so he could lower and rest his forehead on hers. "I worried about you every day."

"I wasn't screwing around."

Why would she tell him that unless…? Was there a chance that she still felt something for him? That she might let him back in? Searching her face, he couldn't figure out if her affection for him was current or nostalgic.

If there was a chance she wanted to try again, he wanted to try too. This wasn't a time for teasing or games.

"Neither was I," he said. "I haven't been with anyone since you."

Worry crossed her face. She tried to withdraw, but he tightened his hold and pulled her back. "I don't know why I said that, Oakley. I'm sorry, I—"

"What are you thinking about right now?" he asked, maybe hoping too much.

Being together was powerful, just sharing space was intense. Evie curled her lower lip into her mouth in a way that strengthened his optimism, it was only increased further when her attention drifted to his.

She'd said she was better, that she was together, that she was happy. Tipping her head back, he angled her to receive his mouth and as soon as their lips touched she gasped in a desperate mew of need.

Damn. She was still his. It might not make sense to her how he could still love her like he did, but it made no sense to him how she could doubt it.

Tasting her tongue with his own, he withdrew at the same time her fingers curled into his shirt. "Thirteen?" he asked, strengthening his grip on her face.

He hauled her close and threw an arm around her. The ragged way he said her name and their mismatched breathing intensified the air crackling around them.

Gasping in, she tried to find his mouth, but he kept her away and sought her consent. "Ding, ding," she sighed out.

He'd never heard such a beautiful sound.

Picking her up, he carried her to the bed they'd first made love in and stripped both of them down slowly. She had a tenderness in her touch that was unfamiliar, he'd never felt so cherished as he did when he slid himself inside her. Her whole body yielded to accept him.

But she felt good, like his warm, willing woman had never left him, not really, not in spirit. She'd always belonged to him and here she was giving herself to him in a way more wholly than she had before. Oak felt it was his responsibility to bring her to climax over and over, begging her without words to need him, to trust him, to stay with him.

When he reached his own crescendo, he saw

tears in her eyes that terrified him, not because of their sorrow, but because of their adoration and gratitude.

Evie was here with him, the same Evie she'd always been, but a more enhanced version, a better version, one who was more at peace.

Oak didn't know how long they lay in the sheets staring at each other. A good long while. But he didn't want to leave the moment and so stayed completely silent. It was Evie who spoke first.

"Oak," she said, "what do we do now?"

"Now," he said, punching the pillow that was under his head to elevate it enough to see both her eyes with both of his. "I make a commitment."

Her smile bred his and they laughed. "Oh," she said and sighed as she stroked a hand down his chest. "I can't deny that I love you. I can't do it… But I'm not sure it would be fair of me to put you through all that again."

"You said you were cured… as cured as a person can be."

"And I am," she said, watching him take her hand from his chest to kiss his fingertips. "But I put you and Taylor through a trauma of your own… How can you look at me without….?"

"Seeing you pointing a gun at me?" he asked. "Sweet, the moment lasted ten seconds… You got with it and… I trust you. Can't you trust that I love you and want to be with you? Nothing has changed."

"I don't have a job," she said.

"You have one at MatchMate just like I always wanted," he said. "How are you at spending the night?"

"I haven't spent the night with a man," she said. "But I've spent the night in rehab and in my new apartment without traps… We did a lot of work on my issues and I spent the night in dorms with other people."

"So you'd be willing to give it a try?"

"You think we just jump straight into this?" she asked. "We don't miss a step or date, we just... live together and get married and—"

"Why not?" he asked, infused with hope. "Give me one good reason why not? I love you. You love me. You've worked hard to go from traumatized victim to empowered survivor. I'll support you, just like I always did before. I'm not going to throw our whole relationship away because of twenty minutes one night... Shit, I've been with women who've got themselves so drunk they've waved knives in my face. Sometimes people flip out, and I appreciate that what you went through wasn't like that, but that makes you a more secure bet."

"A more secure bet," she said, squashing her hand to his face.

"We never got a real shot if you weren't ready. I want that shot now..." He looked up and then back at her. "If that's the right choice of words." When he released a laugh, so did she. He kissed her. "I'm going to get a drink, you want one?"

She nodded and stayed in bed as he got up and grabbed his shorts to pull them on as he went through to the bar. He'd just opened his beer when the suite door opened. Shit, he hadn't even known it was unlocked.

"Okay, shout at me if you're going to shout at me," Taylor said, storming toward him. "I've been in my room stewing, expecting you to call and yell at me. So, yell at me, I can't stand the silent treatment."

Lowering his beer bottle from his lips, he cleared his throat. "Yell at you for what? Did you forget to overnight those contracts I gave you?"

She snapped her mouth shut then croaked. "I... No, I... shout at me about Evie, you idiot. You weren't mean to her, were you? She's been through enough and it's not right of you—"

"Can I have three olives?" Evie asked, opening the bedroom doorway then freezing. "Oh."

"Yes, Sweet?" he asked as if she was referring to him.

"No, I mean… oh," she said, stepping forward and smoothing her fingertips down the line of buttons on his shirt that was draped over her body, though he noted she'd only done up the bottom two so her abdomen and cleavage were on show. "Taylor, I… I'm sorry, I didn't—"

Taylor screamed so loud that even he jumped. "What the fuck, Tay?" he barked, opening his mouth wide to pop his ear.

His sister ran over to Evie and pulled her into a hug then grabbed her hand to drag her over to the bar. "Oh my God! You're back together! You're back together, right?"

"We were just talking about that," he said and looked at Evie. "Are we giving it a go, Thirteen? Are you ready for the love and romance bullshit that comes with being fucked good and hard?"

She didn't seem to get it, but she looked at Taylor's hopeful grin and his face that had to be full of expectation and smiled.

"You do make it very difficult, Mr. Orion," she said and came over to drape herself against him as she begged for a kiss.

"Is that a yes?" he asked, hesitating.

Grinning, she pouted and lowered her voice to a simper. "It's a sad, unavoidable truth. It's not a dream you're going to wake up from. I am actually your girl now. It's completely real."

Thank you for reading this tale!
If you can, please take the time to review.

~

Ask your local library for more Scarlett Finn novels!

~

For all things Scarlett Finn
check out:

www.scarlettfinn.com

CHECK OUT

OUT NOW!